Duty and Dishonor

"Sizzles with excitement."   —Nora Roberts

"Exceptional . . . fresh and unique. . . . Powerful
[and] passionate."   —*Romantic Times*

"Lovelace's command of the plot is impressive . . .
intense and evocative . . . [an] unusual and well-
written story."   —*Gothic Journal*

"A great yarn told by a masterful storyteller. It
could have happened!"
     —Brigadier General Jerry Dalton, USAF (Ret.)

Line of Duty

"Brilliant . . . fans of Tom Clancy and Scott Turow
will love Merline Lovelace . . . exciting . . . gutsy . . .
powerful."   —*Affaire de Coeur*

"Lovelace has created an interesting background for
this sizzling romance. The sparks explode off the
page."   —*Rendezvous*

"Evocative . . . high-energy . . . moves at an
incredible pace . . . keeps the suspense taut and the
romance hot. . . . A high-flying suspense novel from
an obviously accomplished writer."   —*Gothic Journal*

"Strong, action-packed stuff from Lovelace."

     —*Publishers Weekly*

"Fabulous . . . fantastic . . . dazzling . . .
extraordinarily powerful . . . has bestseller written all
over it."   —*I Love a Mystery*

DARK SIDE
OF DAWN

Merline Lovelace

A SIGNET BOOK

SIGNET
Published by New American Library, a division of
Penguin Putnam Inc., 375 Hudson Street,
New York, New York 10014, U.S.A.
Penguin Books Ltd, 27 Wrights Lane,
London W8 5TZ, England
Penguin Books Australia Ltd,
Ringwood, Victoria, Australia
Penguin Books Canada Ltd, 10 Alcorn Avenue,
Toronto, Ontario, Canada M4V 3B2
Penguin Books (N.Z.) Ltd, 182–190 Wairau Road,
Auckland 10, New Zealand

Penguin Books Ltd, Registered Offices:
Harmondsworth, Middlesex, England

First published by Signet, an imprint of New American Library,
a division of Penguin Putnam Inc.

First Printing, January 2001
10 9 8 7 6 5 4 3 2 1

This book is dedicated to the men and women I served with in the 1550th Combat Crew Training Wing—they gave me a true appreciation of that unique breed of warriors who fly in both the vertical and horizontal planes.

My special thanks to:

Lieutenant Colonel Brian Page, USAF, 1st Helicopter Squadron, who worked with me back in those final, hectic days of AFSC— never dreaming he'd one day provide the gritty detail for a thriller.

Captain Dona Zastrow, USAF, Special Missions Instructor Pilot, as sharp an officer as she is an aviator. Thanks for showing me the 1st Helo Squadron at its finest, Dona.

And most particularly,

Colonel Bob Sander, USA (Ret.), friend, comrade-in-arms, and repository of great war stories and chopper disasters. Keep those hairy details coming!

Chapter One

Air Force Captain Joanna West was just congratulating herself for catching a brisk tail wind and making up the twenty minutes lost due to her passenger's late arrival at the State Department's helo port when disaster struck.

The devil-red Ferrari didn't look like disaster when Jo first spotted it from the cockpit of her UH-1N. It looked like the fine piece of machinery it was, eating up the winding country road below with the ground-hugging grace of a predator. She identified the Italian sports car easily. With five brothers, each of whom considered himself the penultimate car guy, she'd been taught early to appreciate the beauty of a machine that could streak from zero to sixty in 5.3 seconds. This particular machine was headed south, cutting through the rolling green hills of Virginia's famed horse country at just about the same speed as her helo.

"Jesus!" Her copilot's reverent voice came over the cockpit intercom. "Look at that baby."

"I'm looking."

"How much do you think something like that costs?"

"More than we'll ever be able to afford," Jo replied dryly. "Something over two-hundred thousand, if I remember correctly."

With the ease of long practice, she kept one eye on the instruments, the other on the gleaming red Ferrari as it sped along the curving road. The bright September sunlight glinted on its windshield. Its chrome trim sparkled as if polished with diamond dust. Lord, what a beautiful piece of workmanship!

Her hands and feet light on the controls, Jo tipped the chopper's nose a few degrees to keep the Ferrari in sight. Known affectionately as the Huey to the two generations of military aviators—and not quite as affectionately by a number of other names—the UH-1N responded like the tried and true workhorse it was. The Vietnam-era helo was an old airframe, older than Jo herself and she'd be hitting the big three-oh in a few weeks. But it had been regularly modified over the years. Even more to the point, its proven reliability, easy maintenance, and superb safety record made it a joy to fly.

Jo knew the bird's moves almost as well as she knew her own. She should. She'd been flying Hueys for more than five years, first with a Rescue Squadron based out of California and now with the prestigious 1st Helicopter Squadron at Andrews Air Force Base, just across the Potomac from Washington, D.C. She'd been handpicked for this assignment and counted herself fortunate to wear the patch of the Fabled First.

Of course, the fact that she'd darted in under police sniper fire last spring to pluck Major Carly Samuel and former hockey star Ryan McMann from a raging flood might have had something to do with her current position. Carly's grateful mother, a powerful member of the U.S. House of Representatives, had "suggested" to the Air Force that they reward Jo's heroic actions by moving her to the Washington-based unit. A component of the 89th Wing, which provided airlift for the President and high-ranking VIPs, the 1st Helo Squadron accepted only the best of the best.

Jo had jumped at the assignment when it was offered. Career-wise, it was a great move. What's more, it had come at exactly the right point in her personal life. She'd just ended an engagement to another pilot, and welcomed the change of scene to help blunt the hurt of their breakup. She'd packed her bags, piled them into her cream-colored MG, and driven across country from her California base without looking back.

So here she was, ferrying passengers like Mrs. Beth Adair to high-level meetings and conferences. The tall, flame-haired Secretary of State and her entourage were now strapped in the seats behind Jo and her copilot, going over their notes for the speech Mrs. Adair was scheduled to give at the University of Virginia in Charlottesville.

The size of the Secretary of State's entourage had surprised Jo when she'd received the information for preflight planning, as did the fact that her passengers included a Secret Service detail. She'd been in the job long enough now to know that the Secret Service normally provided protection only for the President, Vice President, visiting heads of state, and their families. Although Jo wasn't privy to the specific rationale for this exception to the routine, she guessed the extra protection had to do with the Secretary's

tough-minded foreign diplomacy. News reports indicated that at least one terrorist group had targeted
Mrs. Adair personally.

Who woulda thunk it? Jo thought wryly. A small-
town Wisconsin girl rubbing elbows with the movers
and shakers of national and international policy. Four
months ago, she'd been flying rescue missions off the
coast of California. Now she was cruising along beside the smudgy purple peaks of Virginia's Blue Ridge
Mountains, peering through her helmet's sun-visor at
a bright red Ferrari as it cut through a patchwork of
green pastures, white rail fences, and windbreaks of
maple and oak ablaze in fall colors below.

She was taking a last admiring look at the Ferrari's
sculptured lines when it whizzed passed a tree-lined
side road. The moment the sports car sped by, a white
van pulled out. Within seconds, the van had nosed
up directly behind the speeding car. Their bumpers
almost kissed, then the Ferrari leaped forward in another burst of speed. Exhaust plumbed from the van
as its driver, too, laid the pedal to the metal and gave
chase.

Jo's copilot leaned into his shoulder harness and
squinted downward. Lieutenant Charlie Fairbanks
had logged only half the flying hours Jo had, but kept
a light hand on the stick. Jo had been pleased to draw
him and Staff Sergeant Mike McPeak, the flight engineer riding in the rear with the passengers, for this
mission.

"What the heck are they doing?" Charlie exclaimed.

"I don't know. Playing tag, maybe."

"Not too smart on these narrow roads."

Shrugging, Jo eased the stick to the left to tip the

aircraft into a turn. Suddenly, her hand froze on the controls. The Ferrari had headed into a turn as well, but too widely. Far too widely!

While Jo watched with her breath in her throat, the driver tried to cut his angle, overcorrected, and fish-tailed wildly across the road.

"He's going to hit!"

Charlie's grim prediction was no sooner out of his mouth than the Ferrari sideswiped a guard rail. Sparks flew as metal scraped along metal. For a moment, only a moment, it looked as though the driver might regain control. Then the car spun away from the rail and off the opposite side of the road. Its right side tipped high in the air. The left side dragging dirt, it crashed through a white fence and plowed a trench through a lush green pasture.

Either unable or unwilling to halt its own forward momentum, the white van sped right past the shattered fence. It didn't stop, didn't even slow, as a horrified Jo watched the Ferrari's wheels tip higher in the air. The sports car rolled, then rolled again, landing on its roof.

From her ringside seat, Jo couldn't miss the flames that licked at the front tires. Instinctively, she took the Huey into a steep bank, bringing it down for a closer look. Already startled by the careening Ferrari, a half dozen sleek Thoroughbreds grazing at the far end of the pasture took off at full gallop.

She was still making the sharp, descending turn when the senior Secret Service agent jumped onto the intercom. "What the hell's going on?"

Her eyes on the deadly fingers of fire licking at the front wheel wells, Jo keyed her mike. "A car just below us went off the road and rolled. I'm going down to take a look."

She instructed her copilot in the next breath. "Get on the net to the control tower. Ask them to notify the state troopers."

Charlie was already reaching for the bank of radio switches. "Roger."

"Tell them we'll stay on the scene until they arrive."

Jo's throat closed, almost choking off her words. Horrified, she spotted the Ferrari's driver, trying desperately to wiggle out the side window. He wouldn't make it! The flames now dancing around the front wheels had already generated a funnel of black smoke. The tires were burning. It was only a matter of moments . . . seconds . . . until the fire reached a fuel line.

Jo had only those seconds to weigh her responsibilities. First and foremost, she had to protect the VIP aboard her aircraft. That was her mission, her charge, her sworn duty. Yet she couldn't just sit back and let a man die when she had the means to save him.

"The driver's trapped in the vehicle," she advised the Secret Service rep. "We've got fuel suppressant fire extinguishers on board. I'm taking us down."

"That's not your decision to make!"

"I'm in command of this aircraft."

"And I'm in charge of Mrs. Adair's security detail. What if this is a setup? A terrorist ploy to draw her down into a trap?"

A burning vehicle? A trapped victim? Jo didn't think even the most sophisticated terrorist could stage a scene that precisely. But her passenger's safety had to remain a primary concern.

"The copilot will stay with the aircraft and lift off at any sign of danger," she informed the agent.

"I can't take that chance. I won't take that chance."

"I will." Mrs. Adair's authoritative voice came over the mike. "Take the chopper down, Captain."

Jo didn't need the sideways look Charlie shot her to know Beth Adair's concurrence wouldn't relieve the pilot-in-command of responsibility for this decision. She'd have to answer to her Director of Operations when she returned to Andrews Air Force base.

"Advise Andrews that I'm putting us down," she told Charlie tersely.

She banked and brought the Huey to earth far enough away from the wreck to protect both the aircraft and its passengers from the explosion that appeared more and more likely with each passing moment. Bright tongues of fire danced along the Ferrari's undercarriage. Black smoke billowed from its front end, drenching the fall afternoon in the scent of burning rubber.

Eyes stinging, nostrils pinched against the acrid stench, Jo threw her legs out of the cockpit and jumped down. Her one-piece resistant flight suit covered her in fire-resistant Nomex from her neck to her ankles. Her leather-palmed gloves would protect her hands, the helmet and visor would shield most of her face.

"Stay with the aircraft," she shouted to Charlie. "Keep the engines at one hundred percent."

"Roger."

She caught the extinguisher the flight engineer tossed her on the run. Sergeant McPeak jumped out and followed with the second extinguisher. Together they raced toward the burning vehicle. Her stomach clenching, Jo saw that it could go at any moment.

They aimed extinguishers at the dancing flames. Foam sizzled and spit on hot metal. Smoke billowed a dirty gray instead of black. For an anxious second or two, Jo thought they'd doused the fire. She'd barely dragged in a breath of relief when tiny tongues of red flickered anew inside the right front wheel well.

"Get back!" she shouted to the engineer. "I'll pull him out."

She didn't consciously weigh the fact that Sergeant McPeak was married with two small children, one of whom was on the waiting list for a kidney transplant. Jo had brought her aircraft down. The risk was hers and hers alone. Throwing up an arm to shield her face from the fierce heat, she darted in and bent to grab the driver's wrist.

Under more controlled circumstances, she would have assessed his injuries before attempting to move him. The present circumstances were about as uncontrolled as Jo ever wanted to experience. Digging both boot heels into the lush green pasture, she yanked on his arm.

He grunted, the sound barely audible over the blood roaring in her ears.

"Push!" she yelled. "Push!"

He lifted his head, his face white and strained, his jaw locked tight. "My . . . foot's . . . caught."

Cursing, she dropped flat on the ground beside him. She needed only one look to see that the Ferrari's roof had crumbled, pinning the driver's right leg between it and the steering wheel.

Jo carried a Swiss Army knife with the other survival gear in the pocket of her flight suit, but there wasn't time for an emergency amputation, even if she had the guts to perform one under these conditions.

Grappling through the window for a hold, Jo got a one-handed grip on his pants leg right above his ankle and yanked. His foot didn't budge.

"No . . . good. I'm . . . stuck." Sweat ran down his temples. "You'd better . . . get . . . back before . . . she . . . blows."

Ignoring the desperate croak, Jo put everything she had into another brutal pull on his trapped leg.

"Push, dammit!"

For a heart-stopping moment, nothing happened. Beneath her fingers, Jo felt his calf muscles bunch as he gathered himself for another, all-or-nothing push.

He came free with a grunt. White-faced, he tried to crawl away from the car.

Jo scrambled up and traded her death grip on his leg for one on his arm. Panting, her breath stabbing into her lungs, she dragged him away from the heat and the choking smoke.

An ominous hiss warned her the Ferrari was about to go. Flinging herself facedown, Jo covered its driver with her body. A half-second later, the world exploded around her.

Chapter Two

"Jesus! Captain! You okay?"

Jo barely heard the frantic shout above the roar in her ears. Sprawled atop the Ferrari's unmoving driver, she managed a shaky nod. She couldn't speak. Could hardly breathe. The explosion's percussive force had squeezed every ounce of air from her lungs. Swallowing convulsively, she sucked in several sharp gulps. The nauseous stink of burning rubber and gasoline stung her nostrils.

Craning her neck, Jo shot a quick glance over her shoulder. Flames engulfed the gleaming sports car—what was left of it. Heat rolled from the wreck in waves. A column of black smoke rose against the sky, desecrating the crisp autumn afternoon.

Only then did she shift her attention back to the man lying facedown under her. Turning her back on what could easily have become her funeral pyre, Jo pushed to one knee. She tugged off her helmet, tossed it aside, then peeled off her leather-palmed gloves and felt for a pulse in the side of the driver's neck.

It galloped almost as fast as hers. Shuddering with a combination of relief and delayed reaction, Jo sat back on her haunches. She was dragging in another long, shaky breath when the man stirred.

"Don't move until we check you for injuries," she instructed. "Mike, give me a hand here."

McPeak dropped to his knees beside her. Like most of the crew members selected for the 1st Helo Squadron, McPeak had several tours in combat rescue under his belt. While not trained to the same level of medical expertise as the teams who parachuted in to rescue downed crew members, both he and Jo had picked up enough of the basics to know they shouldn't move the victim until they'd ascertained the extent of his injuries.

With McPeak working beside her, Jo performed a quick visual of the prone driver. She spotted no awkwardly bent limbs, no protruding bones or external wounds staining his camel-colored sports coat.

"Can you move your head?"

"Yes. "

To prove his point, he lifted his cheek and turned toward her. When his gaze collided with hers, Jo felt the air leave her lungs a second time. She'd met some handsome men in her time. Even a few she'd classify as first-class hunks. None of them carried half the sheer male firepower as this one, however.

She formed a swift impression of coal black hair, slashing brows, a square jaw, and a sexy, dimpled chin. Blood from several small cuts streaked his face. A bruise was already forming on his temple. But it was the intensity of his eyes that grabbed her by the throat and refused to let go. The irises were a steely blue-gray, ringed at the edges with a band of darker midnight. Jo saw herself reflected in his pupils. They were normal, fixed, focused. Thankfully, he hadn't gone into shock.

"How about your arms?" she asked. "Can you move them? Your legs?"

"I'm okay."

"Take it easy. Let us roll you over."

With McPeak at his hips, Jo got a grip on his shoulders. He sported some hard muscle under that soft-as-angel's-hair jacket. Cashmere, she guessed. It would have to be cashmere to go with the Ferrari.

Slowly, gently, alert for any sign that the movement might aggravate possible internal injuries, Jo and the flight engineer eased the victim onto his back. The controlled movement took more effort than she'd expected. He packed some solid weight than his lean, elegant frame would suggest.

His shoulders had no sooner touched the clover than a shadow came up to block the sun. Those penetrating blue eyes sliced to the Secret Service agent looming over him. With a single glance, the driver took in the tense expression, the tailored suit, and the discreet wire trailing from the man's earpiece to disappear under his collar.

Under Jo's hands he went as taut as a steel cable. "Take it easy," she murmured. "He's one of the good guys."

His jaw hard, he sank back on the thick clover. "That's a matter of opinion."

She was still digesting that when the agent hunkered down on one knee beside her. "You okay, sir?"

"Yes."

"The state troopers and EMTs are on the way."

"I'm okay, I said."

Ignoring Jo's caution to remain still, he rolled onto a hip and got a knee under him. The agent rose, reaching out to help the other man up.

Ignoring the offer, the driver pushed to his feet. When he put some weight on the ankle that had been trapped by the Ferrari's crushed roof, white lines bracketed his mouth. He shrugged off the discomfort with an obvious effort and settled his elegantly tailored sports coat over his shoulders with a hitch of one shoulder.

"As soon as we ID'ed your license tag, we got on the net," the agent informed him. "Headquarters has notified your grandfather."

"Shit!"

Fury flashed in the driver's eyes. Those jet black brows slashed down. For a startling second or two, his classically handsome face hardened into something almost ugly.

"Dammit, you know my grandfather's condition."

"Yes, but—"

"You also know I've refused all Secret Service protection. I neither need nor want your agency's interference in my life."

The operative's jaw jutted. "Judging by what we just saw from the air, you might want to reconsider that position."

"Hell will freeze over first."

Totally lost by the terse exchange, Jo swept up a hand to clear the honey-blond strands that had straggled loose from her French braid and were now stuck to her forehead.

"Excuse me? Would someone care to clue me in here? Not that it particularly matters, you understand, but it might be nice to know who I almost went up in flames with."

The driver wiped the hostility off his face. It happened so smoothly, so swiftly, that Jo could only admire his rigid self-control. Her own temper rarely came to full boil, but when it did, her brothers had learned the hard way to stay out of her way until it cooled.

"Sorry," he said with a lopsided smile that set off a queer little pinging just beneath Jo's breastbone.

Good grief! The man ought to come packaged with a warning label. Handsome. Obviously rich. And too damned sexy for any woman's peace of mind.

He held out his hand. "I'm Alex. Alexander Taylor."

His strong, warm grip had enfolded hers before she made the connection.

Alexander Taylor! Former lieutenant governor of Virginia. Only grandson of John Tyree Taylor, who, according to those who tabulated such esoteric matters, was one of the richest men on the planet and, oh by the way, a former president of the United States.

Vague images from her childhood jumped into Jo's mind. Of TV cameramen crowding the participants in a White House Easter egg hunt. Of the proud, aristocratic President Taylor showing off his grandson to the American public. Alex had been a toddler then. Three or four. Just about Jo's own age. She remembered envying him for the fact that he got to scarf up all those candy eggs.

Her memory bank churned up a kaleidoscope of images of a grown Alex Taylor. Most were gleaned from the tabloids and magazine cover stories that invariably touted his ancestry along with his devastating good looks. She remembered reading, somewhere that he'd attended Princeton, that he'd married an heiress, was elected Virginia's lieutenant governor on his first try, and was thinking of running for governor.

Then, three years ago, his wife had died after a short, tragic illness. He'd served out his term, she remembered, then disappeared from the public eye. Or at least from the tabloids.

Somehow, Taylor had managed to live the past few years of his life outside the vicious media glare that spotlighted every move made by other famous progeny like John Kennedy Jr. and the British royals. But not without extraordinary effort, Jo soon learned. Stunned, she heard him berate himself for endangering both her life and his own in a stubborn attempt to elude the media.

"You think that's who was chasing you in that white van?" she gasped. "Paparazzi?"

"I don't think," he bit out. "I know. That son of a bitch has been on my tail for the past . . ." He caught himself, once again exercising that awesome self-control. "Please excuse my language. I guess I'm still a little ragged around the edges."

Jo was still a little ragged, too. She unraveled even more when he caught her hand and lifted it to his lips.

"I owe you my life. It's a debt I may never be able to repay."

Before she could make it clear she wasn't expecting payment, he brushed a kiss across her knuckles.

"Thank you."

The old-fashioned gesture was at once absurd and astonishingly elegant. If Jo hadn't been standing with her boots ankle deep in clover and her hair no doubt flying all over the place after parting company with her helmet, she might have imagined herself a debutante in virginal white, crowned with a wreath of roses.

Feeling her face heat up, she glanced helplessly at Taylor, at the Secret Service agent, at Sergeant McPeak, at Taylor again.

"You're welcome."

Those fascinating, light-dark blue eyes trailed down her face and neck to the name patch attached with Velcro to her flight suit.

"Jo West," he read in a soft murmur. "Captain, United States Air Force."

"That's me." She eased her hand out of his hold. "And this is Sergeant Mike Mc—"

"Alex!"

The Secretary of State's crisp New England accent cut through Jo's introduction of her flight engineer. Flanked by the rest of her security detail, Beth Adair rushed forward.

"I couldn't believe it when I heard that car belonged to you. Are you all right?"

Taylor took her outstretched hands in both of his. "I'm fine, Beth. Thanks to Captain West."

"And Sergeant McPeak," Jo put in quickly. "Mike McPeak."

If there were any thanks to spread around for this save, she wanted them to include the flight engineer. Any criticism, she'd handle herself.

Releasing Ms. Adair's hands, Taylor took a step to-

ward McPeak. "You have my most profound gratitude, Sergeant. I..."

He broke off, grimacing, as his right leg buckled.
Jo, two Secret Service agents, Beth Adair, and the flight
engineer all jumped forward. They were just lower-
ing him to the ground once more when the wail of a
siren sounded in the distance.

Within moments, three police cars had converged
on the scene. They were followed in short order by an
ambulance ablaze with flashing lights, two fire trucks,
another police car, and a black-and-silver Bronco. Suddenly, the quiet field overflowed with emergency response personnel. Police radios crackled. Red and blue
strobes flashed a dizzying pattern.

It hadn't taken long for word to spread that the
Secretary of State and the grandson of a president had
made unscheduled stops in the area.

Jo and her flight engineer found themselves edged
to the sidelines by the chief of Ms. Adair's security
detail. Jo might be in command aboard her aircraft.
The burly Secret Service agent left no doubt that he
was in charge on the ground.

Her copilot joined them a moment later. "I gave
the Operations Control Center an updated report."

"Thanks, Charlie."

He slanted her a sideways glance. "Ops Control re-
layed a message from the DO. He wants you to report to his office as soon as we return to base."

"Why doesn't that surprise me?"

Jo could just imagine the reams of reports this little incident would generate. Sighing, she waited pa-
tiently while the paramedics gave Taylor a thorough
once-over. Beth Adair countered his objections to

being strapped onto a stretcher and convinced him to let the medical crew take whatever measures they deemed appropriate.

Appropriate turned out to be immediate transfer to the local hospital for X rays and treatment for superficial lacerations, bruised ribs, and a possible broken ankle. A uniformed trooper climbed into the ambulance to take Taylor's statement during the ride in.

Another trooper approached the flight crew. After jotting down their names, addresses, and phone numbers, he cut to Jo.

"Mrs. Adair's security detail wants to get her back in the air as quickly as possible, so I'll make this brief and follow up by phone if necessary."

"Good enough."

"I understand you witnessed the accident?"

Jo nodded.

"Will you describe what happened in your own words, please?"

He scribbled furiously as she related the series of events. When she mentioned how the white van had almost crawled up the Ferrari's trunk, he shot her a swift look.

"Did this van actually impact Mr. Taylor's car? Force him to swerve or take evasive action?"

"I didn't see any actual contact. Taylor hit the gas to pull away, then took a corner too wide."

"That's the story he gave us, too," the trooper remarked, as if disappointed he didn't have something more sensational on his hands. "You didn't by any chance get the van's license tag?"

"No."

Neither had the copilot nor the engineer. The trooper

took their statements, as well, before giving in to the unspoken pressure exerted by the Secret Service. Tipping two fingers to his hat brim, he advised them he'd get in touch if he needed more detail.

Fifteen minutes later, the blue-and-white Huey lifted off. The half dozen police officers and accident investigation personnel still in the field clamped onto their hats in the vicious downdraft. Jo's last glimpse of the scene was the blackened remains of the once gleaming Ferrari.

The Secretary of State gave a gracious, if somewhat abbreviated speech in Charlottesville. They made the return to the capital without incident, bucking the wind that had cut so much time off the trip out.

By the time Jo put the skids down on the Andrews Air Force Base ramp just after 4:00 P.M., she was feeling the effects of the long flight and the desperate rescue. In addition to the mental fatigue that came with hours at the controls, her arms ached from her elbows to her shoulder sockets from the strain of pulling Taylor out of the burning vehicle. She'd washed up during the wait in Charlottesville, but the smell of burning rubber clung to her hair and flight suit. The smoke she'd inhaled had burned a raw line down the back of her throat.

She croaked out the after-landing and engine shutdown checklist, wishing she could climb out of the chopper, complete the aircraft forms, conduct a quick crew debrief, and head for her car. Instead, she gave Ops Control a detailed update on the flight deviation and logged the event in the Flight Log Book, then reported to the Director of Operations.

The DO was waiting for her. Most of the administrative personnel had already left, so Jo rapped once on the door frame and poked her head inside his office.

"You wanted to see me, sir?"

Lieutenant Colonel Marshall's head jerked up. His bushy brows snapped into a brown, furry line. Since those thick brows constituted the only hair on his otherwise bald head, the effect was instant, direct, and disconcerting.

"Yes. Come in and grab a seat."

Edging past the helo seat from Lyndon Johnson's Huey, which occupied a sizable portion of the paneled office, Jo dropped into one of the chairs spaced around the conference table in front of the colonel's desk.

"What the hell happened down there this afternoon, West? We've been fending calls from everyone from the White House Press Secretary to the Undersecretary of State to the editor of the *National Enquirer.*"

"You're kidding! The *Enquirer* is already onto this?"

"Unfortunately," he grumbled. "All right, Captain, report."

Succinctly, Jo ran through the sequence of events from the moment she spotted the Ferrari to liftoff from Charlottesville. Marshall didn't speak during the briefing, but his brows dropped lower and lower by the second. When she finished, he leaned forward, threaded his knuckles together on the cluttered desk, and fed the pertinent details back to her.

"Let me get this straight. You deviated from your approved flight pattern with a Code Two on board. You overruled her security chief's objections and made an unscheduled landing. In the process, you saved the life of the grandson of an ex-president of the United States."

"That about sums it up."

"You don't do anything by halves, do you, West?"

"No, sir."

He thumped his thumbs on his folded hands. "You know you violated both Secret Service and FAA directives this afternoon."

"Yes, sir."

"From what you've told me, I think you exercised sound judgment in doing so."

She blew out a relieved breath. Too soon, it turned out. Colonel Marshall's thumbs thumped again. Once. Twice.

"Unfortunately, you also caused a small stampede."

"Stampede? Oh, the horses." She'd forgotten all about them.

"Not just horses, West. Thoroughbreds. Worth collectively several million dollars, or so the owner claims."

A sudden premonition of disaster curled in the pit of Jo's stomach. Only last year, a low pass over a Maryland turkey ranch had frightened the birds into a wild charge. They'd crushed up against the wall of their pens in a big, feathery mass. Hundreds had suffocated, and while the crew dogs all joked about it now, the poor pilot involved at the time had been charged with failure to operate his aircraft at an altitude and airspeed that precluded damage to property or persons on the ground.

"Please don't tell me one of those million-dollar Thoroughbreds broke a leg," she begged.

"No. It fell into a ditch and broke its neck."

Jo groaned. Seconds ticked by. She braced herself for what was coming.

"Because of the deviations from FAA and AF directives and the potential claims against the government, I'll have to pull you off flying status while we conduct an informal inquiry."

She gulped. "Yes, sir."

Marshall's furry brows lifted an inch or so. Although he had to maintain an impartial objectivity, encouragement and sympathy flickered in his dark eyes.

"You saved a man's life, Captain. That counts for a hell of a lot more than a horse in my book. I'll see that the inquiry is conducted as expeditiously as possible."

"Thanks."

"Now go home, get some rest, and report to the Training Office tomorrow. Captain Kastlebaum will keep you occupied while the inquiry's in process."

Jo's heart sank. Being grounded was bad enough. Being detailed to work with the one person in the squadron she actively disliked made it even worse.

"Yes, sir."

Twilight was starting to descend when she walked outside a few minutes later. She couldn't believe that only seven hours had passed since the last time she'd exited the same building . . . or that her life had taken such a dramatic turn in the same short time.

She'd never been grounded before. Never been the subject of an inquiry, informal or otherwise. Having her wings clipped made her heart thump hollowly in her chest.

She'd been born to fly. She'd recognized that fact the first time her dad took her up with him in the twin-engine Cessna he piloted while covering his farm-checkered Wisconsin territory for the American Dairymen's Association and let her pretend to take the controls. She'd earned her private pilot's license at sixteen, and received offers for an appointment to both West Point and the Air Force Academy while a senior in high school.

Having grown up the only daughter with five rowdy and all-too-protective brothers, Jo had no desire to subject herself to the predominantly male environment of the military academies. She'd opted for UW instead and thoroughly enjoyed four years of Badger football, frat parties, and freedom from brotherly interference, all subsidized by a generous scholarship and the part-time job she'd stumbled into her first year in Madison.

After hearing about Jo from a friend, a chopper pilot with a local TV station had offered to teach her the thrills of operating in both the vertical and horizontal planes, with the promise of a job on the news crew if she didn't crack up and kill herself first. She'd jumped at the offer, and was hooked from the first time she'd climbed into the cockpit of a rotary-wing aircraft.

Unlike flying a fixed-wing aircraft, piloting a helo required an instinctive coordination that relatively few people possessed. It had nothing to do with athletic ability or training or even intelligence. You either had it, or you didn't.

With a control for each hand and foot, any action by one appendage required a corresponding action on all other controls to maintain attitude. Even more to the point, the aerodynamics that governed fixed-wing flight didn't play with choppers. When you increased power, natural forces would cause the whole helo to spin unless you also increased power to the tail rotor to keep it in trim.

As Jo learned her first time up, an airplane wants to fly. A helo doesn't. It was that simple. And challenging.

It hadn't taken her long to realize that the military offered her the best opportunity to hone her skills as a chopper pilot. She'd signed up for AF ROTC, been commissioned after graduation from UW, and gone through undergraduate pilot training at Fort Rucker in Alabama. After five years flying helos, first in Rescue, now at the Fabled First, she couldn't imagine doing anything else.

She didn't want to do anything else.

Trying not to give in to a fluttery feeling of panic at the thought of being grounded, Jo crossed the parking lot. A brisk wind had swept away the tang of aviation fuel that usually hovered over the flight line area and replaced it with the scent of autumn. Just enough chill invaded the air to make her wish for the leather aircrew jacket she'd left in the backseat of her car this morning.

Helmet bag slung over her shoulder, she made for her car. Dry leaves crunched underfoot. She was halfway across the parking lot before she noticed the figure lounging against the black Chevy Blazer parked next to her MG. Arms folded, the collar of his leather flight jacket turned up against the chill, Captain Deke

Elliott gave her one of his patented, lazy once-overs as she approached.

"Hey, Wonder Woman."

She bit back a rueful smile at the nickname her fellow pilots had given her after word of her daring rescue of Major Samuel last spring.

"Hey yourself, Elliott."

"Heard you added another notch to your belt this afternoon."

"Yeah, well, Wonder Woman just got grounded because of it. Someone else will have to fly her glass plane for a while."

He cocked his head. "The DO's going to direct an inquiry?"

"You got it." Unlocking her car door, Jo tossed her gear bag into the backseat. "What are you doing here this late?"

"I thought you might need a beer after you got through with Marshall."

She hesitated, all too aware of the glint in his hazel eyes. If she'd been the least inclined to fly in close formation with anyone in the squadron, Deke Elliott would be her first choice. Tall, rangy, and leather tough, he filled out a flight suit the way it was meant to be filled. His sense of humor and the slow-as-sin Wyoming drawl he switched on and off with such devastating effect were even more attractive.

But Jo had traveled down that road once. Somehow the love she'd been so sure would last forever had gotten all tangled up in conflicting schedules and differing career goals. In good-natured rivalries for ratings, for schools, for additional responsibilities and challenges. After a while, the rivalry had grown a little too keen, the competition a little too cutting. Finally, Jo had opted out—out of the competition, out of the squadron, out of her brief but disastrous engagement.

The breakup had been mutual, but when she remembered the rosy dreams that had accompanied the emerald-cut diamond solitaire Brian had slipped on her finger, she still felt a sting of regret. Regret, and a determination not to subject herself to that kind of hurt again.

On the other hand, she could use someone to talk to right now. She was still debating the matter when Deke's mouth tipped.

"All I'm offering is a sympathetic ear and a cold Heineken, West."

Dammit, he must have known she couldn't resist the challenge in that mocking grin.

"I'm from Wisconsin," she tossed back. "Care to change that to a Schlitz?"

"'The beer that made Milwaukee famous?' Sure."

"I'll meet you at the Officers' Club."

Chapter Three

Jo woke to hazy daylight and a muffled sound outside her bedroom window. She shot upright in bed, eyes wide and unfocused, clutching the down-filled quilt Granny Modl had hand-stitched and folded into her only granddaughter's as-yet unneeded wedding chest.

The abrupt movement caused the room to tilt. Groaning, Jo dropped the quilt and put up a hand to message her temples.

Damn Elliott for goading her last night!

And damn her own, built-in competitiveness!

Just because she'd never backed down from a dare tossed at her by any one of her five brothers didn't mean that she had to beat *every* male at *every* endeavor, Mortal Kombat included.

She and Deke had limited themselves to two beers at the Officers' Club. Neither of them harbored any desire for a DUI that would terminate their respective careers. But one mocking challenge inevitably led to another, and somehow Jo had found herself taking him on in a series of no-holds-barred, knock-'em-dead video games.

Deke certainly knew how to operate a joy stick,

she'd discovered. Hunched over the machine, his flight suit molding those broad shoulders, he'd zigged in answer to every one of Jo's zags, and fired off a steady stream of killer electronic bullets.

He also, she remembered, massaging her aching forehead, didn't take kindly to having his butt kicked. Pointedly, Jo had suggested that he should think twice in the future before challenging someone with five brothers to a video-duel.

She'd called a halt sometime after midnight, exhilarated by her final championship win. They'd parted company in the O Club parking lot, Deke still smarting from his defeat and Jo still smugly triumphant. The long day had caught up with her on the drive home. Vaguely, she recalled decompressing as the MG wound along darkened Maryland roads to Fort Washington, the sleepy suburb on the Potomac where Jo had rented a house. The bedroom door had barely closed behind her before she'd stripped down to her black cotton sports bra and high-on-the-thigh black panties, and nose-dived into oblivion.

She might still be out cold if something hadn't jerked her into consciousness. Frowning, she lowered her hand and squinted at the scraggly rays filtering through the miniblinds. She had almost convinced herself that she'd imagined the noise when she heard it again.

A small scrape, like a tree branch hitting the window. Only there weren't any trees that close to the bedroom.

Shoving aside the quilt, she swung out of bed and padded across the room. Goose bumps danced along her thighs and midriff, her bare skin registering the chill.

If Jo had been thinking about something other than the slap of cold linoleum against her naked feet or the headache that bored straight in from either side of her temples, she might have had the sense to peek around the edge of the blinds. Like a fool, she simply pulled on the cord enough to allow her to peer out . . . and allow the stranger standing right outside her window to peer in.

For a startled second they gaped at each other, Jo in her skimpy underwear and the outsider in a yellow plaid shirt, royal blue down vest, and a red-and-gold Washington Redskins ball cap. The stalemate broke when the stranger whipped up a camera.

His finger had started pumping before Jo could do much more than let out an indignant yelp and jump back.

"Pervert!"

Her furious shout didn't faze him. He clicked away as she grabbed for the cord and yanked. To her dismay, the hard tug brought the miniblind out of its brackets and down on her head. Spitting a stream of curses, Jo tossed aside the crinkling aluminum.

The blinds hit the linoleum with a clatter. Tight-jawed, she spun away from the still madly shooting cameraman and rushed for the door. She'd lugged her brother Dave's baseball bat around with her ever since she'd left home for college. This seemed like as good a time as any to put it to use. The pervert and his expensive-looking camera were dead meat.

Charging down the hall, she dug into the closet for the bat and a flannel-lined denim jacket and raced for the front door. She had one arm in the jacket sleeve and the bat in the other hand when she got the door open. A blast of cold air hit her. Fingers of frost rose from the ground.

That was all Jo noticed before she stopped dead on the front stoop, stunned by the sight that greeted her. At least a dozen vehicles crowded the minuscule front yard. One van sported the NBC peacock, she noted with disbelief, another the black-and-white CBS eye. A small crowd milled outside the vehicles, talking, stomping their feet against the early dawn chill, holding paper cups of coffee. Suddenly, one of them spotted her.

"There she is!"

The shout went up, almost like a baying call of hounds alerted to a fresh scent. Before Jo's astonished eyes, coffee cups went flying, van doors were yanked opened, reporters and camera operators grabbed for their equipment.

"Captain West!" A dark-haired female in a red jacket and silky black pants pounded toward her, mike in hand. "Is it true you pulled Alexander Taylor from a burning car yesterday?"

"I, uh . . ."

"How badly was he hurt?"

"Can you tell us exactly how the accident occurred?"

"What was Mrs. Adair's reaction when you put your chopper down?"

The questions were thrown at her from every direction. One distinguished, gray-haired reporter savagely elbowed his way to the front of the pack.

"Why won't Air Force Public Affairs release the details of yesterday's incident?"

At that point two salient facts finally penetrated Jo's stunned brain. One, a half-dozen TV cameras were now capturing her with hair uncombed, teeth unbrushed, and jacket dangling half off one arm to expose a wide expanse of bare flesh. And two, the Air Force wasn't talking, which meant she'd better not, either.

"Sorry." She grabbed behind her for the door. "I have no comment at this time."

"Come on, Captain, give us a break here!"

"At least tell us if you think Taylor was drunk or on drugs when he rolled his car."

"No, I can't comment on . . ."

She broke off, her heart jumping as she caught sight of a red-and-gold Redskins ball cap. It sat atop the head of a photographer who at that moment darted around the corner of her house and aimed for a white van parked on the grass—the same white van that had almost crawled up the trunk of the Ferrari! Jo was sure of it!

"Hey! You!"

She tried to catch his attention over the clamor of the reporters still tossing questions at her. When that failed, she jumped up a few times in a futile attempt to snag the numbers from the license plate. She succeeded only in snagging a boom mike on the temple.

"Ouch!"

"Hey, watch the mike, lady!"

Shooting the man at the other end of the boom an evil glare, she backed inside the house, slammed the door, and slumped against the sturdy panel.

Good grief! Was this what the Alexander Taylors of the world went through every time they ventured beyond their secluded, secure domains? Was this what Princess Diana had endured for so many years before her tragic death?

Thoroughly rattled, she made her way around the small house, closing the blinds she hadn't bothered with late last night.

She'd grown careless living in her little rented place, she realized belatedly. The tiny, two-bedroom home was set back, well off Riverview Road, several miles from the million dollar residences that had sprung up farther down the Potomac. The brick and clapboard structure had been built in the 1930s, when the Maryland side of the river was still dotted with small truck farms. Tall shade trees surrounded the house, and the open fields behind it that had once produced acres of sweet, silver-peg corn had long since stubbled over.

The original owners had deeded the property down through the family to its current owner, a former member of the 1st Helo Squadron. Convinced that the acreage with its view of the Potomac would only increase in value over time, he'd held on to his inheritance and rented it out to a succession of 1st HS personnel. Luckily, Jo had been tapped for her assignment to Andrews the same week the previous renter received orders to Hawaii. She'd negotiated a one-year lease over the phone, sight unseen.

To her delight, the tiny house gave her the feeling of living in the country while still allowing her to enjoy the benefits of the sophisticated capital just across the river. She loved the gold-leafed birches edging the fields, the silvery Potomac glistening less than a hundred yards away. She loved even more the winding side roads to the base that bypassed the traffic-clogged Beltway.

At this particular moment, however, the house's isolation presented a real challenge. The prospect of dodging reporters and camera operators while she made her way to the detached garage, then backed her MG through the throng was a bit daunting. Maybe they'd all give up and depart the premises by the time she showered and dressed.

No such luck. The media was still camped outside when she grabbed her car keys and her black leather clutch purse. Angling her flight cap over her forehead, Jo drew in a deep breath and let herself out the back door.

Head up, a smile fixed firmly in place, she waded through the swarm that buzzed around her within seconds of stepping outside. It took some doing, but she stuck to her "no comment" and managed to back out of the drive without flattening anyone.

She didn't breathe easy until she'd left the Potomac behind, cut across Indian Head Highway, and hit Allentown Road. Only a few of the most persistent reporters still followed, probably hoping to grab an interview on base. Fine. She'd let the wing's public affairs officer handle them.

Twenty minutes later, she joined the streams of traffic pouring in through Andrew's West Gate. The guard checked her decal and saluted her through. Since the primary mission of the 89th Wing was to provide transport for the President of the United States, the vice president, cabinet members, and other high-ranking U.S. and foreign government officials, security at the base always remained tight. When Air Force One was being readied for flight or world events turned especially nasty, security got even tighter.

Cutting past the three-story, semicircular headquarters building set at the end of flag-draped Command Drive, she headed for the flightline that bisected the base from north to south. As the MG crawled along at the mandated 25 mph, Jo's satisfaction at eluding the media slowly seeped away. The closer she got to the hangar housing the 1st Helo Squadron, the glummer she felt at having to report to the Training Office instead of to Operations to pick up her next mission.

Nor did her mood improve when she walked into the Training Section and found the chief already in his favorite position. Boots crossed on his desk, toothpick protruding through the gap between his front teeth, Captain Henry Kastlebaum grinned at her.

"Hey, West. Marshall told me you hot-dogged yourself right into an inquiry board. Way to go, sweetcakes."

The master sergeant updating a status board on the other side of the room rolled her eyes.

Jaw set, Jo decided she might as well get things straight. "Since we're going to be working together for a few days—"

"A few weeks, babe. These things do take time."

"Since we're going to be working together for an unspecified period of time," Jo amended, praying he was wrong, "let's deep-six the cutesy nicknames and keep it professional."

"Don't get your buns in a pucker." Unperturbed,

Kastlebaum folded his hands across his stomach. "What's the scoop on this Taylor jerk? Did he really roll a Ferrari?"

Jo tossed her purse onto an empty desk. "Yes."

"I couldn't believe the pictures when I saw them. What a waste of a gorgeous machine."

"What pictures?"

"In the *Post*."

Her jaw sagged. "The *Washington Post*?"

Grinning, Kastlebaum thumped a folded newspaper with his boot heel. "Morning edition, sweetcakes. Front page."

She nailed him to his chair with a lethal glare. "Call me sweetcakes one more time and you'll be chewing on that toothpick from the inside out."

Striding across the room, she jerked the paper from under his boot heel. Her first reaction was astonishment at the clarity of the pictures that took up half the front page. Her second, fury.

There she was, her face scrunched with intense effort, dragging Alexander Taylor through a cloud of black smoke. The shot was so close-up, so fine-grained, that she guessed immediately it had been taken with one of those gargantuan telescopic lenses by the same creep who'd all but run Taylor off the road. Evidently he'd pulled over and doubled back to shoot pictures of a man about to burn to death.

The bastard!

No doubt he'd crowed all the way back to D.C. over his exclusive scoop. If Jo ever, *ever*, spotted that white van again, she'd do a little running off the road herself.

Disgusted, she tossed the paper back at Kastlebaum. She wouldn't even dignify the story by reading it.

"You want to tell me what I can do around here for the next few days?"

"Weeks, West. Weeks." Still grinning, he pushed to his feet and tugged his flight cap out of his leg pocket. "Tobias will fill you in on what needs to be done. I've got a check ride this morning. See you around, babe-ettes."

"Asshole." Master Sergeant Tobias made the observation under her breath before turning a smile on Jo. "Welcome to the Training Section, Captain. It's a pleasure to have you here."

Jo wished she could say the same. The best she could manage was an answering smile. "Thanks."

"Grab a cup of coffee and I'll show you the drill."

A petite blonde and one of the youngest Air Force NCOs to sew on Master Sergeant stripes, Gretchen Tobias was a recognized expert in the training business. She'd recently spent a month down at the headquarters of the Air Education and Training Command in San Antonio, helping revise the proficiency modules for enlisted aircrew members. It was common knowledge that she ran the 1st Helo Squadron's training program with little input either asked for or received from her nominal boss, Henry Kastlebaum.

Under normal circumstances, Jo would have enjoyed learning the intricacies of the system that kept both support and aircrew personnel up to speed in their various specialties. These were hardly normal circumstances.

She crossed to the coffeepot and filled a mug decorated with 1st Helo Squadron's patch. She was on her way back across the room when the photo in the *Post* attracted her gaze once more.

The idea that someone could photograph such a desperate act and not even try to help made her feel ill. It also killed any thought of cooperating with the media or handing out interviews. Her no comment would stand as just that. Public Affairs could handle any inquiries that might come in regarding her involvement.

Which is what she told the wing PA officer when he called twenty minutes later to request that she report to his office to help respond to the calls and requests for information that were flooding in.

"I'll be happy to give you the details. You can dole them out to the media as you see fit."

"They want to talk to you."

"I'm facing a board of inquiry. I'm not talking to anyone until that's behind me."

"All right, all right. Just get up here to fill me in."

"Have you cleared this with Colonel Marshall?"

"Christ!"

From the muttered exclamation, Jo gathered the wing PA wasn't having a fun morning. Tough. Neither was she.

"Yes, Captain, I've cleared it with your DO. Now get in gear."

Jo's day went from bad to worse.

Stories started popping up on the local news stations, featuring stills of Alexander Taylor, footage of an incinerated Ferrari, and vivid shots of an Air Force captain wearing little more than her underwear and

a look of owlish surprise. Kastlebaum, of course, rode
her unmercifully.

Afternoon brought the late edition of one of the
more notorious supermarket tabloids, with even more
revealing photos taken from right outside her bedroom window. The caption over the pictures suggested a nauseating "cosmic bond" between reclusive
Alexander Taylor and his curvaceous rescuer.

The paper made the rounds of the squadron at warp
speed. For the rest of the afternoon Jo got a chorus of
hoots and catcalls from her fellow aviators—not particularly known for their sensitivity—whenever she
walked down the corridor.

Even Deke Elliott smirked when he strolled into
the training office later that afternoon, a newspaper
folded conspicuously under one arm.

Jo's eyes narrowed. "Do *not* say a word."

"That's going to make it kinda tough for me to ask
for a Mortal Kombat rematch."

His Wyoming twang was out in full force. Jo
rounded her vowels and shot back in her Wiscon-
sin/Minnesota deep woods accent.

"Ooooh, and do you want me to give you another
shellacking, then, big fella?"

A gleam she couldn't mistake jumped into Deke's
eyes. She knew then that a shellacking wasn't all he
wanted from her.

Alarms starting clanging like crazy up and down
Jo's nervous system. With every feminine instinct in
her body, she sensed that she and Deke were fast ap-
proaching what the old SAC bomber crews used to
call the failsafe point, the point of no return. She could
either put the skids on their banter—and the sim-

mering physical attraction neither had yet acknowledged—right here, right now, or follow them through
to their natural conclusion.

For the rest of her life Jo would wonder whether
she would've decided to go or to no-go. Before she
could make up her mind, the decision was snatched
out of her hands by Gretchen Tobias. Her face alight
with excitement, the senior NCO poked her head into
the office.

"You'd better grab your hat and come outside, Captain."

"Why?"

"Just grab your hat. I don't want to spoil the surprise."

"What surprise?" Jo eyed her warily. "There isn't
another crowd of photographers lying in wait for me,
is there?"

A sympathetic smile flitted across the sergeant's
mouth. No woman likes being photographed with uncombed hair and a naked face.

"No, it's nothing like that. Come on, Captain.
You've gotta see this."

Still suspicious, Jo shagged her hat from the zip-
pered leg pocket of her flight suit. With Deke right
behind her, she followed the sergeant down the corridor. Moments later the three of them stepped out
into the parking lot, where a stretch limo sat with engine idling. A uniformed chauffeur leaned against the
gleaming black monster, chatting with the crowd of
Air Force personnel gathered around him. When
someone pointed out Jo, he pushed off the fender.

"Captain West?"

"Yes," she answered, still wary.

"I'm Patrick Smith, ma'am. Mr. Taylor's driver. Mr. Alexander Taylor," he clarified, separating the grandson from his famous grandfather. "He sent me to pick you up."

"Pick me up for what?"

"If you have time, he'd like to see you. To thank you privately for saving his life."

Chapter Four

Jo lounged in a cloud of soft leather as the stretch limo glided across the base, out the front gate, and onto the Suitland Parkway. Crystal tumblers tinkled in their holders. A single white rose in a silver vase gave off a delicate perfume. The slow, powerful strains of Dvořák's New World Symphony filtered through the limo's speakers. Jo knew the piece well, having suffered along with the rest of her family until her brother Matt finally gave up his misguided goal of becoming a tuba virtuoso in favor of high school wrestling.

"Now this," she announced to the driver sitting what seemed like half a mile away, "is the only way to fly."

He grinned at her in the rearview mirror. Lifting her Champagne flute in a toast, Jo let the bubbles tickle her nose before taking another sip. She didn't recognize the label of the dew-streaked bottle resting in a crystal ice bucket, but then, she rarely indulged in Champagne. Wisconsin born and bred, her preferences ran to beer and thick frou-frou drinks like the grasshoppers and White Russians so popular in the pubs around the University of Wisconsin's Madison campus.

But this particular brand of bubbly wasn't bad.

Not bad at all.

Nor was the town house the limo glided to a halt in front of some forty minutes later. It was located in the heart of old Georgetown, where brick-paved sidewalks undulated over the roots of ancient oaks and real estate cost more than the average mortal would earn in a lifetime. The three-story residence ruled the quiet street like a dowager queen, tall, stately, with generations of ivy draped like lace against its white facade. Golden light spilled from wavy-paned windows. The gas-lit brass lanterns mounted on either side of the front entrance glowed a welcome.

The limo pulled into the pillared port cocherie, lit by a massive carriage lantern suspended overhead. Fallen leaves skittered along the otherwise immaculately swept drive, crunching under Jo's boots as she climbed out of the limo.

"So this is where the rich and famous hang out," she murmured, more than a little awed by the understated splendor.

Smith smiled an assent. "When they're in town."

She stood on the brick-lined drive for a moment, breathing in the scent of damp leaves and chrysanthemums. Someone had a fire going. The tang of burning wood hung on the night, along with a crisp chill that made her glad she'd lifted her leather jacket out of her car before climbing into the limo.

"I thought I read somewhere that Mr. Taylor lives in the country."

The chauffeur's smile faded, leaving his expression

a bland mask. "Mr. Taylor does prefer the farm at Chestnut Hill, particularly since his wife died," he confirmed.

His reference to that tragic affair was almost lost in the rustle of leaves as a night breeze teased the oaks on either side of the drive.

"This way, Captain."

He ushered her up the stairs toward the black-painted door, which swung open as they approached. Handing Jo off to the butler with a promise to return her to the base whenever she was ready, the driver melted back into the shadows.

"Good evening, Captain West."

The butler or majordomo or whatever this dignified individual was called led Jo inside. She stepped into a black-and-white tiled foyer, illuminated by a chandelier that sprouted what looked like a thousand or so crystal drops. Waterford, she guessed, and not of recent vintage.

"Mr. Taylor is waiting for you in the library. This way, if you please."

Her first impression of the high-ceilinged room was one of dark wood and ancient treasures. Bookcases filled with leather-bound volumes lined three walls, interspersed at intervals with still lifes done by old masters and narrow windows draped in midnight blue velvet. A massive fireplace dominated the fourth wall, its flames leaping brightly.

Her second impression was that the library was the perfect backdrop for the men who occupied the wingback chairs placed before the fire. The older of the two rose at her entrance. With his horn-rimmed glasses, feathery fringe of white hair, and leather elbow patches on his gray wool jacket, he looked at home amid the fine antiques.

The younger sat with his bandaged ankle propped on a tapestry footstool. In contrast to the scholarly looking older man, Alexander Taylor's black sweater molded his lean frame with the elegance of handwoven Persian mohair and his tan slacks had obviously been tailored by the hand of an expert.

It was the man who captured Jo's interest, however, not his clothes. As before, his potent masculinity grabbed her right by the throat. Those odd, intense eyes, made even more vivid by the backdrop of the blue velvet drapes, seemed to pierce right through her.

"Please excuse me for not rising, Captain. It's still a bit difficult, even with the crutches."

She took the hand he offered. "You're excused. I'm just glad to see you're not sporting a cast."

"There was some debate about that for a while, but cooler heads prevailed."

"Yours?" she guessed.

"Mine," he admitted, his mouth curving above his strong, indented chin. Jo had never paid much attention to men's chins before. Amazing how a Kirk Douglas dimple could make such a statement.

"This is Doctor Martin Russ," he said, indicating his other guest with a nod.

"Hello, Doctor." Jo took the elderly man's fingers in an easy grip. "Sounds like you have your hands full with your patient."

"I'm not Mr. Taylor's physician," he corrected with a smile in his cloudy blue eyes. "I'm his historian."

Jo figured it was an honest enough mistake, given

the fact that she'd never met anyone who employed a personal historian before.

"I'm writing the Taylor family chronicles," the doctor explained. "And," he added, catching his host's glance, "I've taken up enough of his time this evening. It was a pleasure meeting you, Captain."

"You, too."

"Perhaps I could call you sometime and talk to you about what happened yesterday. For historical purposes, you understand. No, no, you don't need to show me out," he said to the attentive butler before Jo could respond. "I know the way."

While one guest departed, the butler attended to the other. "May I take your jacket, Captain?"

He folded the brown leather over his arm with the care he might give a full length sable cloak. Politely, he waited until she'd claimed the chair just vacated by the historian to ask if she'd like a drink.

"If your tastes run to cognac," her host said, lifting a snifter of thin, shimmering crystal, "this is from a keg a great-great-uncle of mine smuggled in a hundred or so years ago."

"You have pirates in your family tree as well as presidents?"

"Some say they're one and the same," he returned with a flash of white teeth. "The Federalists hanged that particular Taylor, but not before he'd stashed away enough contraband to last for generations."

"Enterprising of him."

"This is the last keg. I broached it after my near brush with oblivion yesterday."

"I can't think of a better reason to broach a keg," Jo agreed with a solemn nod.

"It has a bit of a bite, but I think you'll find it palatable."

She eyed the cloud of golden liquid in his snifter, wondering how two-hundred-year-old cognac would mix with the Champagne she'd already consumed. Since all she'd had to eat today was the candy bar she'd downed on the way to the wing's public affairs office this morning, she suspected the combination might prove potent.

"I'd better pass. Two glasses of Champagne on an empty stomach is one more than my limit."

"An empty stomach? We can remedy that. Evans, pour Captain West some cognac, then bring her a tray, please."

"Yes, sir."

Before Jo could protest, the butler splashed a discreet inch or two into a snifter. After handing her the drink, he bowed and left, the leather jacket still draped over his arm.

She cradled the delicate crystal bowl in both hands and took a cautious taste. The first sip convinced her Taylor's great-great-uncle knew whereof he smuggled. The cognac ignited a slow burn from her throat to her tummy.

"Funny we should both have relatives in the business of distilling and distributing spirits," she said with a grin. "My great-aunt Gert brewed up some mean tubs of beer in her day.

Gert had brewed up more than beer for the customers of her rather notorious bawdy house to buy but Jo didn't intend to put that family secret out for public consumption.

"It sounds as though your ancestors are as colorful and enterprising as mine," her host replied.

"Well, colorful anyway." She hesitated, suddenly, ridiculously aware of how different their backgrounds really were. "My dad voted for your grandfather in both of his presidential elections," she said shyly. "He'd vote for him again, if he could. He claims a man of J. T. Taylor's moral fiber is exactly who this country needs today."

The President's grandson stared into his drink for a moment, his eyes shielded. When they lifted once more, Jo experienced another small shock. They were so intense. So penetrating.

"It's not public knowledge yet," he said slowly, "but my grandfather's dying."

"Oh, no!" Regret over the loss of a truly great man tugged at her heartstrings. "I'd heard TV reports that he was ill, but had no idea it was that serious. I'm so sorry, Mr. Taylor."

He nodded once, the movement carefully controlled, as if he'd learned long ago to be wary of the emotion he expressed in public.

"Thank you. And please, it's Alex." His glass tipped in another slow swirl. "May I call you Joanna?"

"Of course, although I'm more used to hearing Jo. With six kids in the house, my dad could never manage more than a single syllable per child."

"Yes, I read you had five brothers."

Jo resisted the urge to roll her eyes. So much for hoping he'd missed the media blitz, including the front page shots of her nearly naked and frog-mouthed with surprise.

"Was there something about my brothers in the newspapers, too?"

"Actually, your family history was detailed in the dossier I had compiled on you."

She cocked her head, not entirely sure she liked being the subject of a dossier any more than a tabloid news story.

"You ran a check on me?"

"On you and Sergeant McPeak. I wanted to learn what I could about the people who saved my life."

"What, exactly, did you learn?"

"About you? Nothing of significance that I hadn't already discovered for myself. You're smart, dedicated, brave . . ."

Her nose wrinkled. "I sound like a Saint Bernard."

"And beautiful."

Jo knew damn well she fell far short of beautiful, but if the man wanted to be polite, she wouldn't argue with him.

"I was fascinated by the clippings about your rescue of Congresswoman Samuel's daughter," he added. "You made the front pages then, too."

"At least I had my clothes on that time."

He looked genuinely contrite, although the smile lingered at the corners of his mouth. "I'm sorry saving my life led to such, ah, embarrassing exposure."

It was a pretty weak pun, but it won him an answering smile.

"That's not all it led to," Jo murmured, wishing the fire in the massive hearth didn't blaze with quite so much enthusiasm. Sweat had started down between her breasts in a genteel trickle.

"What else did it lead to?"

Her mouth twisted in a wry smile. "I'm flying a desk for a few days, pending a review of the incident."

"What?"

"It's just a formality," she assured him, ninety-nine percent certain she was right. It was that one percent that left a little knot just under her sternum.

"I don't understand." A frown slashed across Taylor's handsome face. His brandy snifter hit the table beside his chair with a clunk. "Tell me who's conducting this review and why!"

Disconcerted by his swift transition from genial to imperious, Jo thrust her own jets into reverse. Normally, she wouldn't think of blurting out her problems to strangers. Even to friends. She could only blame the combination of Champagne, cognac, heat, and this man's potent personality.

"It's just a routine inquiry," she repeated. "Mostly concerning collateral damage to the property where I put down."

"I'm the one who drove his car off the road. If there was any damage done, I'll take care of it."

"I appreciate that, but this is something the Air Force will have to look into. I shouldn't have even mentioned it." Deliberately, she changed the subject. "I'm more concerned about that bandage wrapped around your ankle. What's the diagnosis?"

The frown stayed in place, but he followed her lead.

"It's only a pulled ligament. Far more annoying than painful at this point."

Jo knew better. Among them, her sports-mad brothers had pulled just about every muscle and shattered most of the breakable bones in the human body. One had spent the past fourteen years in a wheelchair. A disability was never merely annoying.

A discreet knock on the double doors heralded the butler's return, this time with a wheeled cart and two maids to assist him. When Jo caught the tantalizing aromas drifting from under the array of silver domes, her stomach somersaulted in delight.

"May I serve you, Captain?" Silver chinked as he removed lid after lid and handed them to the waiting maids. "Caviar, perhaps? Crusted brie?"

"I'll pass on the caviar, but no true Wisconsinite ever turns down cheese."

With a small flourish, the butler cut through a decorated pastry shell that in itself was a work of art. The creamy filling spilled over the knife onto a round, wafer-thin English biscuit. Jo munched away while he proceeded to fill a plate with smoked breast of quail, Westphalian ham shaved into thin curls, ginger curried rice, and watercress drizzled with cranberry vinaigrette. After pointing out the selection of chocolates and cream-filled cakes on the cart's lower shelf and adding another inch of cognac to his employer's glass, he and his minions retreated once more.

"Tell me about these brothers of yours," Alex said as she worked her way through the delicacies on her plate. "Are they all as intrepid as their sister?"

"Where do you suppose I got it from?"

"Toughened you up, did they?"

"I don't think I ever heard the word *can't* until I started kindergarten, and by then it was too late."

If he'd been trying to put her at ease, he'd pushed the right button. Between nibbles, Jo regaled her host with selected incidents from her childhood, all highly edited to minimize the mayhem and maximize the ridiculous. It was a habit she'd acquired early in life, one that had frequently protected her adored, adventurous older siblings from their parents' wrath. Looking back, Jo often wondered how she'd survived infancy, much less girlhood.

As if sensing how solidly her upbringing had grounded the woman she'd become, Alex sipped his cognac and appeared genuinely interested in her silly stories. While she rambled on, Jo couldn't help contrasting her youth with his. He was the only child of an only child. His father had died of a massive heart attack just months after his son's birth. His mother had served as ambassador to Belgium before marrying a Danish archduke.

He'd attended private schools. Played polo instead of T-ball. Spent his childhood in the White House with his famous grandfather while his mother flitted about the capitals of Europe until she, too, died some years later in a tragic train accident while she and her duke were on their way to the Italian Riviera.

Try as Jo might, however, she couldn't cast Taylor in the role of poor little rich boy. He was too confident in his bearing, too comfortable in these luxurious surroundings to elicit even a glimmer of pity.

"Your oldest brother is a surgeon specializing in neuropathological research, isn't he?" he asked when she ran out of stories at about the same time she finished the shaved ham.

"Yes. That's Tom."

"Did he choose that specialty because of the accident that left Jack paralyzed?"

She slanted him a look. "You *have* done your home-work, haven't you?"

Once again he made no apologies. "Yes."

His gaze held hers, and for a prickly moment Jo felt even more exposed than she had in front of the cameras this morning. Suddenly, the heat got to her. Sliding her plate onto the cart, she pushed to her feet.

"Thanks for the fireside picnic. I'd better go. It's a long ride back to the base, even in a limo. No, don't get up!"

Ignoring her request, he groped for the crutches propped behind his chair. Instinctively, Jo reached out to help him. The corded muscles under the cloud-soft black sweater didn't surprise her this time. He rose with more grace than she would have in the circum-stances, and smiled down at her.

"I've been trying to think of an appropriate way to express my gratitude to you and Sergeant McPeak."

"I can't speak for Mike, but Champagne and din-ner does it nicely for me."

"It's a start," he agreed. "So is this."

Sliding a hand into a pocket of his slacks, he ex-tracted a small box. Embossed in gold on the maroon velvet lid was the name of one of D.C.'s most exclu-sive jewelers.

"You don't have to give me a gift," Jo protested.

"I know I don't have to. I want to."

The lid lifted noiselessly at his touch.

"Oh!"

Enchanted, Jo fingered the tiny helicopter nestled in a bed of creamy satin. It looked like a sparkling dragonfly, its body spun from gold and its rotors ablaze with crystals. Only when she tilted the box and the blades caught the firelight did she realize those weren't crystals.

Delight, greed, and common sense fought a fierce battle. To Jo's profound regret, common sense won.

"It's gorgeous, but I can't accept it."

"Of course you can."

"No." Firmly, she closed the lid on the box. "I was trained in rescue. It's what I do. Air Force regulations prohibit accepting expensive personal gifts as a result of our official duties."

Annoyance flickered across his face. "Surely there's some way I can express my gratitude."

"Dinner was thanks enough."

"This hardly qualifies as dinner," he protested, obviously unwilling or unused to taking no for an answer. "I hope you'll let me do it right when I get off these crutches."

"Call me then, and we'll talk about it."

"I will."

The soft promise sent a ripple down Jo's spine. The expression in those killer eyes took that tingle and tripled it. Returning the jewelry box to his pocket, he studied her for several seconds.

"You're a remarkable woman, Joanna West."

"Yeah, well, you're not too shabby yourself."

She spent the long drive back to Andrews sprawled comfortably in the back of the limo, her thoughts whirling. Alex Taylor's face hovered in her mind, as mesmerizing as the city lights reflected on the darkened windows.

Jo had never encountered anyone with his combination of breathtaking charm and casual sophistication. Given the circles they each moved in, that was hardly a surprise. Yet she'd felt so comfortable with him after those first awkward moments. Hot and more than a little sweaty, but comfortable. The next time she took a limo to a cozy evening tête-à-tête, she decided, she'd make sure she was wearing something other than her flight suit.

Snuggling down in the leather, she indulged in the harmless fantasy of a next time. In her mind, she glided across a chandeliered ballroom. Diamonds glittered at her throat. Layers of filmy chiffon floated around her ankles. Men glanced sideways as she passed. Women cast her envious looks. And there, at the far end of the room, Alex Taylor waited in white tie and tails.

The pleasant, Cinderella fairy tale lingered during her drive home from the base and followed her into sleep. It was still at the back of her mind when she walked into the squadron on Friday morning to find that Taylor had made a series of calls after she'd left him Wednesday night.

One changed a little girl's life forever.

One left Jo stunned.

And one brought what felt like a ton and a half of Air Force brass down on her head.

Chapter Five

"Captain!"

The cry caught Jo in the corridor outside the Training Office. She spun around to see Sergeant McPeak rushing down the hall, his eyes bright with what looked from a distance suspiciously like a sheen of tears.

"Mike! What's the matter?"

The flight engineer's throat worked. "It's Brenda."

His little girl! Jo's heart clutched. The six-year-old had been on the list for a kidney transplant for almost a year, but the docs had told McPeak her condition wasn't critical enough to move her up.

"Is she okay?" Her nails dug into her palms. "Can you tell me?"

"She was at Bethesda this morning for her dialysis and . . . and . . ." He dragged in huge gulps of air. "The doc caught my wife just as they were leaving. The National Organ Bank called. They've found a kidney for her, Captain!"

"Oh, Mike, that's fantastic!"

"Ops is laying on a medivac bird now to fly us to Philadelphia Children's."

Frustration ate at Jo. "Damn, I wish I could take the mission. Who's got it?"

"Captain Elliott."

That made her feel marginally better. If anyone in the squadron could get Mike McPeak and his family to Philadelphia within the time parameters set by the National Organ Bank, Deke could.

"Do you need me to look after your other daughter?" She searched her memory, trying to remember the name of the bright-eyed cherub she'd met at a squadron picnic some weeks before.

"No, my wife's arranged for a neighbor to watch Lisa." McPeak grabbed Jo's hand and pumped it. "I just wanted to thank you."

"Me? For what?"

"For taking the chopper down the other day."

"But . . ."

"I had my doubts," he admitted on a hoarse laugh. "I thought Taylor was going to fry, and us with him. But you got him out and he got Brenda this kidney."

"Taylor?"

"I don't know how he did it. I don't *want* to know. If the doc at Bethesda hadn't asked a few pertinent questions, we wouldn't have had a clue he was even involved." He gave her hand a final, vigorous shake. "Look, I gotta go, Captain. Just . . . thanks!"

Jo stood open-mouthed long after his pounding footsteps had faded.

"Wow," she murmured to the empty hall. "That was fast work, even for the grandson of the richest man on three continents."

Since a good portion of the lst Helo Squadron missions involved medical airlift of both living patients and harvested organs, Jo understood how the system worked. Intellectually, she respected the priority ranking that gave the organs to the neediest patients. Emotionally, she shared Mike's fierce joy at seeing his child moved up the list.

Still on a high for him, she strolled into the training office. Even the sight of Hank Kastlebaum with his boots on his desk and a toothpick at full mast between his front teeth didn't faze her. The message he delivered in his uniquely obnoxious style grabbed her full attention, however.

"Hey, sweet thang. Someone named Tom called. He said for you to call him back immediately."

"Tom Who?"

"Beats the hell out of me."

She came off her high with a grind of her back teeth. Kastlebaum could move a saint to murder, and Jo made no claims to sainthood. "Did he leave a number?"

The toothpick dipped in the general direction of her desk. "It's on the phone."

"Jerk," she mumbled just loud enough to raise a chuckle from the other officer. Sweeping across the room, she tugged a yellow stickie from the phone. She recognized the area code and prefix immediately. Milwaukee.

Oh, great! The sleazy shots of her in her underwear must have hit the Midwest, too. She could imagine the ragging Tom and the rest of her brothers would give her. She debated not returning the call, but knew that would just delay the inevitable. Might as well get it over with.

Charging the long-distance call to her home number, she got through to her brother's secretary, and then to Dr. West himself.

"You want to tell me what the heck you're doing out there?" he demanded by way of greeting.

"Just the usual. Flying, flying, and more flying."

"You touched down long enough to stir some serious waters, baby sister. I'm still in shock."

Oh, Lord! The coverage must have been bad to shock the once hulking University of Wisconsin linebacker who'd established a well-deserved reputation as a party animal, then stunned everyone by turning down an offer from the Green Bay Packers to enter med school.

"Have Mom and Dad said anything yet?" she asked.

"Not to me. I doubt if they know about it. I just got the call this morning."

"Who called you?"

Her middle brother, Dave, she guessed. Or Jack. Even paralyzed from the waist down, Jack still managed to squeeze in more reading time between his job as a stockbroker and his work with wheelchair-bound kids than her other four brothers combined.

"I think it was . . ." Tom rustled some papers. "Hold on, let me check my notes. Here it is. His name was Stern. Albert Stern."

"Who the heck is Albert Stern?"

A short, pregnant silence followed.

"You don't know?"

"No."

"A guy calls to make that kind of a donation in your name, and you don't even know him?"

"What kind of a donation? What are you talking about?"

"I'm talking about the million dollar grant just handed to the American Spinal Cord Injury Foundation in the name of Joanna West. What are *you* talking about?"

Stunned, Jo flopped into the chair behind the desk. Several seconds ticked by before she could squeak out a reply.

"A . . . million . . . dollars?"

"To be used for whatever research I deem appropriate."

Alex! It had to be Alex.

She loved him at that moment. He couldn't have chosen a better way to thank her than by contributing to the research that might one day help kids injured as severely as her brother Jack to walk again.

But a million dollars!

"What's this all about, Jo?"

Recovering in slow degrees from her stupefaction, she filled Tom in on the highlights of her last mission.

"Good Lord, that was you! Taylor's accident made the papers, but no one out here paid much attention to it."

That was the difference between Washington, D.C., and the rest of the world, Jo thought wryly. Everyone inside the beltway thought the universe revolved around what happened in the nation's capitol. Outside, folks were more concerned with the wheat harvest and high school football rivalries. With a silent prayer of thanks that the seminude shots hadn't made the *Milwaukee Journal*, Jo cut her brother off in mid-sentence.

"I'll call you back. I want to talk to Mr. Taylor before I say anything more. I'm guessing he's behind this grant, but I don't know for sure. Don't say anything until I call you, okay? He may want to remain anonymous."

Still dazed, she hung up to find Hank Kastlebaum unapologetically eavesdropping.

"And don't you say a word about this," she warned. "Not one single word. I mean it, Hank."

He spread his hands. "Hey, would I leak anything about a million dollar grant even if I knew all the juicy details, which I don't, but I'm dying to hear more about?"

"I don't know the details, either. I don't even know if it's legit. Please, for once in your life, keep your mouth shut and your—"

The phone shrilled under her hand. Shooting Kastlebaum another warning look, Jo picked up the phone and received a curt order from the Director of Operations to report to his office immediately.

Now what?

Feeling as though she'd been caught in a whirlwind, she headed down the hall.

Colonel Marshall was pacing his office when she arrived, which took considerable maneuvering since his desk, a conference table, and President Johnson's helo seat occupied all but a few square feet of floor space. The tight line to his furry brows told Jo he wasn't happy.

"Who have you been talking to, West?"

"About what?"

"About the inquiry," he snapped. "What else?"

"No one."

"Is that right?" He took another turn behind his desk. "Then maybe you can explain the calls I've just received via the Pentagon from a gentleman by the name of Sam Peterston."

She felt a "Duh?" rising in her throat and quashed it just in time. "You've got me, sir. I don't know any Sam Peterston."

"Let me give you a clue. He owns a horse farm south of Manassas."

"Oh. I didn't know his name. Why did he call?"

"He wanted to inform me that he'd been adequately compensated for his Thoroughbred and won't file a claim against the government."

Alex again!

"Mr. Peterston wasn't at liberty to disclose the exact amount of the settlement," the colonel said coldly. "Or even who paid him. But we can both guess who took care of it. We can also guess who was behind the call to the Secretary of Defense, which resulted in a communication from the Chief of Staff of the United States Air Force to the commander of Air Mobility Command, who in turn got the Eighty-ninth Wing Commander on the hot line."

Good grief! Jo couldn't remember when she'd heard that many titles strung together in one sentence. She was still reeling when Colonel Marshall stopped pacing and leaned his knuckles on his desk.

"I told you I'd wrap up this inquiry as expeditiously as possible. I don't appreciate having my hand forced like this."

"But I didn't . . . ! Well, maybe I did, but I . . ."

Jo caught herself. She'd learned long ago owning up to a mistake was a lot less painful in the long run than trying to wiggle out of blame. Dragging in a long breath, she started again.

"I did let something about the inquiry slip to Mr. Taylor the other night, but I made it clear this was an Air Force matter. It never occurred to me he'd try to influence the outcome. It should have. I apologize, sir."

Her frank admission of fault soothed a few of Marshall's ruffled feathers.

"Yeah, well, Taylor didn't actually try to influence anything. He just wanted information. In the process, he involved a whole lot more stars in the matter than either you or I needed."

"I'm sorry," Jo said again.

His ire spent, the colonel palmed his shiny forehead. "Just watch what you say until this inquiry's over, okay?"

"Yes, sir." She knew she was pushing her luck, but had to ask. "Any idea when that might be?"

"The inquiry officer was appointed this morning. He should contact you sometime today."

The call to report to Wing Headquarters came just after two o'clock that afternoon.

Jo drove across base to the semicircular headquarters building and ducked into a ladies' room as soon as she was inside. She'd worn her dark blue uniform slacks and light blue long-sleeved shirt this morning instead of a flight suit. She wished heartily for her green bag now. She'd prefer to meet the inquiry officer as a flier, instead of a temporary ground-pounder.

Okay, this was just routine, she told the face in the mirror as she swiped on some lipstick. All she had to do was run through the incident as she remembered it and answer the inquiry officer's questions as clearly as possible.

Her little pep talk helped. She was able to knock on the conference room door with brisk confidence and present herself with a credible show of professionalism to Lieutenant Colonel DeMotto.

To her profound relief, the interview went far easier than she'd anticipated. Evidently Colonel Marshall hadn't communicated the sudden interest from higher headquarters to DeMotto. He kept things relaxed as he reminded Jo that this was a fact-finding process, focusing primarily on the safety of flight operations. As such, the findings would remain cloaked in strict confidentiality to ensure that everyone involved spoke freely.

That didn't, of course, relieve crew members from possible disciplinary action if they'd acted recklessly or seriously violated procedures, but such action would entail a separate process entirely. DeMotto would interview Jo first, she was informed, then her copilot, and Sergeant McPeak when he returned from Philadelphia.

After signifying that she understood the process, Jo related the exact sequence of events, from her first observation of the Ferrari to her return to base. Even now, several days after the incident, she could taste black smoke and the coppery bite of fear.

And, strangely, the tumult of her morning faded with the telling. She and Sergeant McPeak had saved

a man's life. That man wanted to express his gratitude in ways commensurate with his means.

It was as simple as that.

And just as complicated, Jo discovered when she
returned to the squadron and found she'd received
yet another call, this one from Alex himself. Thankfully, she had the office to herself to make the return
call.

When she reached the number he'd given, the
woman who answered introduced herself as Phyllis
Seager, Mr. Taylor's personal secretary.

"Mr. Taylor just left to fly down to Richmond to
see his grandfather," she advised in a softly cultured
voice. "He asked me to relay a message. The doctors
have assured him he'll be off his crutches by next
week. He'd like to make good on his offer of dinner."

The man certainly believed in repaying his debts.
Her thoughts spun once again to Sergeant McPeak's
joyous face and the incredible call from her brother.

". . . a small, private dinner in honor of Krysta Dominick on Tuesday evening."

That brought her whirling thoughts back with a
jolt. Jo wasn't into poetry, but even she recognized
the name of the brilliant, passionate woman recently
named poet laureate of the United States.

"Are you by any chance free Wednesday evening,
Captain West?"

"As far as I know."

"Wonderful," Mrs. Seager enthused, as if Jo had
just made her day. "Mr. Taylor will pick you up at
eight, if that's convenient. May I suggest formal attire?"

Jo performed a quick mental scan of her closet. She'd have to do some serious shopping between now and next Wednesday. The only really formal attire she possessed was her Air Force mess dress uniform. As elegant as that was, she didn't see herself wearing shoulder boards and medals to a private dinner with Alex Taylor.

She hung up, dazed all over again by a day that had taken her from joy, to incredulity, to the throat-closing experience of facing an inquiry officer, right back to incredulity again. Damned if the fairy-tale daydream she'd indulged in during the limo ride back to the base the other night hadn't taken on shape and substance. The American equivalent of a prince had just asked Cinderella to the ball.

She needed to go home and sort things through, she decided. Preferably in a steaming hot bathtub. With a cool beer close at hand. She was on her way out the door when she caught the whup-whup-whup of an incoming chopper. A glance out the window showed a blue and white bird on final. Moments later, it eased into a hover above the four-spot, then rocked down to a feather-light landing.

The special mission scheduled earlier to fly Mike and his family to Philadelphia had just returned. Jo hit the light switch and was headed down the hall before Deke cut the engine and the rotors whirled to a slow stop. She waited impatiently in the Ops Center while he and his crew went through the shut-down checklist and climbed out of their bird.

Black thunderclouds were rolling across a horizon already darkening with the early fall dusk when Deke slung his helmet bag over one shoulder and headed for the Ops Center. He looked tired, she thought, noting the way his broad shoulders slumped just a bit inside his flight suit. Tired, yet imbued with the satisfaction unique to an aviator of one more takeoff and landing successfully completed.

"How'd it go?" she asked after he completed the crew debrief, filled out the flight log, and turned in his equipment.

"Good." He raked a hand through hair flattened by his helmet. "Children's had a whole medical team waiting on the roof when we set down. Evidently the donor kidney was already on site. McPeak said he'd call the squadron as soon as he can to let us know how Brenda's doing."

"I hope the transplant goes okay."

He nodded, falling in beside Jo as they made their way through the Ops offices and out into the hangar. Only a few maintenance personnel remained, pulling late duty to ready the aircraft designated for tomorrow's missions.

Deke slanted her a glance. "Funny how Mike's daughter got moved up the list so suddenly."

"Isn't it?"

"McPeak seemed to think Alexander Taylor had something to do with it."

"So he said."

She wanted to tell Deke that Alexander Taylor might have had a hand in other matters, too, but she'd already been burned once by talking out of school. Colonel Marshall's caution that she keep her mouth shut until the inquiry officer finished his work was still fresh in her mind. Besides, until she confirmed that Alex really had paid off the horse farmer and made the incredible donation to her brother's research foundation, there was no point in adding fuel to the speculation already flaming the squadron.

Wrapped up in her private thoughts, she stepped into the parking lot with Deke. A freshening wind whipped the night. Thunder rumbled in the distance. A storm system was sweeping in off the Chesapeake. One of the howlers that made flying in this part of the country so much fun, according to the more experienced squadron hands.

Deke walked her to her MG, blocking the force of the wind with his body. "Want to catch happy hour at the club? You still owe me a rematch, remember?"

Jo hesitated. The Officers' Club usually jumped on Friday nights. But the events of the day had drained her. She needed to decompress.

"I'd better pass."

"How about tomorrow?"

"Sorry," she replied with a smile. "I've got some serious shopping to do. I intend to be at White Flint Mall when it opens."

Deke rested an elbow on the top of the MG while she unlocked the door. "White Flint, huh? That is serious shopping. What's the occasion?"

Once again, Jo hesitated. The ongoing inquiry didn't preclude her from having dinner with Alex . . . or any other man, for that matter. She just needed to watch what she said. Even more to the point, her brushes with the media and all the ribbing she'd taken from her squadron mates imbued her with a decided urge to keep the appointment with Alex to herself. But her awareness that Deke was ready to take their friendship to the next level demanded an honest response.

"Alex Taylor invited me to a dinner in honor of Krysta Dominick." She tried to pass it off with a cheeky grin. "Imagine, a dairy farmer's daughter from Wisconsin having dinner with the grandson of a president and a poet laureate."

He studied her face for a moment, his hazel eyes narrowed against the brisk wind.

"Yeah," he drawled. "Imagine."

Firmly, Jo quashed a sting of regret as he slid his arm off the MG and tipped her a salute.

"See you around, West."

Chapter Six

"The White House?"

Jo almost tripped over the hem of her emerald satin skirt. Alex slipped a hand under her arm to keep her from ending up in an undignified sprawl on the cement walk in front of her little rented house.

"We're having dinner at the White House?" she asked incredulously.

"Is that a problem? We can cancel and go somewhere else, if you prefer."

Cancel at the last minute on a White House function? She didn't think so.

"No, it's not a problem. But I thought your secretary said this would be a small, private dinner."

"It will. That's the only reason I agreed to attend. I've made it a point to avoid public gatherings in the past few years."

Since his wife died. Sympathy for this intense, darkly handsome man tugged at Jo. If half the stories in the tabloids were true, he'd all but withdrawn from life after his wife's brief, tragic illness. Gathering her rustling skirts high in both hands to avoid the damp leaves fringing the sidewalk, she edged him a quick glance.

In his exquisite formal wear of snowy white and
midnight black, he didn't look like a brooding, near
recluse who fought a constant battle with intrusive
media. He looked, she decided with a silly little thump
of her heart, like every woman's secret fantasy come
to life.

"Ordinarily, I wouldn't attend this gathering
tonight," he confessed, guiding her to the waiting
limo. "It's no secret that my family donated considerable sums to Bob Hayworth's opponent in the last
election. But Krysta was . . . is . . . a close personal
friend of my grandfather. He asked me to represent
him tonight." His fingers were a warm slide on her
arm. "And I thought you might enjoy it."

Jo gave the chauffeur standing at rigid attention
beside the stretch limo a friendly nod as she slid into
its sybaritic confines. As before, a single white rose
crowned the silver vase attached to the frame. Its
haunting perfume added one more exotic touch to a
night that was fast taking on the dimensions of a
dream.

"Speaking of donating considerable sums," she said
when Alex had joined her and the glass partition separating them from the chauffeur whirred up, "your
grant to the Spinal Cord Injury Research Foundation
blew me away."

He didn't bother to deny that he was behind the
grant. Reaching across the seat, he tucked her hand
in his.

"I didn't intend to blow you away. I just wanted
to thank you, and since you wouldn't accept even a
small personal gift—"

"I couldn't accept it."

"I thought a donation to a cause near to your heart would be more acceptable."

"You couldn't have given me a more wonderful gift," Jo admitted. Her throat got tight, the way it always did when she remembered her brother's painful transition from an energetic, hockey-mad kid to an energetic, hockey-mad paraplegic.

"And Sergeant McPeak's daughter. I won't ask how you pulled that off, but he's not going to forget any time soon what you did for Brenda. Neither will I."

"Any more than I'll forget what you did for me."

As he had the day of the accident, he lifted her hand to his lips. Only this time the gesture didn't carry even a hint of old-fashioned courtesy. This time, he turned her hand and pressed a kiss on the inside of her wrist.

Goose bumps popped out all up and down Jo's arm.

"You look exquisite tonight," he murmured, his lips performing a magic act against her skin.

Since this was the first time held seen her in something other than her flight suit, she might have dismissed the compliment with a smile. But in this instance, Jo happened to totally agree with the man. She'd put a serious dent in her savings for this wickedly decadent skirt with its yards and yards of billowing green taffeta. The strapless bustier and matching long-sleeved bolero jacket sewn with beads that sparkled like emeralds in the light had cost even more, but what the heck! Between the gown and the three hundred dollars she'd blown on everything that went with it, including her visit to an exclusive salon this afternoon, she felt like a princess.

Before she let this prince charming sweep her off to the ball, however, she needed to square one more matter with him. Easing her hand from his, Jo searched for a polite way to tell him to back off. She finally decided there wasn't one.

"About the racehorse that broke his neck. I shouldn't have even mentioned that to you, and you shouldn't have paid off the owner."

"Nonsense. Of course I felt obligated to make restitution. I can afford it. Probably more than the Air Force can."

She didn't doubt that for a moment, but the sweeping assertion took her breath away. Or maybe it was his quicksilver grin that caused the sudden hitch in her chest.

"I consider it the height of absurdity that the Air Force grounded you for saving a man's life, by the way."

In her heart, Jo wanted to agree. But she'd flown too many years to dismiss the need for a methodical review of incidents involving safety of flight or damage to civilian property.

"However you feel about it," she replied, "it's Air Force business. Please, don't make anymore calls to the Secretary of Defense."

"I'll agree to that if you agree to keep me posted on the progress of the investigation."

"I can't discuss an ongoing inquiry with you, Alex. Just back off, okay?"

He didn't like being told to butt out. She could see that by the way his jaw set. Prince Charming, she realized, could come across as pretty formidable when he wanted to.

"If that's what you want," he conceded stiffly.

"It's what I want."

Having scored her point, Jo let the small silence spin out between them while the limo glided onto I-295 and headed north toward the Capitol Street Bridge. The lights of Alexandria winked across the Potomac. On this side of the river, traffic flowed in a steady blur of red taillights and white head beams. The smoothly moving vehicles reminded Jo of another subject of great interest to both Alex and her.

"How did you get all the way over from Georgetown to pick me up without the media giving chase?"

"I sent another driver out with a limo a few minutes before I departed," he told her, relaxing once more. "He has instructions to lead any and all interested parties on a long drive to nowhere. We shouldn't face any invasions of our privacy tonight."

Oh, sure! Where were the photographers when she was dressed fit to kill?

Smiling in the darkness, Jo eased back in the seat and let Alex fill her in on what to expect when they arrived at the White House for this small, private affair.

She soon discovered that his definition of both small and private differed considerably from hers. Limos lined up six deep at the security checkpoint, and light poured from every window of the building when they finally arrived at the side entrance. Jo didn't even try to feign a blasé disinterest. She soaked up every detail to relate later to her parents, from the uniformed ushers who escorted them inside to the pair of elegant settees with mahogany arms in the shape of swans' heads inside the foyer. Bemused by the splendor, she kept her hand planted firmly in the crook of Alex's arm as they were led to the Blue Room, where, they were informed, President and Mrs. Hayworth and the guest of honor would soon join them.

Located at the rear of the White House, the oval Blue Room lived up to its name. Sapphire satin draped the tall windows and furnishings. Embroidered eagles decorated the backs of the antique armchairs, and a blue carpet set off to perfection white walls trimmed with gold. Eight or ten couples graced the room, the women sparkling with jewels and the men elegant in white tie and tails.

"I wish my mom and dad could see this," an awestruck Jo murmured to Alex.

"That's easily arranged," he answered with a smile. "Just let me know when it's convenient for them to come to Washington. I'll set up a private tour with the curator. He's an old friend."

The casual reminder that her escort had spent part of his youth in this living museum sent a shiver down her spine. As did the President and First Lady's arrival just moments later. To Jo's secret disappointment, brass trumpets didn't ring out with ruffles and flourishes. A more informal atmosphere prevailed as, couple by couple, the guests were escorted across the room to meet their host.

A lantern-jawed Marine colonel approached Jo and Alex. A rigidly polite smile cut through the granite of his face.

"Mr. Taylor. Captain West. If you'll come with me, please."

Her stomach fluttering, Jo accompanied Alex across the room. She would *not* say anything except yes, no, and it's a pleasure to meet you, she swore fiercely. Maybe not even yes or no. She would *not* make any remark that could get back to the Pentagon, the wing, or the squadron. She'd sip one drink, very cautiously, before dinner, sit tall in her seat through the meal, and let this glamorous mix of politicians and literi toss the conversational ball.

Unfortunately, those swift, silent vows didn't take either her escort or the President into account. A politician to his bone, Robert Hayworth could charm a smile out of a rock when he set his mind to it.

"The Secretary of State briefed me personally after the incident last week, Captain," the President said.

At least he hadn't read about it in the tabloids, Jo thought on a wave of relief.

"That was quite a rescue."

"I've been involved in hairier ones," she admitted. "But not many."

"Leave it to a Taylor to be dragged out of a burning car by a beautiful woman."

"A very beautiful woman," Alex agreed.

Jo was female enough to bask in the undisguised admiration of both men, and just human enough to feel a bit smug over their attention.

After cocktails, the small party flowed from the Blue Room to the Red Room. And it *was* red, Jo discovered. Red satin covered the walls. Red and gold silk upholstered the antique sofas and chairs. Red valences topped the gold draperies. Opulently intimate, the room was perfect for this small, elegant group. Despite her determination to keep her mouth shut, she couldn't resist Alex's skillful maneuvers to draw her into discussions that ranged from poetry to politics and back again.

She offered no opinion on anything that sounded even remotely political, but Sister Mary Margaret had hammered enough appreciation of American poets into the heads of the sixth-graders at Saint Bernard's that Jo recognized Whitman, Frost, and e. e. cummings when she heard them. Her familiarity with the works of Maya Angelou she owed to Oprah Winfrey.

But it was Krysta Dominick's after-dinner recital that caught her by the throat. Elbows on the table, her veined hands cradling a red-and-gold china cup, the silver-haired poet laureate poured out her verse in the smoky voice that had made best-sellers of her CDs. She ended with one of her most famous works, a poem as powerful as it was erotic. The last verse resonated with an emotion that seemed to come from her soul.

Silence gripped her audience when she finished, broken a few seconds later by an earthy chuckle.

"I wrote that the day after I met your grandfather in Paris, Alexander. I fell desperately in love with him, you know. Unfortunately, he was engaged at the time."

A smile played at Alex's mouth. "My grandmother always maintained that the course of history might have changed significantly if J.T. had met you before he did her."

Charmed by this very personal glimpse into the famous President of her youth, Jo stored up every word to share with her folks. Her mental recorder had come close to overload when Alex finally handed her into the limo.

"That," she confessed with a laugh, "was the most exciting and terrifying night of my life."

"Funny, it was the most enjoyable I've ever spent in this house."

She grinned, more than willing to take the compliment as it was intended, and settled back with a rustle of satin skirts into glove-soft leather.

Yanking at the ends of his starched bow tie, Alex let them dangle down the front of his shirt. Another twist of his wrist popped open the top stud. Suddenly, endearingly human, he stretched his legs out beside hers.

"The night's not over yet, Jo. My family's boat is moored at the Georgetown Marina. I have the crew standing by. Shall we take you home via the Potomac instead of the parkway?"

Her heart melted into a puddle of mush. She couldn't imagine a more incredible end to this magical night than standing on the deck of a yacht as it glided past the lights of the city. Particularly with this man standing beside her. Only the sense that she was getting in too far over her head too fast kept her from agreeing instantly.

That, and the casual way Alex reached out to link his hand with hers.

"You're just off your crutches," she reminded him. "You probably shouldn't stand for another hour or two at the rail of a boat."

"It has a glassed-in salon and comfortable chairs on the upper deck, Jo. And three staterooms with king-sized beds below."

The wicked smile in his eyes made her laugh.

"Only three, huh?"

"The main stateroom has slept four presidents and two kings," he added with a waggle of his brows.

"Oh, well, how can I resist adding my name to a roster like that?"

"I'm hoping you can't."

He was serious, she realized with a shock. Under that teasing grin lurked an honest-to-goodness offer of seduction. She was still reeling from that when he slid his hand free of hers and curled it around the back of her neck instead.

"If that doesn't tempt you, maybe this will."

His thumb slid slowly along the line of her jaw. Just as slowly, he tilted her head back. Jo registered a confused mélange of sensations . . . the power of those compelling eyes, the scent of white roses and starched shirtfront, the whispery touch of skin on skin. Then only his mouth, hot and hard on hers.

The man could kiss. Lord, he could kiss! He knew just how to anchor her head, just where to angle that dimpled chin. And he wasn't polite about it. Didn't make any pretense of playing the gentleman. He started off hungry, and soon swept her into greed.

Or maybe she swept him. Within moments, Jo couldn't tell where his kiss ended and hers began. Heat blocked her throat, climbed into her cheeks. She splayed a hand against his chest, wanting the feel of him under her fingers, taking the taste of him with her mouth.

She was shuddering when she drew back. Small, rippling shudders that amazed and embarrassed her.

"Jo?"

"We'd, uh, better skip the boat ride and take the parkway home, Alex."

"Did I move too fast?"

"I think we both did."

"I'm used to going after what I want." His gaze drifted down to her mouth. "I want you, Joanna West."

She gave a shaky laugh. "Hey, don't pull any punches here."

"Does that offend you?"

"No, it doesn't offend me. It doesn't come anywhere close to offending me. But it does rock me back on my skids."

"Why?"

"You don't even know me."

"I know all I need to know." His finger traced a line along her lower lip. "I ran a background check on you, remember? You're smart, dedicated, brave . . ."

"And strong. Don't forget strong." Her laugh was steadier now. She only wished her pulse would stop cartwheeling.

"Strong . . . and beautiful," he finished.

"Well, I didn't run a background check on you."

His finger stilled. For a moment, his smile slipped at the edges, as though the idea that someone might want to check out his credit or credentials had never occurred to him. Jo found his unconscious snobbery amusing.

"I need time," she told him. "To get to know you."

"How much time?"

"You're joking, right?"

"I never joke about what I want. How much time?"

"I don't know." She tossed out a hand. "Days. Hours. Weeks. Whatever it takes."

"All right. We'll start with days and work our way

up to weeks. Come home to Chestnut Hill with me this weekend. It's a farm just north of Lexington. We can ride, or walk the hills, or just stretch out in front of the fire."

It sounded wonderful. Too wonderful. And, unfortunately, undoable.

"I can't. I'm on duty this weekend."

Assuming, of course, DeMotto wrapped up his inquiry in the next few days and Jo returned to flying status in time for her scheduled alert rotation.

"Can't you get out of it?"

The last thing she wanted to do at this point was rock the boat.

"'Fraid not. I'm on alert from nine Saturday morning to nine Sunday."

"Then we'll leave at nine-thirty on Sunday."

"I'd have to be back by seven Sunday night to go into crew rest for Monday's sorties. Are you sure you want to drive all the way to Lexington for a few hours?"

"It's less than forty minutes by chopper."

She had to ask. "What kind of chopper?"

"A Sikorsky. I'm not sure of the designation. It was just delivered yesterday."

"An S-Seventy-six," she breathed. "It's probably an S-Seventy-six, the elite of the executive transports."

She was hooked. Just as he'd known she'd be.

She spent the rest of the ride home contemplating the twin pleasures of strolling through September-colored hills with Alex and getting a firsthand look at the luxury version of the aircraft that had set twelve world records for speed, altitude, and endurance.

The kiss Alex laid on her when he escorted her to

the front door of her little rented house added considerably to her shivery sense of anticipation.

The envelope she found stuffed into her mailbox the next evening almost destroyed it completely.

Chapter Seven

Tired from her long day, Jo turned over the manila envelope she'd just plucked from her mailbox and searched for a return address. The only writing on the outside was her name in a nearly illegible scrawl.

Dropping the rest of her mail on the kitchen table, she wandered down the hall toward her bedroom. On a cold, drizzly night like this, comfortable jeans, a warm sweatshirt, and her fuzzy slippers constituted her first priority. Particularly after a day like the one she'd just put in.

She'd expected to hear from Colonel Marshall that he'd returned her to flying status. Had waited most of the morning for his call. Finally, she'd tracked him down and asked the status of the inquiry. DeMotto had completed his report, Marshall had informed her, but because of the interest generated by Alex's call, it would go up for review at higher headquarters before the findings were announced. So Jo was stuck with Kastlebaum for at least another few days. She only hoped she could make it through those days without inflicting serious bodily harm on the obnoxious captain.

Idly, she wandered into her bedroom, sliding a finger under the flap of the manila envelope. When she reached inside and pulled out the single black-and-white photo, shock slammed into her gut.

She knew at once who'd taken the shot. He'd framed her in the same uncompromising angles as when he'd captured her dragging Alex out of the Ferrari. She wasn't panting with strain and fear in this shot, though. This one showed her in her taffeta skirt and beaded jacket gazing up at an unseen Prince Charming like a moonstruck Cinderella.

The bastard could have softened the contrast. Could have romanticized the setting a little to include the limousine or even the darkly handsome prince. Instead he'd positioned Jo against the front of her little rented clapboard house. Just her, in all her finery. Like a Wisconsin mud hen all dressed up to play with the peacocks.

She grasped the intended message even before she flipped the photo over and read the words inked in a handwriting made almost indecipherable by intricate loops and swirls.

Be careful. Very careful.

Nice of the creep to warn her, Jo thought contemptuously. As if she didn't already know she had stepped into a scary, uncharted universe with Alex. He existed on a different plane, one that included presidents and Ferraris and high speed chases. Which reminded her . . .

Her mouth set, she changed and made for the spare bedroom that doubled as her office and junk room. It took her a few moments to locate the name and num-

ber of the Virginia Highway Patrol officer who'd taken
her statement the day of Alex's accident, and a few
moments more to connect with his unit. After identi-
fying herself to the dispatcher and explaining what
she wanted, she was passed to another sergeant, who
dug out the official report.

"Yep, the investigating officer tracked down the
source of the photos that appeared in papers. According to this, the photographer's a freelancer who
lives in Arlington, Virginia."

"Can you give me his name and address?"

Jo had no idea what she'd do with the information. Call the ghoul and tell him to get a life, maybe.

"Sorry, ma'am. We can't release that information
except to the parties involved or their insurance representatives."

"Did he offer any excuse for what he did?"

"He claimed he didn't cause the accident. He was
just following the Ferrari, which exceeded the speed
limit and spun out of control. We found no evidence
to prove otherwise."

"He saw what happened," Jo protested. "He drove
right past the accident while the Ferrari's wheels were
still spinning. Doesn't Virginia have a Good Samari-
tan law that requires people to aid a motorist in trouble?"

"The law requires citizens to take reasonable and
prudent measures to aid individuals in distress. Not
to risk their own necks by dragging them out of a
burning vehicle. That falls into the category of heroic
actions, Captain."

Jo dismissed her own actions with a flick of her
wrist. "What about harassment? This creep was fol-

lowing Mr. Taylor. He camped outside my house the morning after the accident, and now he's including me in his gallery of mug shots."

"That's something you and Mr. Taylor will have to take up with the local authorities. If you can prove harassment, you could get a restraining order requiring him to keep a specified distance away."

His damned telescopic lenses would defeat any specified distance, Jo guessed.

Frustrated, she thanked the sergeant and hung up. Most of the media frenzy had fizzled out in the face of her flat refusal to give interviews or discuss the accident. The wing public affairs officer was still fielding offers from local talk shows and a few enterprising reporters who wanted to follow up on the "cosmic love" nonsense, but none of them wanted the story badly enough to remain camped outside her house.

Except this guy.

Had he followed the limo last night? Or had he been lurking in the shadows when they drove back from the White House? Was he out there now, watching. Waiting?

For the second time in less than a week, Jo regretted the quiet and isolation that she had so cherished when she first rented the house. Tucked away at the end of its lane, with open fields on either side and the nearest neighbors a quarter mile away, her little retreat from the traffic and bustle of the suburbs now echoed with an eerie quiet.

Well, that was easily fixed!

Within moments, lights blazed in every room and her CD player pumped out the ballads of the great female torch singers like Edith Piaf, Dinah Washington, and Etta James. Her body swaying to the bluesy throb of "What A Difference A Day Makes," Jo poured a tall glass of milk and surveyed the contents of her fridge. A sandwich, she decided. A real jaw-breaker stuffed with sliced turkey, Swiss cheese, tomato, lettuce, and red onions. Lots of red onions.

Awash in the singers' potent emotions and the onion's even more potent aroma, she was sniffling her way to the living room to munch through Headline News when the phone rang.

Jo froze. For a startled moment, her thoughts cut back to the photograph she'd left in the spare bedroom and to the man who'd taken it. Was his white van parked just down the road, out of sight? Had he seen her pull into the driveway, turn on all the lights?

Frowning, she detoured to the CD player to dim the volume. Her brush with celebrity status was making her paranoid. Which was why her greeting held a distinctly cool note.

"Hello?"

After an infinitesimal pause, a now familiar voice came over the line.

"It's Alex, Jo. Did I catch you at a bad time?"

Relief and pleasure bubbled through her as she set her plate aside and curled her legs under her on the sofa.

"No."

"You sounded a little reserved there for a moment. You're not still being harassed by the media, are you?"

As amazed that he'd learned to read her so well in such a short time as by his intuitive grasp of the situation, she gave a little puff that was half laughter, half disgust.

"Only by one. Your friend in the white van."

"Stroder."

He said the name with such venomous lack of inflection that Jo blinked.

"You know him?"

"Not personally. Did he contact you?"

"He left a souvenir in my mailbox. A picture he took when you brought me home last night. The bastard must have followed us."

Or been waiting. Frowning, Jo threw a look at the closed miniblinds. "The picture came with a warning."

There was another pause, this one longer, quieter.

"What kind of a warning?"

"In his unsubtle way, he's suggesting that I'm out of my league with you."

"Mr. Stroder's becoming more than just a dangerous annoyance," Alex observed softly before asking, "Do you agree with him?"

"Yes."

"I . . . see. Does that mean you've changed your mind about Sunday?"

A wiser woman might have said yes. Common sense told Jo to nip her growing attraction for Alex in the bud right now, before it took root. But as any one of her brothers could attest, she reacted to unsolicited and unwanted interference in her life much like a kitten going nose-to-nose with a toad. Her fur went straight up.

"No, I haven't changed my mind about Sunday."

His slow release of breath flattered her enormously.

"I'm glad."

So was Jo. Glad and more than a little turned on

by the hidden currents flowing through those two simple words. He had a sexy voice, she decided. Sexy and smooth, underlaid with the charm of his native Virginia.

A shivery impatience to see him again rippled through her. For a moment she was tempted to tell him that the damned inquiry was still working its way through the system and she didn't have to pull alert on Saturday. They could spend the whole weekend together, as he'd suggested. But she'd learned her lesson. She wouldn't breathe a word to Alex or anyone else about the status of the inquiry.

"You were right, by the way," he added, breaking into her thoughts.

"About what?"

"The new aircraft is a Sikorsky S-Seventy-six. My pilot says he'll check you out on the controls on the way down to Chestnut Hill."

At least she'd get *some* flying in this weekend. Delighted, Jo agreed. "Tell him he's on."

"I'll see you Sunday, then."

"Is that why you called?" she asked on an afterthought. "Just to tell me about the Sikorsky?"

"No, Joanna." The answer was a caress, slow and soft. "I called to hear your voice."

Across the river, Alex replaced the receiver with a deliberation that revealed nothing of the blood pulsing through his veins. It had been so long since he'd felt this swift, hard punch of lust. So long since he'd *wanted* to feel it.

He savored the tight ache in his groin, relished even the frustration of knowing he wouldn't satisfy it tonight. But soon, he thought with fierce satisfaction. Soon.

He'd heard her breath catch just as he'd hung up. Sensed without arrogance that he fascinated her as much as she did him. She was so different from the women he'd grown up around. Less sophisticated, perhaps. More intriguing, certainly. Her refusal of the diamond pin had surprised him. And, he admitted with brutal honesty, challenged him.

He'd deliberated for some days before deciding to take her up on that challenge. She couldn't know the significance of his invitation to Chestnut Hill. She was the first woman he'd allowed into his home since . . .

Since Katherine.

His gaze drifted to a photo in a baroque silver frame. A young, vibrant Katherine, her eyes alight with the teasing laughter that had attracted him from the first moment they'd met that bright, breezy July afternoon.

She'd been his lodestone, his North Star. The only woman he'd ever allowed himself to love. He'd grown up under his grandfather's tutelage, ignored by his jet-setting mother. He hadn't grieved when she and the drunk she'd married died in that train derailment.

But Katherine . . .

He kept the picture here, beside the phone in his study, to remind him of the shock and pain of her loss. Kept others scattered throughout this house and the farm for the same reason. He never wanted to experience that pain again. Never wanted to taste the bitterness of knowing all his millions, all his grandfather's millions, couldn't save Katherine from the abyss.

Shuddering, he thrust away the memory and left the study. Dr. Russ was in the library, waiting with a historian's patience to record Alex's memories of his youth in the White House.

"I'm sorry to have kept you waiting."

The curt apology carried little more than form. Martin Russ was well aware that Alex suffered this invasion into his privacy only because of his grandfather.

John Tyree Taylor was failing fast. He knew it. His grandson knew it. Yet J.T. insisted on editing his only authorized biography even as he approached its final chapter. As a consequence, he encouraged Russ to poke into every nook and cranny of the Taylor family history. So far Alex had resisted the more personal intrusions. Even for J.T., he refused to lay his hurts bare.

Settling into the wingback chair opposite the doctor's, Alex crossed his legs and tweaked his slacks to adjust the knife-edged pleats.

"Before I forget, I won't be available to meet with you Sunday afternoon. I'm going down to Chestnut Hill."

"So Mrs. Seager gave me to understand when I called to confirm our appointment."

Russ's papery thin fingers unscrewed the top of his fountain pen. Immaculate in every other way, the historian could never quite eradicate the ink stains left by the pen on his fingertips.

"Somehow I formed the impression Captain West is going with you."

Those clouded blue eyes didn't miss much, Alex thought with a twinge of annoyance. He'd have to speak to his secretary. She knew better than to discuss his schedule, even with this old family friend.

"I was quite taken with the captain when I met her last week," Russ mused. "She's a beautiful woman. Quite similar to your wife, I think."

Busy tapping the dib of his pen to get the ink flowing, Russ didn't see the sudden tensing of Alex's shoulders.

"On the contrary, I don't think they look anything alike."

"Not in coloring, perhaps. More in . . ." He gave the dib a final tap. "Style. Yes, style. She has a joy to her. And a daring. Much as Katherine had."

Alex drew in a little hiss of breath.

The historian's glasses magnified his blurred blue eyes. "Is that why you're pursuing her with such determination?"

The soft question lifted the hairs on the back of Alex's neck. "I'm not pursuing her."

"Dinner at the White House? A million dollar donation to the research foundation that employs her brother? An invitation to Chestnut Hill?"

Tomorrow, Alex vowed, his annoyance jolting into anger. No, tonight. As soon as he finished with Russ, he'd fire Phyllis Seager. She'd served as his personal secretary for the past five years, but he wouldn't tolerate this kind of lapse.

"Come, come, m'boy," Russ admonished with avuncular familiarity. "I've known you almost as long as I've known your grandfather. Like J.T., you're a man of great deliberation. And, like him, a man of great passion. As Katherine discovered, did she not?"

Alex allowed no trace of his simmering anger to

show. He refused to discuss his wife, refused to open
that dark, private door. They all wanted to feed on
his pain. The reporters. The talk show hosts. Even this
intrusive historian.

"Captain West saved my life, Martin. I'm merely
expressing my gratitude. Now, where did we leave
off in our last session? The trip to Moscow, wasn't
it?"

"Let me see . . ."

Russ thumbed through his handwritten notes. With
a rigid exercise in self-restraint, Alex concealed his icy
fury. Russ operated like some twelfth-century monk,
his ink-stained fingers recording every conversation
in his own arthritic shorthand. Alex would have pitied
the clerical assistants who translated those notes into
computerized text, except the salary his grandfather
paid them more than made up for their excruciating
work.

Swallowing his biting impatience, he talked Russ
through his memories of that headline-making trip,
when his grandfather had met his Cold War rival on
his home ground for the first time and Alex had
recorded with an eight-year-old's eye that slice of history.

Finally, the marble-and-gilt Bruge clock on the man-
tel chimed Alex's release. With a watery squint at the
beautiful timepiece, Russ capped his pen and closed
his leatherbound, three-ring notebook.

"Next week, Alex?"

"I'll have someone call to confirm the time."

Busy gathering his notes, the historian nodded. The
echo of the chimes had barely faded before the butler appeared in answer to a silent buzzer.

"Please escort Dr. Russ out, Evans. Then I have another matter for you to attend to."

"Yes, sir."

While he waited, Alex splashed a generous measure of the smuggled cognac into a snifter. He'd downed only a single fiery swallow by the time Evans returned.

"Mrs. Seager's services are no longer required," he informed the butler. "I want her out of this house tomorrow. You can tell her I'll arrange for her wages and two months severance pay to be sent to her bank."

Evans unbent enough to show a flicker of surprise. He was relatively new, hired after Katherine's death to supervise the staff here in Georgetown while Alex spent most of his time at Chestnut Hill.

"May I tell Mrs. Seager why she's being dismissed, sir?"

"You may tell her *and* the rest of the staff. I won't allow any discussion of my affairs with anyone, including Dr. Russ."

Evans dipped his head in acknowledgment. His contract, too, included a clause requiring absolute discretion and an iron-clad agreement not to publish any personal memoirs of his service. Neither Alex nor his attorneys had considered the gag order unreasonable in view of the exorbitant wages paid to his employees.

"Is there anything else, sir?"

Alex had one more task that needed doing, but this one he'd take care of himself.

"No."

For long moments after the butler retreated, Alex remained still, his only movement the small swirl of his cognac against crystal. With a deliberate effort, he blanked his mind to his residual anger with the employee who'd betrayed him. He needed to think clearly, to decide how to handle the photographer who'd become more than just a dangerous annoyance.

Chapter Eight

Looking back, Jo could never quite pinpoint the exact moment she realized Alex had launched an all-out campaign to seduce her. He stepped up the heat in such subtle increments, slowly at first, then with such consummate skill, that she never noticed the transition from one level to the next. But she soon realized that he'd meant what he said in the limo after they'd left the White House. He wanted her.

She discovered just how much at Chestnut Hill.

It was perfect, that day. Like a series of clippings from a glossy magazine. Each sequence held its own particular pleasure. Even the fact that the inquiry still hung over her like a dark cloud couldn't destroy her enjoyment of the impossibly blue sky, glorious sunshine, and late September chill.

By prior agreement, she met Alex at the heliport in Georgetown where he hangared his chopper. Her heart thumped at the sight of the machine parked on the ramp, then thumped again when she spotted its owner.

She'd seen him in cloud-soft cashmere and white tie and tails, but never in jeans and a cable knit Irish fisherman's sweater that dipped to a V at the neck and emphasized his lithe build. He carried off the casual look, as he did all others, with a combination of inbred elegance and heart-stopping masculinity.

Not exactly sure what one wore for a day at a country house, Jo had opted for sand-colored linen slacks paired with a cranberry sweater shell and matching cardigan. A patterned silk scarf caught her hair back at the nape. When she joined Alex, he smiled a welcome that melted her bones.

"You're right on time. I like that in a woman."

She decided to let that bit of chauvinism pass. "For once, the beltway was wide open."

"Ready to go?"

Was he kidding? Jo couldn't wait to get an inside look at his newest toy.

"She's beautiful," she breathed as they crossed to the waiting helo.

"Yes, she is."

Alex's low murmur swung her head around. He didn't pretend to refer to the Sikorsky. A flush of pleasure heated Jo's skin, but she laughed it off.

"I hope you don't mind if I poke around the cockpit a bit before we launch."

"I expected you to do more than poke. I figured you'd strap yourself in."

She wanted to. God, she wanted to! The aviator in her quivered with a greedy desire to find out how this baby handled. But she was Alex's guest on this trip, and it would be unpardonably rude.

"It's okay." Laughter gleamed in his dark-ringed blue eyes. "Anticipating just such an eventuality, I brought some reading materials for the trip down. But on the way back . . ." His forefinger traced the line of her jaw. "You're all mine."

"It's a deal," she tossed off, utterly charmed by his grasp of what made her tick.

After shaking hands with the pilot, who introduced himself as Doug Brakemen, a former Navy helo driver, she climbed into the cockpit and promptly began to salivate. The S-76 came equipped with the latest high-tech instrumentation and enough advanced digital video displays to thrill any pilot. Like a kid in a candy store, she practically had to sit on her hands to keep from sampling the delights.

Since Brakemen and the ground crew had already completed their preflight, it took only a few minutes to bring the Sikorsky to full revolutions per minute and perform a hover check to confirm available power. Jo soaked in every detail as the pilot reconfigured the lights, transponder, and radio to tower frequency, then taxied from the parking spot to the launch pad.

Moments later, they were airborne. As soon as they'd cleared the metro area and picked up helo Route 1 along the Cabin John Parkway, Brakeman shot her a smile.

"Mr. Taylor tells me you carry a current FAA certification as a helicopter pilot in addition to your military qualifications."

Was there anything about her Alex hadn't uncovered in that background check?

"Yes, I do."

"Want to take over the controls?"

"Does a cat have a tail?"

"Okay, Captain, she's all yours."

The next forty minutes passed in sheer, unadulterated bliss. The Sikorsky responded to Jo's lightest touch. Used to the rattle and roar of the Hueys, she marveled at its whisper-quiet and had to forcibly resist the urge to hotdog a bit to test its instruments.

Hills ablaze with fall color rolled by beneath the wraparound Plexiglas cockpit. In the distance, the purple-smudged Shenandoah mountains poked toward the sky. Even the intermittent glimpses Jo caught of sleek Thoroughbreds grazing in the pastures and paddocks below failed to prick her bubble of enjoyment. She didn't plan to start any stampedes on this flight.

To her joy, Brakeman had her take them in on final approach to Chestnut Hill. Busy with the controls, she gained only a fleeting impression of the sprawling stone house and scattered outbuildings. It's muted glory hit her only after they'd run through the engine shut-down procedures and she accompanied Alex up the brick walk to the house.

It really was a farmhouse, she saw on a beat of delight. She'd expected something more grand, perhaps in the style of the turn-of-the-century mansion John Tyree Taylor owned south of Richmond that was reputed to rival the great castles of Europe.

This place looked as though it had started out as a home for a working family, and grown over the centuries into an amalgamation of character and comfort. Twin chimneys bracketed the central two-story structure, which was flanked on either side by single-story wings. Judging from the irregular line of its casement windows and mellowed yellow stone, Jo guessed the original house must have been constructed in the late 1700s.

"1791," Alex confirmed. "The roof had caved in and rot had eaten through the wall timbers when my grandfather bought it, but he managed to restore most of the original structure."

J. T. Taylor had also added the tiered brick patio and glassed-in pool at the rear of the house, Alex informed her, as well as the stables and the observatory.

"Observatory?"

"There, on that hill."

Leaning close, he pointed over her shoulder. Distracted by his subtle aftershave and the warm breath on her cheek, Jo searched the screen of orange- and red-flamed trees for the little white-domed building a half mile distant.

"My grandfather was an . . ." He stopped, correcting himself with a brief flicker of what could only be pain. "*Is* an avid astronomer. Unfortunately, his illness doesn't allow him to enjoy his hobby as much as he'd like to these days."

Pity rippled through Jo. As the youngest of the West brood, she'd come along late in her parents' life and lost her grandparents to age and infirmity when she was still a young girl. Yet their loss had been buffered by her large, lively family. She could only imagine how painful it would be to watch your only living relative die . . . particularly after you'd gone through the same agony with your wife only a few years before.

Impulsively, she slipped her hand into his. "I'd love to see the observatory, if we have time."

"We'll make the time." His fingers curled around

hers, warm and strong. "I wish you didn't have to be back by seven this evening."

She was tempted to tell him then that she was still grounded and, consequently, didn't have to go into crew rest tonight. Hard-learned caution kept her silent. That and the stutter of her pulse when he lifted her hand and feathered a kiss across her knuckles.

"We'll just have to wring the most from the hours we have," he said.

"Wringing's good," she got out on a fluttery laugh. "Very good."

"So is dining. Are you hungry?"

"I'm getting there."

"Would you like to freshen up first? There's a powder room on the first floor," he told her as he escorted her into a wide foyer. "Or you can use my wife's dressing room upstairs."

The fact that he still referred to the dressing room that way caught Jo's interest. So did the portrait she glimpsed above the sideboard in the dining room.

"Is that your wife?"

His gaze shifted to the life-size portrait. The raven-haired beauty sat wreathed in off-the-shoulder white velvet, her gloved hands folded in her lap, her smile demure yet so teasing that Jo couldn't help but wonder what the joke was.

"Yes, that's Katherine."

The answer came so softly that Jo's chest contracted. She hesitated, unsure how much to intrude.

"She looks as though she enjoyed life."

Those intense blue eyes shuttered. For long moments, Jo wasn't sure he'd respond.

"She did," he said at last. "This portrait always reminds me just how much."

Shaking off his memories with an obvious effort, he gestured to a room filled with bright sunlight and overstuffed furniture upholstered in cheery yellow and blue chintz.

"I'll wait for you here."

Not for the world would Jo admit that it was curiosity spiked with just a touch of envy that made her choose the upstairs dressing room instead of the downstairs powder room. She couldn't be jealous of a dead woman. Couldn't envy her the emotion she still inspired in Alex. All she wanted was a peek at the upstairs.

Yet when she walked through the open doors of the suite at the end of the hall, the eerie sense that Katherine still held her husband in thrall intensified a hundredfold. Goose bumps marched up and down Jo's arms.

If the rest of the house was filled with color and sunlight, this room formed a stark contrast. Everything was white or silver, from the plush carpet to the satin duvet that covered the four-poster bed. A platinum silk gown and robe lay draped across the bed. Silver-topped jars and brushes were scattered with careless abandon on the vanity. The perfume of roses drifted to every corner of the room.

Jo stopped in her tracks, her throat closing at the familiar scent. Turning, she traced it to a crystal vase occupying a low table. Long-stemmed roses filled the vase, at least two dozen, she'd guess, each one as soft as snow, as pale as tears.

Alex must have them brought in every few days,

she thought. For this room and for the bud vases in his limousines. Although Jo couldn't recall seeing any roses during her brief visit to the Georgetown house, she'd bet she'd find arrangements of the same long-stemmed white beauties there, as well.

Stifling the urge to back out and retreat, Jo crossed to the bath. The idea of disturbing anything in this snowy mausoleum was unsettling, to say the least. Only after she'd used the lavatory and swiped the sink dry with a wad of tissues did the total lack of masculine touches in either the bedroom or the bath strike her.

Either Katherine and Alex hadn't shared this suite, or he'd moved out after her death and turned it into a living memorial. Confused by the odd sensation in her chest, Jo made her way back downstairs.

Her confusion dissipated over a long, lingering brunch served outside on the terrace. As soon as Alex seated her at the glass-topped table, Jo discovered she was ravenous. And not just for the Cheddar cheese and sherry soup, Waldorf salad, and chicken divan crepes that melted like butter in her mouth. Basking in the dappled sunlight filtering through brightly col-ored leaves, she scarfed up every sensory detail. The sparkling Champagne in tall-stemmed crystal flutes. The chug-chug of a hay mower in the distance. The swirls of black hair that peeked above the V of Alex's cable-knit sweater.

She stored up the conversation as well, hoarding it as one would a small treasure to be taken out and smiled over on a rainy afternoon. Just like ordinary people, they talked about favorite movies, least favorite foods, and places they'd visited. Alex had jetted to more spots, perhaps, but Jo's never-to-be-forgotten two-week tour of duty at a rescue station north of the Arctic Circle qualified as the most exotic.

They lingered over brunch until well into the afternoon and Alex made good on his promise to show her the observatory.

"It's just a quarter mile through the woods. We can walk or take a golf cart, if you prefer."

"I'd rather walk."

"I thought that's what you'd say. Hang on, I'll find you a jacket. It gets chilly out of the sunshine."

After a brief foray into the house, he returned with a suede jacket. It was butter soft, man-sized, and lined with a rich hunter green plaid. Ridiculously relieved that he hadn't offered her something of Katherine's, Jo wrapped herself in his suede and his scent.

Side by side, they followed a winding path through thick stands of white-barked birch and towering elms. Fallen leaves crunched like popcorn under their feet. Gloriously painted leaves rustled overhead. Her hands pushed in the jacket pockets, Jo matched her stride to Alex's and breathed in the earthy scent of a fall not yet tainted by the damp decay of coming winter.

The observatory was a tiny, time-warped gem, lined with cases displaying an avid enthusiast's collection of astronomical instruments from different ages. Alex pointed out a fifteenth-century astrolobe used by early sailors to calculate their position from the stars and an ancient Egyptian papyrus in a climate-controlled glass display box. Rolled in a crumbling leather carrying case, the scroll purportedly aligned the heavens around their ancient sun god, Ra, with astounding accuracy.

"These pieces should be in the Smithsonian," he admitted, his voice echoing hollowly in the high-domed room. "Perhaps someday."

After J. T. Taylor's death, Jo guessed. Unless his grandson decided to keep the observatory as a memorial to his grandfather, as he'd kept his wife's room dedicated to her.

Shrugging off the morbid thought, she ambled over to the huge brass telescope dominating the center of the circular room. Mounted on a dais that also contained a fixed armchair, the whole apparatus moved by means of a hand crank, swiveling a complete 360 degrees. Another crank extended the telescope's lens almost to the roof. At the same time, a series of pulleys slid back two of the dome's panels to reveal a slice of blue.

At Alex's urging, Jo took the seat and stuck her eye to scope. A bubble of laughter escaped as he tried to convince her the commercial jet liner painting a contrail across the sky was really an alien space ship.

The laughter got trapped halfway down her throat when she dismounted and found herself wedged between the chair and Alex. He stood so close she could see her reflection in those darkly intense eyes, see as well the faint traces of a five o'clock shadow on his strong jaw. Giving in to the urge that had gripped her since she'd first stared down at his face with eyes smarting from smoke, she lifted a finger to trace the indentation in his chin.

"I've been wanting to do this since the first moment I met you," she admitted. "How the heck do you shave without cutting yourself?"

His cheeks creased in a grin. "Very carefully."

"I can imagine."

What she couldn't have imagined was the jolt that coursed through her when he slid his arms around her waist, as naturally as if they belonged there.

"I've been wanting to do *this* since the first moment I met you."

The gleam in his eyes should have prepared her, not to mention the sudden pounding in her veins. Even with those warnings, Jo wasn't ready for her shock of pleasure when he bent and nipped at her throat. Each tiny bite, each scrape of his teeth and chin and cheeks started little fires under her skin.

In startling contrast to her heated flesh, the hand he slipped under her cranberry sweater was cool and smooth. Sliding his palm around to the small of her back, he arched her into him.

With a small thrill, she discovered he was rock hard. Alex allowed her a second, only a second, to register the feel of him before he claimed her mouth. With a hungry growl, he swept her into a river of want.

Her lids fluttered down, shutting out the slice of sky, the domed roof, the storm in his blue eyes. Shutting out everything but the heat of his mouth on hers and the brand of his hand at the base of her spine.

Greed licked at her veins when he dragged his head up. Pupils dilated, nostrils flaring, he stared down at her swollen lips for several moments before pulling in a long, ragged breath.

"This isn't working, Jo."

"Funny," she got out on a surprised laugh, "it was working pretty well for me."

"You don't understand." Curling a hand under her chin, he tipped her head back. "I want more than mere hours with you. More than a few measured days. I want to stretch you out on silk sheets and kiss every inch of your body, without worrying about some damned ticking clock."

That sounded like an excellent plan to Jo, too, but the idea of stretching out with Alex on that expanse of pale, snowy white she'd glimpsed in Katherine's room kept her from saying so.

If and when they made love, she vowed, it wouldn't be in a mausoleum. As if reading her thoughts, he dangled the promise of sunshine and pleasure.

"Come away with me," he urged, smoothing back the tendrils that had escaped the silk scarf. "Next Saturday's your birthday."

She didn't have to ask where he'd gleaned that bit of information. The dossier. No doubt the background check had listed her birth weight and place, as well as the exact minute and hour.

"Spend it with me in Provence," he murmured, punctuating his request with a teasing kiss.

She pulled back, not quite believing he was serious. "Provence, as in France?"

"I bought a villa overlooking the Mediterranean last year, thinking it was time . . ." He stopped, finished on a quieter note. "Thinking I might need a change."

He did, she thought fiercely. He did!

"You'll love it, Jo. The sea sparkles in the sun, and

the front of the house faces fields of red and purple poppies. We'll leave on Wednesday or Thursday, spend a week—"

"Whoa, Alex, as wonderful as that sounds, I can't just take off for a week in France."

The enthusiasm in his eyes dimmed. His mouth took a decidedly displeased downward turn. "No, I suppose not."

Somehow, the idea that one of the richest men in the country could sulk like any other thwarted male made him irresistibly human.

"I'll tell you what. Let me check with Scheduling tomorrow and see what they have on the books. Maybe I can swing next weekend. But," she added when his sulk melted into a knee-knocking grin, "France is out."

"Where would you like to go, then?"

"Maybe it's time I showed you some of my world." She cocked her head, thinking fast. "If I guarantee a total absence of reporters and photographers, can you handle a squadron picnic?"

"I don't know. Can I?"

When he smiled at her like that, Jo didn't doubt he could handle anything she threw at him.

"Just wear jeans and a sweatshirt you won't mind getting dirty and you'll do fine."

She strolled back to the house beside Alex, almost one hundred percent sure she was doing the right thing.

He wanted her, and needed change.

Well, he'd get a taste of both this weekend.

Chapter Nine

The next week couldn't have started off on a better note. Jo arrived at work early Monday morning to find a message directing her to report to Colonel Marshall. She made a beeline across the hangar, answering the greeting from one of the maintenance crew chiefs with a wave but not stopping to chat. As soon as she cornered Marshall in his office, he gave her the news she'd been waiting for.

"Headquarters has completed its review of the inquiry, West."

Her heart thumped. "And?"

"And they concur you stretched FAA and Department of Defense directives to the breaking point."

That sounded ominous. Swallowing, Jo dropped into Lyndon Johnson's chopper seat and prayed for a "but." Fortunately, it came immediately.

"Given the circumstances, however, the board concluded that you acted within your prerogatives as aircraft commander by putting down to assist in an emergency situation."

"Sierra Hotel!"

Marshall's flickering smile indicated that he agreed

with the phonetic abbreviation for "shit hot," the military aviator's all-purpose expression of approval.

"The fact that the Secretary of State weighed in with a written endorsement didn't exactly hurt your case," he added dryly.

"Mrs. Adair wrote to the board?"

"She did. She's also recommended you for an Airman's Medal."

"No kidding?"

Jo shook her head, amazed at how her career had ping-ponged from almost in the toilet to a possible award for heroism in a few short seconds.

"Now get out of here," Marshall directed, "and put yourself back on the flying schedule. You're going to have to hump to make up the hours you lost this month."

Only too happy to comply, Jo made Scheduling her next stop. In an age of computers and scanners, the NCOs who manned the section still relied primarily on their wall-sized grease pencil board to match crews to projected sorties.

"Colonel Marshall says to put me back on the board, troops. Double me up wherever you can. I need to make up some air hours."

The NCO in charge turned away from the board, grease pencil in hand. "Great timing, Captain. We just got word one of our birds PL'ed in a high school soccer field halfway to Norfolk. Ops is generating another sortie now to pick up their passengers."

So one of their helos had flashed a PL—a precautionary light—and had to put down. From past experience, Jo would bet the stranded crew was killing time while they waited for maintenance by giving the high-schoolers an impromptu tour of the chopper. In the process, they'd engage in some on-the-spot recruiting.

"It should be ready to go within a half hour. We can put you on if you weren't out carousing too late last night."

Jo's lingering guilt over allowing Alex to believe she'd needed to go into crew rest last night evaporated on the spot. The aviation gods must have intended for her to reject Alex's tempting offer to stay at Chestnut Hill.

"Nope," she told the sergeant with a cocky grin. "I was home last night, sleeping the sleep of the pure. I'll take the sortie. Who have you got for copilot and engineer?"

"We're working on them now."

"Okay, I'll go get my gear and start the mission planning. Tell whoever you line up to meet me in the briefing room as soon as they can."

Humming happily, Jo headed for the training section. Life was good. Better than good. Her wings were no longer clipped. She'd strap herself in for at least one sortie today, maybe more tomorrow. And a check of the alert schedule showed it had already been filled for the coming week. Barring unforeseen disasters or late-generating missions, she could give Alex the whole weekend she'd promised him.

Even the sight of Henry Kastlebaum in his customary pose—boot heels on desk, newspaper in hand, and toothpick at full mast—couldn't pierce her bubble.

"I'm outta here," Jo announced cheerfully.

Toothpick rolling, Kastlebaum lowered the paper. "Got your wings back, babe?"

Jo took a mental ten count. If she didn't believe in handling matters herself, she might have considered slapping the jerk with a sexual harassment charge. But growing up in a family of boys had taught her patience and cunning. Sooner or later, fate would hand her the means to cut this cretin's legs out from under him. She'd wield the ax with pleasure.

Grabbing her helmet bag, she decided to empty the borrowed desk of her few personal items later. "See you around, Kastlebaum."

"You, too, West. You looked good on TV last night, by the way." His eyebrows waggled suggestively. "Real good."

"What are you talking about?"

"Guess you didn't catch the late-night news."

Obviously not, or she wouldn't be asking. Impatient to start planning for the sortie, Jo almost brushed him off.

"It wasn't your best shot," he added with a gap-toothed smirk. "Not like the one of the wanna-be soap opera star with the world-class tits who went skinny-dipping with a very married senator a few years ago. Now *that* photo was a work of art."

Jo vaguely remembered a scandal involving a grossly overendowed starlet and a legislator, but couldn't figure how that story involved her.

"Okay, I'll bite. What's the connection between me and Miss Silicone?"

The toothpick took another roll. "The photog, sweet thang, the photog. Eric Stroder, I think his name was."

Stroder!

The bastard who'd sped by a car crash, then doubled back to capture the carnage on film. The same bastard who'd camped outside her bedroom the morning after the accident, then waited in the chill darkness to take that picture of her after dinner with Alex at the White House. Surely he could not have made his way onto the grounds of Chestnut Hill yesterday!

Disgusted, Jo shook her head. "What did a sleaze like Stroder do to warrant a TV spot?"

"Evidently he got crosswise of a mugger or car-jacker last night. The park rangers found him with his brains splattered all over his van and his expensive equipment ripped off. The local news carried the story, and included a little retro of some of his more, shall we say, artistic shots."

Jo tried to work up some sympathy for the man. Remembering the warning scrawled across the back of that black-and-white glossy, the best she could manage was the fleeting thought that Stroder should have followed his own advice and been more careful. She wouldn't wish that kind of end on anyone, even him.

Leaving Kastlebaum to his toothpick and his paper, she slung her helmet bag over her shoulder. An hour later, she and her crew stepped out to their aircraft.

The gray, scurrying clouds to the north didn't dampen her pleasure at the sight of the blue and white helo waiting for her on the ramp. The Huey might have a good twenty years on Alex's slick new Sikorsky, but it had more than proven itself in flight and in combat. Jo couldn't wait to get back in the seat, her hands on the controls and her feet on the pedals.

Happily, she stowed her helmet and bag in the cockpit and completed the required walk-around. The wind whipped at her hair and rustled the forms clipped to the board. Jo noted the fire bottles stationed beside the Huey, then, with her engineer, checked every moving part from the skids to the rotor blades. She was grinning when the crew chief closed and latched the engine cowling.

"Okay, boys and girls, we've kicked the tires. Let's light the fires."

The rest of the week zipped by. Two of Jo's flights were canceled due to the weather that rolled in on Thursday, blanketing the coast from Washington to Boston with rain and fog, but she still managed to make up a good chunk of the hours she'd lost during her time flying a desk.

Luckily, the front swept through and Saturday dawned clear, with the temperature registering a brisk thirty-six degrees but projected to climb into the mid-sixties by the time the squadron picnic kicked off at two. Perfect weather for coed flag football, kiddie pony rides, and hot dogs burnt to a crisp over a charcoal grill.

Perfect weather, too, for Alex to get a glimpse into the lifestyles of the not-so-rich-or-famous.

Turning on the shower taps, Jo chewed on her lower lip while she waited for the hot water to make its way through the pipes. She didn't kid herself about why she wanted him to see the real Jo West in her natural setting. Despite her initial desire to take things slow between them, matters had heated up considerably last weekend. Her skin still tingled at the memory of his hands roving her back. And, yes, she'd indulged in a few fantasies this past week, most of which took place in a sun-washed villa high atop a cliff over-looking the Mediterranean.

She had no idea where this simmering attraction would take them, wouldn't let herself even imagine the possibilities. Before they took the next step along that uncharted path, though, she needed to be very, very sure Alex knew the woman she was.

Or, more correctly, the woman she wasn't.

Unlike Katherine, she didn't spring from a mon-eyed background. She hadn't graduated from a seven-sisters college, and certainly hadn't done the debutante bit. Nor could she exist in a rarefied at-mosphere devoid of the noisy companionship she'd grown used to with her boisterous family and equally boisterous friends.

In short, Jo decided, wrinkling her nose at the face in the mirror, she wasn't the white rose type.

Still, her conscience pinged her as she finished her morning routine and padded back into the bedroom to pull on jeans and her favorite fuzzy purple sweater. She buttoned it slowly, doubts surfacing like unin-vited guests.

By his own admission, Alex had shunned large gatherings since his wife's death, going to great lengths to keep out of the public eye. Now Jo was pushing him right back into it.

Maybe she'd overstepped herself. Maybe he wasn't ready for this kind of event. Maybe, she thought on a gulp, the afternoon would prove a total disaster.

They'd only stay for a few minutes, she decided, yanking on a sneaker. Just pop in for a beer and a hot dog.

Or not go at all.

By the time she finished dressing and downed a bagel and juice, she'd almost convinced herself that not going was the best option.

To her surprise, Alex didn't agree.

Jo was leaning against the fender of her MG, waiting for him, when he drove up to the house a little past one. He was behind the wheel of a gleaming new Ferrari—this one a midnight blue. The car was a work of art, but it was the man who climbed out of the beast who set Jo's pulse to booming.

He'd taken her at her word, she saw, and wore a faded black-and-orange Princeton sweatshirt with the sleeves pushed up to his elbows and jeans every bit as snug as hers. Sunglasses and a black ball cap shaded his face, but nothing could disguise that sexy, dimpled chin.

She managed not to drool. Barely.

"Hi. You're right on time. I like that in a man."

To her delight, he recognized the echo of his own words and flashed her a grin.

"I'll assume that's a compliment, although I suspect I'm being paid back in kind for a bit of unintended sexism."

"It is, and you are. Clever of you to pick up on it."

He slid his arms around her waist, bringing her mouth to his in a long, hard kiss before answering.

"Clever is my middle name."

"Alexander Clever Taylor," she got out when the sky had stopped swirling and her breath had returned. "Catchy."

"Almost as catchy as Joanna Sylvestra West."

Jo gave a strangled groan. "As far as I knew, my

birth certificate is the only place that name was ever recorded. Whoever compiled your blasted dossier certainly did his homework."

Laughing, Alex tugged playfully at a strand of her hair. "I pay well for my information, Miss West. Remember that if you ever try to hide anything from me."

"I will."

"Are you ready?" he asked, releasing her. "Do you want to drive us to this picnic of yours, or shall I?"

Her earlier doubts resurfaced with a vengeance. "Maybe we should skip the picnic, Alex."

"Why?"

"I know how much you value your privacy. I shouldn't have put you on the spot by inviting you to this kind of public function."

"I wouldn't have agreed to it if I didn't want to."

"I know, but . . ."

He put his own spin on her change of heart. "Did word leak out? Are you worried we'll be besieged by reporters?"

"No, I haven't told anyone you're coming. We should be able to make it through the afternoon relatively unscathed. Unless you were followed."

"I made sure I wasn't."

She swept the fields around the little rented house, hugging her arms as a small shiver raced over her skin. She couldn't imagine living her life in a fishbowl the way Alex did, with someone always waiting, watching.

"At least you won't have to worry about Stroder anymore," she murmured.

"What do you mean?"

The sharp question jerked her head around. Alex's

sunglasses shielded his eyes, but she couldn't miss the sudden tensing of his body.

"I didn't see the news story, but I understand the guy got caught in a mugging or car-jacking that went bad."

"Well, well." A small, unpleasant smile played at his lips. "Someone just saved me a great deal of money."

"What?"

Shock jolted through Jo. An incredulous thought sprang into her mind, dark and unsettling. Surely Alex didn't . . . Surely he wouldn't . . .

He must have read the horror on her face. His smile twisted into a wry grin.

"No, I didn't put out a contract on him."

Jo was just chiding herself for her ridiculous doubts when he added a kicker.

"I considered it. Several times over the past few years, if you want to know the truth. When he began harassing you, I decided it was time to take action."

"What kind of action?"

"Money talks, even in this town," he replied with a cynical shrug. "I told my lawyers to put out the word that I was considering a lawsuit against Stroder and any newspaper or magazine that published his pictures. Just the prospect of defending against that kind of legal action is enough to make an editor think twice."

Under that well-bred, elegant exterior, Jo thought, he was as ruthless as a shark.

But far more fascinating. Not to mention sexy as hell. Her whole body rippled with pleasure when his hand curled around her neck and tipped her face to his.

"So, my darling, I suggest we go to your picnic. As you so correctly pointed out, you've seen my world. We'll spend the afternoon in yours . . . and the night in one we create for ourselves."

That 'darling' alone almost melted Jo on the spot. His understanding of her need for him to know who she was finished the job. Looping her arms around his neck, she drew him down for a kiss that promised more, so much more, in that special place they'd create.

Her pulse was racing when she pulled back. Deciding they'd better get it in gear or they'd never make the blasted picnic, she suggested she drive.

"If you show up in the Ferrari, you'll have a hundred kids with sticky hands climbing all over it."

"It's just a car, Joanna."

"Ha! Try convincing any other male over the age of ten of that."

She reached for her car door, only to have Alex stay her with a hand on her arm.

"Wait. Before we go, I want to give you your birthday present."

"You just did," she answered with a grin.

His face softened. His long, supple fingers caressed her arm through her sleeve.

"I haven't begun to show you how I feel about you, my darling."

There it was again, that low, seductive endearment. She might grow tired of it, she decided, in a couple thousand years or so.

"This belongs to you." Sliding a familiar maroon

velvet box from his pocket, Alex clicked it open. "You wouldn't accept it before. I hope you will now."

Her sigh was one of complete surrender. She'd used up her supply of nobility when she'd turned down the jeweled helicopter the first time he offered it. No way she could refuse it again.

"Here, I'll pin it on for you."

"Alex! I can't wear diamonds to a picnic."

"Yes, you can," he countered, his knuckles warm on her skin as he worked the pin into the ribbed neck of her sweater.

"I might lose it," she worried. "What if the clasp comes loose?"

"Then I'll buy you another."

His lack of concern shouldn't have surprised her. Nor should she be disappointed by the realization that he didn't attach any particular sentiment to the exquisite piece.

It was a gift, she told herself as they drove the winding back roads to the base. A thoughtful, beautiful gift, one he wanted her to have. Of course it wouldn't mean as much to him as it did to her.

Only after they'd arrived at the picnic did she realize that his beautiful, thoughtful gift was also a brand.

Chapter Ten

Not five minutes after they arrived at the pine-edged recreation area known as Camp Springs Lake, Jo knew she should have listened to her gut instincts and scrubbed this whole idea.

The picnic proved a total disaster. Word of Alex's identity spread like wildfire. Heads turned as they wove their way through the noisy throng. The spouses who had begun to draw Jo into their friendly circles kept their distance. Crewmates who ordinarily would have popped a beer with her and joked about the latest absurdities coming from higher headquarters seemed to feel they had to watch their manners around the grandson of a President.

Seemingly relaxed, Alex didn't appear to notice the looks aimed his way. He even smiled and agreed to pose for the giggling preteens who asked if they could take a picture with him. To Jo's embarrassment, one photo op led to another and then another as kids went for parents, parents for their cameras, and a line formed.

"I'm sorry," she murmured between takes. "I promised you no photographers."

"I don't mind," he assured her graciously, although

she could tell he was as relieved as she when the line finally dwindled. She could only hope that no one decided to sell their shots to the tabloids.

With the feeling of having run a gauntlet, Jo turned. The broad-shouldered figure coming toward them made her realize she had one more challenge yet to face. Her stomach sinking, she introduced Alex to Deke Elliott.

The pilot's eyes were cool, but he transferred his beer to his left hand, swiped the dew from his right on the leg of his jeans, and took Alex's hand in a friendly enough grip.

"Glad to see you didn't sustain any serious injury in that car wreck, Taylor."

"Thanks to Jo. She's quite something."

"Yes, she is." Deke's hazel eyes flicked to the pin adorning her sweater. "And so well-dressed, too. Nice piece, West."

"It is, isn't it? It's a birthday gift."

She didn't kid herself. She knew exactly what drove her prickly need to explain the sparkling diamonds. Deke had come so close, so dangerously close, to breaking through her self-imposed restrictions against getting involved with someone in her unit. If she'd taken him up on his offer of a video combat rematch, if she hadn't met Alex when she did . . .

Firmly, Jo pushed the traitorous thoughts aside. She wasn't the kind of woman to play two men against each other. She didn't have the inclination, the energy, or the skill for those kinds of games. Still, she couldn't suppress a little spurt of relief when Deke slipped into his usual, laid-back self.

"Which birthday is this, West? Thirty-one? Thirty-two?"

"Hey, let's not rub salt in the wound. I'm thirty and proud of it . . . not that you need to broadcast that information around the squadron."

"My lips are sealed," he promised with a glint in his eyes that suggested otherwise.

"I offered Jo a trip to the south of France to celebrate the momentous occasion," Alex said, sliding an arm around her waist. "Unfortunately, her schedule isn't as flexible as mine."

Deke didn't miss the message conveyed by Alex's words or his casually possessive hold.

"I'm sure you'll work something out," he drawled, his Wyoming twang out in full force. Lifting his beer, he tipped the bottle toward a couple ensconced at a table in one of the pavilions.

"You'd better introduce your guest to the boss, Jo. He's been shooting glances this way."

"Yes, I guess I'd better."

"Maybe we'll get a chance to talk again, Taylor."

"Maybe."

Jo hadn't grown up surrounded by brothers without learning to recognize the signs of two males circling each other to determine just where one's territory ended and the other's began. The fur was up. The smiles had taken on the predatory edge of bared teeth.

Sure enough, Alex slanted her a narrow glance as they made their way to the pavilion.

"Am I poaching on Elliott's preserves?"

"Deke and I are just friends."

"Not by his choice."

It wasn't a question, but it deserved an answer.

"No, not by his choice."

"Good. That saves me having to take him out of the competition."

"You're not in a competition, Alex. Wherever we go from here is between us. Only us."

"Us, and the United States Air Force."

Since Colonel Marshall and his wife were within earshot, Jo chose not to respond to Alex's dry reminder that her job constraints kept getting in his way. Instead, she introduced him to the director of operations and his vivacious spouse.

If Marshall had any opinion about Jo's obvious involvement with the man who'd generated such a flurry of phone calls from higher headquarters, he didn't show it. He greeted Alex with the same careful politeness the others had displayed.

Jo bit back a sigh. Where the heck did she get the crazy idea that inviting Alex to this gathering would bridge some of the gap between their worlds? She might have come to regard him as a fascinating, complex individual, but the rest of the squadron saw him only as a VIP. They hauled the bigwigs where they needed to go, but didn't socialize with them. Jo had crossed an invisible line and felt it.

The colonel's wife, however, didn't seem worried about any lines. An economics professor at the University of Maryland, Eve Marshall proved no more immune to Alex's blue-eyed charm than Jo. He soon had Eve laughing at a highly unlikely explanation of how the university had chosen the terrapin as their mascot.

The 1st Helo Squadron's commander and his wife drifted over to join them some moments later, bringing along the brigadier general who commanded the 89th Wing. General Orr had stopped by the picnic as a show of support for the squadron, as he did for all the units under his command, but evidently decided to stay for a while. He was dressed casually in a knit shirt and slacks, his handheld radio squawking occasionally with the normal weekend business of the busy base. His greeting to Alex contained the confidence of a man used to welcoming the presidents and dignitaries who flew aboard Air Force One and the rest of the wing's aircraft.

"It's a pleasure to meet you, Mr. Taylor. I had the honor of flying your grandfather some years ago. I was the pilot on the aircraft that flew him to India when he represented the United States at the funeral of the former Prime Minister."

"He was a great admirer of Mrs. Gandhi," Alex explained with a smile that charmed the women and put the men at ease. "Although he did his best to sway her from her stubborn neutrality toward the Soviet Union, he appreciated the problem of having the Soviet Bear for a neighbor."

"Didn't he help broker a truce between India and Bangladesh when war almost broke out over a border dispute a few years ago?" Eve Marshall put in. "I remember reading that he was nominated for a Nobel Peace Prize."

"The dispute was actually more of a religious one between the Hindus and Muslims than a territorial one, but J.T. managed to exert some behind-the-scenes pressure and put the lid on it before it flared into war."

"If only he could exert some behind-the-scenes pressure with Pakistan," General Orr commented.

With only a superficial understanding of the shifting political sands that now aligned the United States and India, often at odds in the past, Jo wisely kept silent. The conversation flowed around her, fast and fascinating, until a raucous cheer drew her attention away.

A flag football game had kicked off in the grassy area beside the lake, pitting maintenance against operations. Charlie Fairbanks, Jo's copilot on the memorable flight to Charlottesville a few weeks ago, streaked down the field with the football tucked tight under one arm and yellow streamers trailing from the waistband of his jeans. Evading pursuers decked with red streamers, Charlie made it halfway down the field before a petite, determined maintenance officer planted herself squarely in his path. Charlie whirled left, collided with another defender, and executed a wild lateral pass just before hitting the grass.

Deke Elliott leaped up and caught the football one-handed. With the agility of the first-string receiver he once was, he dodged one opponent, spun away from another, and shot across the goal line. His teammates followed, whooping, and piled on top of him in the exuberance that characterized the game.

Jo found herself grinning and wishing she was down there in that heap. She loved football. Like most Wisconsonites, she followed the Green Bay Packers with singled-minded devotion, although she'd developed a soft spot for the Redskins in recent months. And as she'd proved on previous occasions, she could more than hold her own in this freewheeling version of the game. Her brother Tom had taught her how to drill one hell of a pass before he abandoned football to enter med school.

Idly, she considered asking Alex if he wanted to join the fun. As quickly as the notion came, she dismissed it. She'd learned a valuable lesson this afternoon. Wealth and privilege didn't mix as readily as she'd hoped it would with rough and tumble.

"Is it true President Taylor's taken a turn for the worse?" Eve Marshall asked, pulling Jo's attention back to the ongoing conversation just in time to catch Alex's swift frown.

"I don't discuss my grandfather's health."

The terse response froze Eve Marshall's smile on her face.

Jo could understand where the curt reply had sprung from. Alex's feelings for his grandfather, like those for his wife, were rooted too deeply to discuss their loss with outsiders. That understanding didn't prevent her from wincing inwardly as Eve flushed with embarrassment.

"I'm sorry. They mentioned it on one of the talk shows recently. I didn't realize—"

"I hope you don't believe everything you hear on talk shows, Mrs. Marshall."

Eve's flush deepened. "No, of course not."

Distinctly uncomfortable, Jo stepped into the breach.

"My own recent brush with the media has given me a new appreciation of what Alex and his grandfather live with every day. I don't think I'll ever open my blinds again until I check to see if someone's looking in from the other side. And *certainly* not until I comb my hair and put on some lipstick."

Her attempt at humor raised a few polite chuckles, but the damage was done. Looping her arm through Alex's, Jo beat a hasty retreat.

"If you'll excuse us, I promised Alex a hot dog and a beer before we leave."

"Are we leaving?" he asked as they wove through the crowd to the two huge, black-barrelled grills that served the squadron for everything from pig roasts to soft shell crab boils.

"Yes." Jo forced a smile. "This wasn't one of my more brilliant ideas. I'm sorry about the kids and the cameras, Alex."

She couldn't bring herself to apologize for Eve Marshall, though. The woman hadn't deserved the terse response Alex had given her. He recognized that fact himself. There, in the midst of the crowded picnic grounds with the sound of kids screeching and the sizzle of hot dogs and hamburgers filling the September air, he opened a part of himself to her.

"I had to throw up barriers to protect myself after Katherine died, Joanna. The vultures who feasted on her death would have picked my bones clean, too, if I'd let them. They'll try to do the same when my grandfather dies."

"I know, Alex."

"No, you don't. You can't. I wish I could spare you that part of my life. I wish I could shut you away in an ivory tower and keep you safe from the Stroders of the world."

This wasn't the time or the place to tell him she

had no desire to live in an ivory tower. Later, she vowed. They'd talk later.

"Why don't we skip the hot dogs?" she suggested. "I can pull a couple of steaks out of the freezer, zap them in the microwave, then fire up the grill at home to give them that genuine charcoal flavor."

"Sounds good to me. I do a mean Caesar salad, if you have the makings."

"Everything but anchovies."

The idea of Alex going to work in her tiny kitchen helped dispel a good bit of her disappointment over the picnic. They'd eat in the dining room, she decided. Or maybe on the living room floor in front of the fire. With no butlers, no maids, and no kids or parents with cameras to interrupt them.

Not until she'd climbed into the MG to drive them back to her place did Jo realize she'd already begun bricking in the walls of their solitary tower.

After the disaster of the afternoon, the evening promised pure magic.

It was four-thirty by the time they pulled into Jo's drive, and close to five when Alex polished off the glass of Merlot she poured him. Shedding his ball cap, he fashioned an apron out of a red-and-white checkered dish towel.

"Behold the master at work."

She dropped into a chair, one leg tucked under her, content to watch while he arranged the assembled ingredients to his satisfaction on the counter. He soon had her laughing helplessly as he wielded a long knife with the dramatic flourish of a Samurai warrior. The wooden chopping board rattled with each swipe. Romaine leaves flew into the air. Some even made it into the salad bowl.

"Aren't you supposed to rub the sides of the bowl with garlic before you add the greens?"

"Only if I want to ward off vampires, along with the woman I haven't kissed in the past three hours. Correction . . ." The knife paused long enough for him to check his ultrathin Swiss watch. "Three hours and seventeen minutes."

Chuckling, Jo sipped her Merlot. "It's been that long, huh?"

"Seems like a lifetime." The lettuce took another leap into the air. Alex batted it into the bowl with the skill of a major league pinch hitter. "So are you going to just sit there or come over here?"

"Well . . ."

Bringing her wineglass with her, she offered him a sip. He smiled at her over the rim. Jo thought she'd never get used to the way those dark-ringed eyes seemed to cut into her soul.

Or the way his mouth moved so hungrily over hers.

It always startled her, his swift transition from erudite sophisticate to pure male. As if he shed his outer layers with the contact and loosed the inner being. The kiss consumed her. Fired her. That she could ignite such swift, intense passion in him thrilled her.

Gasping, she pulled back. Alex held her for a long, shuddering moment, one hand buried in the hair at her nape and the other holding the knife disconcertingly close to her cheek.

Sliding his fingers free of her nape, he wrapped them around the stem of the glass she still clutched in her fist and tipped it to her mouth.

"Drink your wine, my darling, while I fix the salad. Then we'll eat, stretch out before the fire, and continue what we've started here."

As if she could force anything down her throat now! She tried to tell him so, but he'd already turned back to his masterpiece.

He knew how to play the game to maximum effect, Jo soon realized. That soft promise acted as no aphrodisiac ever could. Anticipation sang in her blood all through dinner. Little licks of heat seared her skin and fanned a slow, steady flame. Each glance, each smile, each casual touch added another spark to the fire.

Yet even the most intense blaze would eventually burn itself out. Over a bowl of Ben and Jerry's double chocolate fudge, Jo's shivery anticipation took on an edge of impatience.

The candles she'd lit all around the living room gave even her little rented house a seductive atmosphere. The place might not compete with a villa in France in the long run, but for tonight it would do. More than do.

Shadows danced on the cream-colored walls. Eartha Kitt crooned her signature "Smoke Gets in Your Eyes" from the CD player. It was time, Jo decided. Past time.

Sliding the ice cream bowl off its resting place on the flat plane of Alex's stomach, she replaced it with her hand. Her fingers slipped under his sweatshirt to tug at the knit shirt underneath. Before they found the warm flesh they sought, however, Alex surged up on one elbow and tumbled her onto the pillows.

"Oh, no, Joanna. I've been thinking about this for weeks. Planning every touch."

Impatience flicked through her once again. She was all for setting the scene, but there was something to be said for a little spontaneity, too. She buried the thought in a determination to enjoy the moment.

Smiling, he started on the buttons of her fuzzy purple sweater. The first button bared the hollow of her throat to his mouth. The second, the soft skin of her shoulders.

"You taste like white chocolate."

Her stomach quivered on a laugh. "I think that may be Ben and Jerry you're tasting."

Slowly, so slowly, he slid the rest of the buttons through the loops and peeled back the sweater. His lips left small brands. His teeth gently scraped her nerve endings. Under her scoop-necked bra, Jo's nipples hardened.

Alex's hand closed over her breast, exploring its shape, teasing the rigid center with thumb and forefinger.

"I've been fantasizing about this since I saw those pictures of you in the tabloids."

"I thought you didn't read the— Oh!"

Gasping at the nip of his teeth on her engorged nipple, she arched under him. Pleasure streaked from her breast to every finger and toe. Pleasure, and a small thrill of pain.

The sensations were still jolting through her system when Alex lifted her just enough to drag the bra over her head. It caught at her elbows, binding her arms behind her back. Jo tried to pull them free, but Alex's weight combined with her own to push her into the cushions, her arms still twisted behind her back.

"I can't touch you," she protested, half embarrassed and wholly aroused by the glitter in his eyes as he unzipped her jeans.

"I don't want you to touch me, my darling. Not yet."

His palm splayed on her belly, pushed down her jeans and panties. Not all the way to her ankles. Barely to her knees. Just enough to give him room to slide a hand between her thighs. His palm cupped her mound, his fingers found the hot center it protected.

They'd go for spontaneous next time, Jo decided on a wave of pure sensation. This scripted seduction was erotic, so foreign and exciting. She'd never made love like this, sprawled across a pile of cushions, exposed, entangled, unable to reciprocate. Never been made love to with such intense deliberation.

His fingers explored her with a nimble skill that soon had her wet and trembling.

"Alex . . ."

"Just enjoy, my darling. Learn. . . ."

"Learn?"

She wasn't exactly a neophyte, although she'd never played the game in quite this manner.

"How I like it," he murmured, bending to rake her nipple with his teeth again.

It took a few moments for that husky "I" to penetrate the pleasure coursing through her body. There should have been a "we" in there somewhere, she thought. Awash on a wave of tingly sensation, she suddenly needed to play in the game, too.

"I want to touch you," she panted. "Raise up a little so I can untangle my arms."

"No, not yet. You're not ready."

Her pleasure ebbing sharply, she tugged at her bound arms. "Let me up."

"Not yet."

"Alex, I don't like this."

"You will," he promised in a silky whisper. "Katherine did. Whatever else we disagreed about, she always liked this."

The hairs on the back of Jo's neck stood on end. Katherine! He was making love to Katherine. It was his wife he held pinned to the pillows, his wife he intended to pleasure in an erotic ritual of dominance and submission they'd obviously raised to an art form.

Before she could gasp out that she wasn't Katherine, that she'd love him in her own way or not at all, he covered her mouth in a savage kiss.

Surprise held her immobile for a heartbeat, maybe two. Then her brain kicked into gear. Fury whipped through her. Fury, hurt, and disappointment.

But not fear. She'd learned too many moves from her childhood and her various Air Force survival and self-defense courses to doubt her ability to end this scene. It was *how* she'd end it that engaged her thoughts while Alex engaged her mouth.

Before she could decide, an alarm pierced the harsh, pounding thunder of her heart.

Not an alarm, she realized after Alex dragged his mouth from hers. A phone. His phone.

His brow slashing into a frown, he rolled to one side. "I'm sorry, Jo. I have to take it."

"Sorry isn't the word for it," she muttered, trembling with the force of her rage.

While he dug a slim cell phone out his back pocket, she yanked her arms free of the black spandex and snatched up her sweater. She was fumbling with her jeans when Alex's sharp exclamation snapped her head around.

"How bad is it?"

He shot to his feet, his face draining of all color.

"Have the jet ready. I'll be there in fifteen minutes."

Flipping the cell phone shut, he spun to face her.

"It's my grandfather," he managed, his skin stretched tight across his cheekbones. "He's had another stroke. They don't know . . . The doctors . . ."

He stopped, his throat working.

Pity found its way through Jo's bubbling anger. She'd almost lost a brother once. Even now, after all these years, she could remember the long, silent vigils by Jack's hospital bed.

"I have to leave, Jo. I'm sorry," he said again.

She couldn't lay her own tumultuous feelings on him now. Not with his face taut with worry and his thoughts already winging to the bedside of the only person in the world he had left.

"I'll call you," he promised on his way out the door. "As soon as I know how he is, I'll call you. . . . And thanks for a wonderful day."

Chapter Eleven

Shivering in the damp chill that had swept in with October, Jo unlocked her back door Monday evening just as a sharp ring broke the silence inside her house.

Alex.

He'd called last night. Twice. She'd been on alert, standing in for another pilot who'd come down with the flu, but the message he'd left on her answering machine had wrung her heart. His grandfather's stroke had robbed him of all movement and much of his speech. Alex planned to stay with him indefinitely. He'd left a number, asked her to return the call.

Jo had intended to . . . as soon as she figured out what the heck she wanted to say to him. Goose bumps still popped out on her skin whenever she thought of those moments by the fire.

The phone's ring cut through the air once again. While she hurried through the kitchen, the answering machine kicked on and rattled off her breezy leave-a-message instructions. She plucked the cordless phone from its charger cradle and was just about to stab at the talk button when a deep, rich baritone jumped out of the recorder.

"Joanna, this is Alex."

Her finger hovered over the button.

"Call me. I need to hear your voice."

The request took on a bite.

"Tonight, Joanna. The number is—"

She punched the key. "Hello, Alex."

"You're there?"

He sounded surprised, as if the possibility she might listen to his message and not pick up had never occurred to him. Jo guessed few people failed to answer when Alexander Taylor called.

"I just came in the door and heard you on the machine. How's your grandfather?"

"The same."

"I'm so sorry." Unzipping her brown leather flight jacket, she dropped into the chair beside the phone. "What's the prognosis?"

"Not good, I'm afraid."

"I'm sorry," she said again, recognizing the inadequacy of the words. A small silence spun out, broken by Alex a moment later.

"I called you last night. Where were you?"

She blinked at the abrupt question. Just in time, she swallowed her instinctive retort: It wasn't really any of his business. Her brothers might shrug off that kind of knee-jerk response from the little sister whose life they'd insisted on poking their collective noses into. Alex deserved better.

"I had to pull alert for another pilot who got bit by the flu bug. I was going to call you tonight."

"I don't like not being able to reach you. I'm going to give you a specially configured phone, similar to the one I carry. It's small enough to fit in the pocket of your flight suit and keyed directly into my private number."

"That's not necessary."

"Not necessary, perhaps, but eminently convenient. We can speak to each other at the press of a single button."

"And what happens if you press that button while I'm cruising along at three thousand feet and a hundred plus knots? The wrong kinds of electronic transmissions could screw up my radio signals, maybe even send my aircraft into a dive."

"Don't joke about something like that!"

The whip in his voice earned him a cool reply.

"I wasn't joking, Alex. I never joke about flight safety."

He drew in a ragged breath. "I'm sorry. I can't handle the thought of losing you right now, even in the abstract."

Her fingers tightened on the phone. *Tell him*, her conscience urged. Tell him he lost you two nights ago, in front of the fire . . . not that he'd ever really had you.

They'd come close, though. So very close. For a few brief, shining moments she'd almost let herself believe the prince and the dairyman's daughter might find that happily ever after.

"Can you come down to BellaVista?"

His request jerked her out of her thoughts. "I don't think that's a good idea."

"I need you, Joanna."

Tell him.

"I can't."

"Is it your work?"

Impatience bit at his voice. He needed her. He wanted her. In his mind, that took precedence over such mundane matters as her job.

"If your schedule's a problem, I can take care of that with a single phone call."

"Alex, we agreed! That night in the limo coming home from the White House, remember? No interference in my career."

She felt him reigning in, could almost hear him exercise his formidable control.

"You're right. Forgive me. My grandfather's condition has shaken me more than I realized and . . ." He paused, as if weighing his words. "There's no one here I can talk to."

An ache opened in her chest. She could only guess at how much it cost him to admit that.

"No one to share the long, endless nights with," he added.

"I'm not sure I'm the right one to share them with you," she said slowly.

"I'm sure, my darling."

The endearment that had so thrilled her when he'd first used it didn't carry quite the same impact at this particular moment.

"Alex, listen to me. The other night, here at the house, I wanted to make love with you."

"I thought I'd made it clear I wanted the same thing." He chuckled, putting his own spin on her odd remark. "If that message didn't come through, I'd better brush up on my technique."

Tell him now!

"Your technique doesn't need practice. You've honed it to a fine art. You and Katherine."

The name produced a stark silence. Swallowing a sting of regret, Jo forged ahead.

"You said her name, Alex. When you were making love to me, you said her name."

And you showed me her portrait, she thought on a silent sigh. I saw her bedroom at Chestnut Hill, as white and still as a marble tomb.

"You don't understand, Joanna. No one does."

"No, I don't think I do."

"Come to BellaVista," he said quietly. "Let me tell you about Katherine. Please. Let me try to make it right between us."

Jo played with the zipper of her leather jacket. Up. Down. Up again. Thinking about his request, wondering how he could ever make those moments before the fire right. She owed him the opportunity, she decided. Owed herself the opportunity.

"I'll check with Scheduling tomorrow and see what I can arrange."

"Good."

"Even if I can clear the flying schedule, I wouldn't be able to make it down there until Wednesday afternoon," she added, remembering the call she'd received only that morning from Colonel Marshall.

The Air Force had approved the award of the Airman's Medal, he'd advised her, based on the personal recommendation of the Secretary of State. Mrs. Adair wanted to pin on the medal personally at a ceremony Wednesday morning before she departed Andrews on a flight to the Middle East.

Having won her agreement, Alex shrugged aside the few extra hours delay. "I'll look for you Wednesday afternoon. Fly the Sikorsky down. I'll have my people get in touch with you to make the arrangements."

"All right."

"I knew I could count on you, Joanna. Thank you."

His relief flowed through the phone, accompanied by a need he didn't try to disguise.

Scheduling was willing enough to help her juggle her flights the next morning. Jo had made up enough hours to close out September still current and had the whole month of October yet ahead of her. By taking both her planned afternoon sortie, a night training flight later in the evening, and delaying her next flight until the weekend, she cleared Wednesday afternoon as well as all day Thursday and Friday.

Now all she had to do was get Colonel Marshall's approval for a leave to go out of the area. Since the director of operations had taken a bird up himself this morning and wasn't due down until noon, Jo filled the hours with the last of the preplanning for her night training flight.

When lunchtime rolled around, she declined an offer of a run to the on-base Burger King and opted instead for the dubious delights of the vending machines in the crew lounge. A pine-paneled room filled with the usual motley collection of Formica-topped break tables, a few sofas, a big-screen TV and the inevitable Nintendo hook-up, the lounge ebbed and flowed with green-suited crew members. Pepsi cans littered the table. Boots were propped on handy chairs. Hoots and catcalls punctuated a talk-show host's earnest attempts to convince a currently reigning beauty queen to confess her supposed affair with another woman.

Leafing through an issue of *Rotor Review* that one of the pilots had brought back from a visit to a Navy helo unit, Jo tuned out the ribald comments. She'd long ago defined her own comfort level with this kind of testosterone-induced irreverence. No woman could operate successfully in a primarily male field without learning where to draw the line . . . and how to draw that line without becoming a martyr or a dweeb.

She'd become so absorbed in a Navy pilot's first-hand experience with autorotation—his helo's aerodynamics after total engine failure—that she didn't register the owner of the boots propped beside hers on a handy chair until Deke's distinctive drawl pierced her consciousness.

"All set for your command performance, West?"

"What command performance?"

"The award ceremony tomorrow." The skin beside his eyes crinkled. "We're all planning to turn out to watch Wonder Woman get another gold star."

She tried to shrug it off. "Don't bother. It's no big deal."

"Right. It's such an un-big deal that the Secretary of State herself is pinning the medal on your chest."

"C'mon, Deke. You and I both know I came as close to taking a serious career hit over that incident as I did to getting a medal."

"Yeah, well, I'm glad it worked out this way for you."

The sincerity behind the simple statement warmed her. Like Jo, Deke understood the vagaries of their profession. No mission was ever routine, despite the many checklists, procedures, and extensive training. Every flight contained the potential for either glory or disaster.

"I'm glad it worked out this way, too," she replied, tossing the magazine aside to hook her fingers across her stomach.

Funny how comfortable she felt sitting here beside Deke. More comfortable than she had in weeks. Not for the first time, Jo regretted the wall she'd erected between them. Deke walked the same walk she did. He talked the same shorthand of technical terminology, military acronyms, and slang so incomprehensible to anyone outside the flying fraternity. They shared so many common points of reference. Too many, she'd worried.

Now . . .

Now her relationship with Alex was providing an entirely new perspective. As difficult as it had been for Jo and her former fiancé to juggle the demands of their military careers, she'd discovered that it was even more of a challenge to balance that career with an outsider's demands on her time and attention. Particularly an outsider like Alexander Taylor, who possessed the resources and the will to arrange his world to suit himself.

Life, Jo decided on a wry inner grimace, had a way of complicating itself.

As if reading her mind, Deke slanted her a considering glance. "Is Taylor going to grace us with his presence at the award ceremony?"

"No. His grandfather took a turn for the worse."

"I'm sorry to hear that. When did it happen?"

"Over the weekend. That's not for public consumption, okay?"

Sudden howls of laughter from the other crew members drowned Deke's reply, but Jo knew she could trust him.

"When did you hear?" he asked when the noise died.

"Alex got the call at my place Saturday night and flew down to Richmond to be with him."

A touch of frost chilled the friendliness and concern in Deke's green-brown eyes. "At your place, huh?"

Jo cursed her slip. She hadn't intended to rub his nose in her confusing relationship with Alex.

"Are you open to a few words of advice, West?"

"It depends on what the advice pertains to."

"Watch yourself with Taylor. I suspect he doesn't fly by the same rules as ordinary mortals."

Jo had already figured that out for herself, but she didn't intend to discuss Alex with Deke, any more than she'd discuss Deke with Alex.

"I've got both hands on the controls, but I appreciate your concern." She pushed off the sofa. "I'd better go check weather. I'm first off the spot this afternoon."

His jaw grinding, Deke watched her stride away. Concern, hell!

Concern didn't figure anywhere in the feelings Jo West generated within him. Desire, yes. Frustration, definitely. And adding fuel to the combustible mix was his instant, instinctive dislike for Alexander Taylor.

Deke didn't kid himself. He knew exactly what

drove that dislike. He'd waited too long to make his move.

Taylor, on the other hand, hadn't waited at all. He'd seen what he wanted and gone after it. The arm he'd banded around Jo's waist at the picnic had marked her as his possession as much as those diamonds flashing on her sweater.

Deke hadn't missed Jo's flicker of embarrassment when he'd commented on the pin. It hadn't been hard to guess that she wouldn't have worn something like that to a picnic if Taylor hadn't pressed it on her. His kind, Deke thought sardonically, always pressed.

And given his way, Taylor would press everything that made Jo West so unique right out of her. There was no way he'd adjust his lifestyle to Jo's. No way he'd accept a schedule that kept her from jetting off for a trip to the south of France. Jo couldn't continue her military career and maintain a relationship with one of the world's richest men. The lady thought she was flying straight, but she was riding for a fall.

Deke was damned if he was going to hang around to watch it. His boots hit the floor with a thump. Scooping up his helmet bag, he abandoned the lounge. He'd driven into work at five A.M. and flown a four-hour sortie. The rest of his day was clear. He'd finish the paperwork, debrief his crew, and get the hell out of Dodge.

He was headed through the mission planning area when one of the administrative troops from the front office escorted a civilian down the hall. Deke recognized both the man and his gray uniform. Taylor's chauffeur. The same driver who'd whisked Jo off in a mile-long limo a couple of weeks ago.

Deke's step slowed as Jo sailed out of the mission planning room to greet the driver with a warm smile.

"Patrick. What are you doing here?"

"Mr. Taylor asked me to deliver this to you."

He handed her what looked like a high-tech, ultrathin flip phone the size of a credit card.

"It's coded to ring only his private number," the chauffeur said helpfully. "You can reach him at any time, day or night."

As if realizing the interest that statement raised among the aircrew members milling around the area, Jo flushed.

"Mr. Taylor asked me to give you this, as well," the driver added, reaching inside his uniform jacket to extract a white envelope. "He indicated it was urgent."

Obviously expecting a note with news of Alex's grandfather, Jo's face clouded with sympathy and concern as she slid a finger under the flap and pulled out a fat document. Those emotions gave way to surprise as she unfolded several legal-sized, gold-bordered pages.

"What is this?"

"I believe it's the title and a copy of the registration for the Sikorsky, Captain West."

"I don't need to see a copy of the title and registration. I've already had the pleasure of flying aboard that baby. I know she's airworthy."

"Mr. Taylor was very specific. He felt you should have them in your possession before the flight to BellaVista tomorrow afternoon."

Deke stiffened. As determined as he was to butt out of Jo's affairs, the knowledge she was joining Taylor in Richmond tomorrow ground glass in his gut. His jaw tight, he turned away.

"Mr. Taylor instructed me to tell you to contact his lawyers if you have any questions about the title transfer."

"Transfer?"

Deke stopped in his tracks and spun around in time to catch the sudden incredulity that flashed across Jo's face. He had an idea of what was coming even before she scanned through the pages, one after another.

She found what she was looking for on the last page. Disbelief widened her eyes. The papers rattled like dried leaves in her hands.

"He transferred the helicopter's title to *me*?"

The last word was a squeak, echoed by a long whistle from the crew dog who leaned over her shoulder to peer at the document.

"Holy shit! It's yours, West. All yours."

"This is a mistake."

"Hey, when you hang up your uniform and start piloting yourself and your boyfriend all across the country, think about hiring me on as your copilot. I could use one of those million-dollar bonuses Taylor hands out like candy."

"Shut up, Cassidy!"

Refolding the papers, she shoved them in the envelope and thrust them at the chauffeur.

"I can't accept these."

His hands spread apologetically. "I'm just the messenger, Captain."

"Well, you can messenger these right back. He can't really be serious."

"You'll have to talk to Mr. Taylor about that."

The standoff continued for another second or two before Jo conceded defeat. "All right. I will."

Unzipping one of the pockets on her flight suit, she stuffed the envelope inside. When she straightened, her eyes caught Deke's. Lifting one brow, he sketched her a sardonic smile.

"Glad to see you've got both hands on the controls, West."

Chapter Twelve

Still in shock over Alex's transfer of the Sikorsky to her, Jo retreated to an empty office, slammed the door, and flipped open the thin phone. A message marched instantly across the digital display, informing her that a private, precoded number had been entered.

Alex answered within mere seconds. "Hello, darling. I see Patrick got hold of you."

"Yes, he did. I can't believe . . . I can't imagine . . ." She shoved her feathery bangs off her forehead, struggling for breath. "How could you think I would accept the Sikorsky as a gift?"

"I hope you'll accept it, just as I hope you'll accept everything else I want to give you."

"Alex—"

"I'm sorry, darling," he inserted before she could explode. "I can't discuss it with you right now. I'm with the doctors. I'll call you later, all right?"

A glance at the wall clock killed the notion she could straighten this out by phone. "I've got missions this afternoon and evening. I'm not sure when I'll be down."

"Then you call me."

Jo could hear the worry pulling at him. Sighing, she let him off the hook. "We can talk when I get there tomorrow."

Flipping the phone shut, she slumped against a desk. Outside, the aircraft prepped for the afternoon's sorties were lined up on the ramp. The noonday sun glistened on their blue and white paint scheme, but instead of the solid, dependable Hueys, Jo saw only the sleek little tan and white S-76.

She couldn't believe Alex had deeded the helo to her! The gesture overwhelmed her. Mortified her. What in the world had she done or said that would make him think she would accept such a gift?

Well, for starters, her conscience pinged, she'd accepted the diamond pin. Then there was that million-dollar grant to the American Spinal Cord Foundation. And let's not forget about rolling around in front of the fire, getting next to naked with the guy.

A bitter taste rose in the back of Jo's throat. She'd known Alex less than a month and here she was, raking in the prizes like a greedy game show contestant. The picture she painted in her own mind didn't flatter her. She could imagine how it must look to outsiders, even to her friends and coworkers.

Like Deke.

The scorn in his eyes a few minutes ago had stung. All right, it still stung. Her jaw set, Jo crossed her arms and glared at the waiting Hueys. Dammit, she didn't owe Deke any explanations. Didn't owe *anyone* explanations, even if she had them, which she didn't.

The truth of the matter was that her relationship with Alex confused the heck out of her. She liked him.

More than liked him. His insistence on showering her with gifts embarrassed her, however, and his fixation with Katherine had shaken her . . . almost as much as those shivery moments before the fire, when he'd pinned her to the cushions.

That experience more than anything else made her suspect that Alex had never learned to relinquish or even share control. His wealth and privileged background had laid the foundation for the power he wielded like an autocratic potentate. Now he wanted to exercise that control over her. Any one of Jo's brothers could have told him that nothing raised her fur faster.

Looking back, she realized she'd been kidding herself to even imagine she could juggle her work and his demands on her time and attention, much less find some intermediate plane between her world and his. More to the point, she had no desire to play the submissive sexual role he seemed to want from her.

Tomorrow. She'd tell him so tomorrow afternoon, when she returned the diamond pin, the cell phone, and the registration papers for the Sikorsky.

She pushed off the desk, relieved that she felt so right about the decision. This was one fairy-tale romance that wouldn't have a happy ending.

The sense of rightness stayed with Jo for the rest of the day, but took a hit from the message Alex left on her answering machine that evening. He couldn't wait to see her. Couldn't wait to hold her. He needed her, more than she'd ever know.

Guilt tugged at her, but she knew she had to break it off before they got in any deeper. With that thought in mind, she got up early to wash her hair. The award ceremony was scheduled for 8:00 A.M. in the rotunda of the Wing Headquarters building. Jo would have preferred a less ostentatious setting, but no one had seen fit to consult her in the matter.

Getting ready for the ceremony took longer than expected. Not only did she lose track of time while she mentally rehearsed what she wanted to say to Alex this afternoon, drying her hair proved a real challenge. She'd let the thick, honey-colored mass get too long, she realized after a good twenty minutes wielding the dryer. Twisting it into a smooth knot at the back of her head, she applied her makeup with a quick hand.

Luckily, she kept her service uniform set up and ready in her closet. Laying the dark blue coat and skirt on the bed, she checked the accouterments. Her captains bars gleamed on the shoulder epaulets. The silver U.S. insignias were perfectly angled on the lapels. A quick adjustment aligned her shiny silver wings over her two rows of colorful ribbons.

Pushing aside her standard black cotton sports bras and briefs, she fished out some panty hose and ecru undies trimmed in lace. The slide of silk against her skin felt wonderful for a change. Another quick glance at the clock had her shoving her feet into black leather pumps.

Since she wouldn't have time to drive back down to her Fort Washington house to change before meeting Alex's pilot at the helipad, Jo fished a pair of black slacks and a red turtleneck sweater from the closet. Draping a red and black plaid Pendleton wool blazer over the hanger, she grabbed her purse and her flight cap and raced through the kitchen for the door.

She had one hand on the knob, ready to twist, when the memory of her charge out the front door, baseball bat at the ready, to confront a battery of TV cameras and reporters hit her. Jo snatched her hand back, a hitch in her chest.

Just as quickly, she gave herself a mental kick. Her stubborn refusal to issue anything but the one formal statement through Public Affairs about the rescue had just about killed the media's interest in her. Besides, the most persistent of Alex's stalkers was dead.

Still, she sucked in a deep breath before she stepped outside. A quick scan of the fields around the house, awash with early-morning mist, revealed no uninvited visitors or parked vans.

She wouldn't have to worry about reporters or photographers after word leaked that she and Alex weren't seeing each other anymore, she thought on a spurt of guilty relief. In its own small way, that cemented another layer of brick in her decision to end things between them.

An idle comment by the Secretary of State an hour or so later added another layer.

Mrs. Adair personified graciousness as she presided over the award ceremony. With only a half hour to spare before she boarded the aircraft that would carry her and her entourage to Africa in a last-ditch effort to curb the excesses of a murderous dictator, she took the time to describe in her own words Jo's actions the day of the accident.

"Captain West exercised extraordinary heroism in the face of overwhelming odds."

The loudspeaker built into the podium magnified Beth Adair's soft voice and gave it the authoritative ring that had become so well known throughout the world's hot spots.

"Not only did she risk her own life to save another's, but she did so without losing sight of her responsibilities to her passengers and crew."

Standing at rigid attention in front of a bank of flags, Jo kept her eyes trained over the heads of the wing staff and 1st Helo Squadron members who'd gathered for the ceremony. She knew darn well the chief of Mrs. Adair's security detail disagreed with that last statement. He'd said so, in writing. Luckily, DeMotto had weighed his statement against Mrs. Adair's own concurrence and written account of the situation.

Jo almost missed thanking the Secretary for that endorsement. After pinning a gold medal suspended from a blue and gold striped ribbon to Jo's uniform, Mrs. Adair shook her hand, then stepped aside to allow her squadron mates to congratulate her. Along with their congratulations, she also received a good number of suggestions on how to keep from incinerating herself should she ever decide to try something so stupid again.

She shook the last hand and edged around the crowd just in time to catch the Secretary of State at the front entrance to the headquarters building. "Mrs. Adair!"

The Secretary paused just inside the glass doors. Jo hurried across the inlaid marble foyer.

"I wanted to thank you for the letter you wrote, as well as for the recommendation for this medal."

"You're more than welcome. I fully concurred with your decision to take the chopper down, and wanted to make sure the inquiry officer knew that."

She pushed open the door and started down the steps, the morning light flaming her hair into a coppery nimbus.

"By the way, tell Alex I appreciated his call. I wouldn't have even known that you were facing an inquiry if he hadn't notified me."

"He called you?"

"Yes, right after you two attended some function at the White House. He mentioned he'd hoped to catch me there, but I was in Japan at the time."

After the White House function?

Jo managed a smile and a friendly, noncommittal response, but inside she'd gone tight. Dammit, he'd promised! That night, in the limo on the way to the White House, Alex had *promised* he wouldn't interfere or make any more calls. Yet the very next day, he'd contacted the Secretary of State and solicited a personal letter on Jo's behalf.

Frustration piled on top of her anger. Toe tapping in her black leather pump, she eyed the flags lining the wide boulevard. Did it make sense to feel this stinging irritation with a man who'd used his powerful connections to her benefit? The same man who'd transferred a brand new helicopter into her name?

Yes, it did. Jo didn't appreciate behind-the-scenes manipulation any more than the next person. More to the point, she was fast coming to the conclusion she couldn't trust Alex to keep his promises when they conflicted with his own agenda.

She carried that thought with her through the rest of the morning and out to the civilian helipad early that afternoon.

She'd changed into her civilian clothes at the squadron. Her uniform she'd leave in the car. Tucking the envelope with the Sikorsky title and Alex's cell phone into her purse, she climbed out of the MG. A stiff breeze whipped at her hair and blazer as she crossed to the flightline.

Alex's chief pilot, Doug Brakeman, had the Sikorsky preflighted and ready to go. Jo's heart thumped at the sight of the sleek tan and white bird. For a moment, maybe two, her determination to refuse the extraordinary gift dissolved in a puddle of want.

She could keep it, a little devil whispered in her ear. She *should* keep it. Alex's life was certainly worth the price of a helicopter.

But hers wasn't, Jo thought on a sigh. She couldn't allow Alexander Taylor to seduce her with extravagant gifts and promises he had no intention of keeping. Nor could she afford to maintain something like the S-76—which she suspected Alex had factored into the equation.

Brakeman met her at the side of the aircraft, a cheerful grin creasing his weathered features. "Congratulations, Captain. I understand you're the new owner of this little lady."

"For the moment, anyway."

"Mr. Taylor told me to send the paperwork into the FAA to change the registration from GenCorp to you."

"GenCorp?"

"It's one of Mr. Taylor's subsidiaries. Deals mostly in international oil leases, I think. I waited to fill out the paperwork, in case you want to change the tail number."

"Hold off on sending in any paperwork, would you? I've got to talk to Mr. Taylor about this first."

He threw her a considering glance, but was too much of a professional to pry into his employer's affairs. "Are your bags in the car, Captain? I'll have one of the ground crew load them."

"It's Jo," she told him, "and I didn't bring any bags."

His brow wrinkled. "I was under the impression you were going to RON at BellaVista."

Jo had planned to RON—remain overnight, in military parlance. Her plans had changed drastically with the delivery of the deed to the Sikorsky.

"I'll be returning tonight," she told Brakeman. "I'm not sure what time. You'd better call ahead to arrange for refueling and turn-around clearance."

"Can do easy, Captain—Jo. Hang loose while I check tonight's weather and give my crew at Bella-Vista a heads-up."

They lifted off twenty minutes later with Jo in the pilot's seat and Brakeman riding shotgun. Despite her mixed emotions about her coming meeting with Alex, she thoroughly enjoyed her first and last flight as owner/operator of the S-76.

The Virginia countryside rolled by below, already browning in patches where the leaves had fallen and the grass had felt the first bite of winter. For the most part, their route followed I-95 as it cut south. Eight lanes wide for a good distance, it narrowed to six and then four past Richmond.

J. T. Taylor's mansion was nestled in the hills halfway between Richmond and Fredericksburg. The original antebellum plantation home had been completely destroyed during the Civil War, Brakeman informed her as they swooped in from the north and circled the Taylor property. But the former president's family had restored it to its former glory.

"And then some," Jo breathed as she caught sight of the pale gray stone castle.

That was the only way to describe it . . . a castle, richly ornamented, multistoried, and capped with a pitched slate roof. An arched gateway led into a central yard surrounded on three sides by the house itself. What looked like fifty chimneys sprouted from the various wings.

"President Taylor's grandparents pulled out all the stops when they rebuilt the old place in the 1880s," Brakeman related with a grin. "It has more than a hundred rooms, fifteen of them bathrooms, although I have to admit I've never tried to make an actual count. Pretty impressive, isn't it?"

"You got that right."

Jo had seen pictures of the estate in magazines, of course, and vaguely remembered a televised tour of the interior during J. T. Taylor's presidency. No photo or retransmitted image could compare to viewing the actual splendor of the stone masterpiece from the air, however. Awestruck, she banked the Sikorsky into a slow turn.

"Frederick Law Olmsted designed a series of gardens that could be seen from all the rooms," Brakeman informed her.

"Hence the name?" Jo guessed.

"You got it. BellaVista . . . beautiful sight. Supposedly, these gardens rival those he designed for the Biltmore Estate in North Carolina."

They certainly rivaled anything Jo had ever seen. Acres of manicured lawns, gravel walks, and trimmed hedges defined the terraced areas behind the house. Chrysanthemums in rich purples, yellows, and reds provided bright flags of fall color. Scattered throughout the gardens were classical temples and statuary, with a bridge in the same gray stone arching over a small stream.

The helipad and private landing strip had been carefully situated to keep their twentieth-century functionality from impinging on the estate's nineteenth-century elegance. Screened from the house by rows of tall beeches still fluttering with gold leaves, the airfield facilities included a hangar, a small operations center, and quarters for the crews who flew and maintained the Taylor fleet of corporate jets and helicopters . . . one of which, Jo saw after she brought the Sikorsky down in a featherlight landing, was configured as a medical ambulance.

She'd flown enough rescue missions to appreciate the 135-degree hinged doors that allowed easy litter loading and the dams in the grooved floorboards to contain body fluids.

Brakeman caught her sideways glance at the other chopper. Waiting until they'd completed engine shutdown procedures, he confirmed her guess as to its function.

"We've got an EMS crew on twenty-four-hour standby. President Taylor wants to remain at home as long as he can, but we're prepared to transport him to an intensive care facility if necessary."

Jo nodded, her chest tightening at the reminder of Alex's bedside vigil. For a cowardly moment, she regretted giving in to his urgent plea to join him here. The last thing he needed during this crisis was her careful explanation of why she thought it best to cut their relationship off now, before they got in any deeper.

She'd let him talk her into it, however. She was here now. She'd just have to find some way to explain her decision before she left tonight. Slinging the strap of her purse over her shoulder, she walked over to a crewman waiting beside a Jeep.

"Frank will take you up to the house," Brakeman said by way of introduction. "Have someone call down to the hangar when you're ready to head back to D.C. We'll get your aircraft fueled and ready to fly."

She felt odd leaving all the postflight chores to someone else. Odd, too, being driven up a road lined with gorgeous flowers to the front entrance of a castle, where a uniformed maid greeted her.

"Mr. Taylor's waiting for you upstairs, ma'am. He thought you might want to stop in and say hello to President Taylor before I show you to your suite."

President Taylor! Jo hadn't envisioned a bedside meeting with the stricken hero of her youth. Gulping, she followed the maid through a tall, vaulted foyer that might have graced a medieval nobleman's hall. Paneled in oak polished to a golden hue, the entryway boasted graceful alcoves, settees upholstered in rich tapestry, and original works of art. Trailing fingers along a stone railing so smooth it felt like silk, she followed the maid up a wide, branching staircase.

It wasn't Alex who met her at the top of the stairs, however.

Jo recognized the historian she'd met at Alex's Georgetown mansion by his tortoiseshell glasses and feathery fringe of white hair. But it was the expression on the man's face that revved her pulse up a few rpms. She thought she saw desperation, almost fear, in his rheumy blue eyes as he stepped out of an alcove to intercept her.

Chapter Thirteen

"Captain West! May I speak with you a moment?" With some effort, Jo pulled the historian's name from her memory bank.

"Of course, Dr. Russ."

"Mr. Taylor is waiting for her, Sir," the maid interjected.

"I'll escort the captain to President Taylor's bedside."

"But my orders were to bring her right up."

"I'll take care of it."

Waving a thin hand, the historian shooed the young woman away. She threw a worried glance down the hall, but didn't protest further.

"What is it?" Jo asked, catching the nervous look the professor sent in the same direction. "Has President Taylor . . . Is he . . . ?"

"He's holding on by a thread."

Grasping her elbow, Russ drew her toward a bench tucked inside the alcove. Vases of bloodred gladiolas on marble pedestals flanked the crimson brocade bench. Trapped by the low, shell-shaped ceiling, the flowers' scent combined with that of the historian's tweed jacket to thicken the air in the little space.

"I didn't know you were coming down until this morning," he began, his shaggy white eyebrows twitching. "I had no idea you and Alex had become so intimate that he would invite you to attend his grandfather's deathbed."

Taken aback by his blunt intrusion into what she considered a private matter, Jo didn't answer.

"There are matters you don't understand, Captain. Matters I've become privy to as I've chronicled the affairs of this family."

"I don't consider my relationship with Alex Taylor a matter for the family chronicles."

"You must . . ."

He broke off, his clouded blue eyes narrowing at the sound of a door opening at the far end of the hall. He cocked his head, caught the firm tread of footsteps on the hardwood floor. Frowning, he extracted an old-fashioned fountain pen and spiral-bound notebook from his jacket pocket.

"We'll speak later," he murmured, scribbling hurriedly with fingers stained blue-black at the tip. "If not here, perhaps in Washington. Here's my home phone. Call me. We'll arrange a meeting."

He tore the sheet out, folded it, and slipped it into the pocket of Jo's blazer.

"Call me," he urged. "It's most important."

As the footsteps neared, he wiped any trace of urgency from his voice and all expression from his face except a mournful respect.

"I know, my dear. President Taylor's legacy will impact this country for generations. I've truly been privileged to . . . Oh, hello, Alex."

Astounded by the professor's swift about-face, Jo swiveled on the bench.

A small shock raced along her skin as Alex's eyes cut into her like lasers. Even now, after all the hours she'd spent with the man, those dark-ringed blue eyes still disconcerted her. The fact that they came framed in such a stunningly handsome face only added to their impact. Alex looked every inch the aristocrat today, his shoulders square in a navy blazer sporting double rows of monogrammed gold buttons, a silk scarf folded into a loose ascot at the neck of his white shirt.

Expecting a welcome, Jo found herself surprised for the second time in as many minutes when he ignored her to pin the historian with a cold look.

"I was told you'd waylaid my guest, Martin."

"We met on the stairs," the professor said airily. "I took the opportunity to reintroduce myself to the captain, and invite her once again to get in touch with me. I still wish to record her firsthand account of the tragic accident that almost took your life."

He gave her hand an absent pat and rose. "Call me, dear."

Alex's solid presence blocked his exit from the alcove. Jo saw only the back of Russ's head, his pink scalp showing above the fringe of whispy white, but Alex's face was clearly visible. His jaw was clamped so tight that white showed around the dimple in his chin. After a moment or two, the younger man backed up a step to allow the elder to pass. His eyes followed Russ's progress down the hall.

"Is that what he wanted?" he demanded, swinging back to Jo. "To talk to you about the accident?"

She pushed off the bench, disconcerted once again by his lack of welcome. "Hello to you, too."

An emotion Jo couldn't quite define rippled across his face. Annoyance? Irritation that she would take him to task like that? Before she could decide, his lips curved in a rueful smile.

"I'm sorry, Joanna. Russ hovers over me like a preying mantis, trying to delve into parts of my life that have no place in history. I tolerate him for my grandfather's sake, but I won't allow him to harass you."

"He wasn't harassing me."

He'd startled her, yes, and confused her with his almost furtive secretiveness. Jo would have to decide later whether she'd agree to his request for an interview. At the moment, Alex demanded her full attention.

He drew her into his arms, his eyes glittering now in unmistakable welcome. "I've missed you, my darling. So very much."

With that, he bent and ground his mouth down on hers.

That was Alex, she thought on a cynical note. So sophisticated in manner and speech, so savage in his needs. His rough magic didn't thrill her as much now as it had before. If he noticed her lack of response, he gave no indication. Heat flushed his cheeks when he drew away.

"I'm glad you're here."

"Alex . . ."

"We'll have time for each other later. First, I want you to meet my grandfather."

She hung back, hesitant to intrude on a man so

gravely ill. "It would be an honor, but he doesn't need strangers hovering over him at a time like this."

"You're not a stranger." He tucked his arm in hers and drew her down the hall. "I've told him all about you. Where you were born, what you do in the Air Force, our plans for the future."

Jo stumbled, her mind bouncing back and forth between the astounding fact that one of the most influential men of the twentieth century knew where she was born and the equally astounding fact that Alex had talked to him about their supposed future.

She had to stop this freight train before it careened completely out of control, she realized in dismay. With that thought echoing through her head, Jo was ushered into the President's sickroom.

She'd encountered death on only a handful of occasions in her rescue career, but those few were enough for her to sense its presence the instant she stepped into the shadowy chamber. Crimson brocade drapes shielded its tall windows, filtering out all but a few determined sunbeams. An inch-thick Persian carpet muffled their approach to the massive bed adorned with ornately carved walnut head- and footboards, but nothing could mute the rhythmic clack of an oxygen machine or the soft beep of life support equipment. The team of medical personnel attending the President stepped aside at Alex's approach.

Eyes closed, John Tyree Taylor lay propped against a bank of pillows. Above the clear plastic oxygen mask, his skin stretched gaunt over hollowed cheeks and sunken eye sockets. Jo might not have recognized him if not for the shock of wavy hair. Only

after she and Alex moved closer did she see that the
trademark silver mane she remembered so well from
her youth had dulled with age and illness.

Jo cringed inside, feeling like a voyeur at the ceremonial passing of a king. She didn't belong here,
didn't want to intrude on the last moments of someone who deserved peace and privacy. She was about
to say so when J. T. Taylor's veined eyelids fluttered.

Slowly, so slowly, they lifted, revealing the same
distinctive eyes he'd passed to his grandson. He
stared unseeing at the wall opposite his bed until
Alex moved into his line of sight.

"Hello, J.T."

The President dragged his gaze to his grandson's
face. Those fragile lids beat like butterfly's wings,
struggling to ward off the darkness.

"I've brought Joanna, J.T. Remember, I told you
about her? She's the woman who saved my life . . .
in more ways than one."

With a tug on Jo's hand, Alex drew her into the
dying man's field of vision.

"It's an honor to meet you, Mr. President."

He regarded her for long seconds with eyes barely
comprehending above the oxygen mask. In an agony
of embarrassment for having been thrust on him like
this, Jo forced a smile.

"My aunt Gert still talks about the time your train
made a whistle-stop in Milwaukee during your first
campaign. According to her, you washed down a
giant-sized bowl of ice cream with what she swears
was a gallon of beer. You've been her hero ever since."

For the barest instant, an answering smile softened

the gaunt lines of Taylor's face. One side of his mouth moved in an indistinct mumble.

"I . . . washed down . . . more than ice cream . . . to win that . . . election."

The smile faltered and his lids dropped again, as if the few words had used what little strength he had left. Alex laid his hand gently over his grandfather's.

"I'll come back shortly, J.T., as soon as I get Joanna settled."

Thin, clawlike fingers caught at his grandson before he could withdraw.

"Keep . . . this . . . one."

The plastic oxygen mask muffled the order, but it was still audible to Jo. As was Alex's soft reply.

"I intend to."

The imminence of death left Jo subdued, but Alex had faced it long enough now to summon a smile as he escorted her from his grandfather's suite.

"Would you like a sherry before I show you around?"

Jo had only experimented with sherry once before. That taste had convinced her to stick to beer. Since sherry was all that was offered, however, she accepted with a nod. The visit to President Taylor left her feeling shaken. As did the way Alex tucked her hand in his with a casual, unconscious propriety.

"I had them put you in the west wing," he told her as they neared the stairs. "It has the best view of the gardens. The maids should have unpacked your bags by now, if you'd like to freshen up first."

Jo pulled in a deep breath. She'd hoped for a more

private setting to break the news that she wasn't staying, but this would have to do.

"I didn't bring any bags."

His step slowed. "Why not?"

"I can't stay."

A muscle jumped under the sleeve of his navy blazer. She felt the sudden tension even as red surged into his cheeks.

"This is absurd. If those idiots at the base won't let you take off a few days to visit a dying former President, it's time they were replaced."

Jo blinked, as astonished at his sweeping indictment of her entire chain of command as by his assumption he could eradicate them at will.

"Perhaps it's time for you to think about leaving the military, as well."

"Excuse me?"

"I need you, Joanna. I want you with me, and not just for the few hours you can wring from your job."

He said it with such finality, as if his needs took precedence over all others, that it took her breath away. It was just seeping back into her lungs . . . along with a healthy tide of anger . . . when a maid appeared at the top of the stairs, her arms laden with folded linen. She took one look at her employer's face and murmured an apology.

"Excuse me, sir."

Ignoring her, Alex gripped Jo's arm and steered her toward the stairs. "We'll talk about this in the garden room."

With a wrench, Jo pulled free of his bruising hold.

Damn straight they'd talk about this in the garden room. They'd talk about several things.

More than a little pissed, she followed him down the wide stone stairs to a glass-roofed sanctuary at the rear of the central wing. Under any other circumstances, the antique rattan furniture grouped amid profuse displays of exotic indoor plants would have delighted her. As it was, she barely registered either the furniture or the marble fountain crowned by a bronze goddess bubbling in the center of the room. Shoving her hands in the pockets of her black slacks, she waited while Alex poured them both a sherry.

Red still rode in his cheeks as he handed her the small crystal goblet filled with amber liquid.

"I'd planned a toast to our future. Perhaps we should just toast my grandfather's continuing hold on life?"

"Perhaps we should."

He tipped the rim of his goblet to hers and took a swallow. "All right, Joanna. What's this all about?"

She abandoned her carefully rehearsed speech. "I'm sorry, Alex. I know how stressed you are right now about your grandfather, but—"

"But?" he echoed stiffly.

He was hurt, and wanted her to know it. She got the message. She only hoped he'd get hers.

"I tried to tell you when you called the other night. This relationship isn't working."

He stared down at her, his black-lashed eyes flat as he processed her words. "It's Katherine, isn't it? You're still upset that I said her name while I made love to you."

"You were making love to her, Alex, not me."

"I knew exactly who I held in my arms."

"Did you?"

He answered her question with one of his own.

"You think I'm still enthralled by her?"

"Given the fact that you keep her pictures all through your house and made a shrine out of her bedroom at Chestnut Hill, I'd say that's a pretty good guess."

His stark expression reminded Jo of all he'd lost . . . all he was about to lose. Softening, she laid a hand on his arm.

"I'm sorry I'm not Katherine, Alex. I couldn't be her if I tried, and I don't want to try."

Deliberately, he took another sip of his sherry. Just as deliberately, he set it on a glass-topped table. Feeling wretched, Jo bent to place her goblet beside his.

"I hated her."

Her hand jerked, splashing sherry on the cuff of her blazer. Certain she'd mistaken him, she carefully placed the fragile crystal on the table and faced him.

"What?"

"Toward the end, just before she died, I'd come to hate her almost as much as I loved her."

Speechless, Jo stared at him.

"She was going to leave me," he continued in the same emotionless voice. *"Just like my mother.* No one knew, not even my grandfather, although I think he suspected."

His gaze drifted to the vista framed by the glass wall. Jo knew he wasn't seeing the magnificent gardens beyond, but the raven-haired Katherine.

"She said I was strangling her, that she couldn't

take another damned hundred-dollar-a-plate dinner or boring speech. She wanted excitement."

His lips stretched in what might have been a smile or a grimace.

"I tried to give it to her. She liked it rough. Liked the kind of games we played, even came to crave them. Still she wasn't satisfied."

"Then she got sick," Jo whispered.

"Then she got sick," he echoed, his voice empty. "It struck her so fast. An infection of the myocardium. One day she was laughing and raking her nails down my back, the next . . ."

Jo didn't want to hear the intimate details, didn't need to probe this private agony, but Alex continued, lost in his memories.

"The next, it seemed, her heart muscle gave out and she collapsed in my arms. She needed me then. She cried for me to hold her, begged me to keep the shadows at bay while we searched for a donor heart."

A fist wrapped around Jo's throat. How sad, how unbelievably sad, that Alex could arrange for Sergeant McPeak's daughter to receive a kidney transplant, but all his millions couldn't buy his own wife a heart.

She kept silent, hurting for the man next to her, but more convinced by the moment that she wasn't the one to erase his painful memories.

Alex didn't agree. That much was evident from the way he turned to her and reached out, his knuckles white as he grasped her hands.

"I won't make the same mistakes with you I did with Katherine."

"Alex—"

"You won't be bored, I promise! We'll travel. We'll ski St. Moritz, cruise the Aegean. I'll get back into politics when, and only when, you're ready." His fingers gripped hers. "Before his last stroke, my grandfather was pressuring me to run for governor. But I've told him what I do with my life depends on you."

Appalled that she'd somehow let matters reach this state, Jo tried to find a graceful way to tell him that the idea of exchanging her flight suit for designer gowns seriously turned her off.

"I'm not now nor will I ever be first-lady material. I'm a helicopter pilot. It's what I do. What I love."

Graceful, she was discovering, didn't work with Alexander Taylor.

"The two professions aren't incompatible," he replied, his eyes glittering. "The only difference is that you'll pilot your choice of aircraft from your own fleet."

He thought that inducement would sway her, she realized incredulously. He really believed she was so materialistic as to marry a man just to acquire a fleet of aircraft.

As shamed now as she was appalled, she tugged on her hands. He released them, only to slide an arm around her waist and haul her up against his chest. Jo planted her palms against the navy blazer, holding him off.

"Alex, listen to me. I came down here today to return the title to the Sikorsky and the phone you sent me. Everything happened between us too fast. I'm

not ready to give you what you want from me. I'm
not sure I have it to give."

"Oh, but you do." He leaned forward, forcing her
to bend back against his arm. "You have exactly what
I want."

"No!"

"Yes, my darling."

"Dammit, I said no, Alex!" Anger flared again, hot
and swift. "I'm not playing games with you."

"Of course you are. And I play this one well,
Joanna. Very well."

She'd forgotten his strength. Forgotten the hard
muscle under his hand-tailored clothes. Steel banded
her waist, cutting off her air.

"Don't make me hurt you," she warned, her voice
dangerous.

If he hadn't laughed then, or grabbed her wrist
and tried to twist it behind her, she might not have
brought him down with quite so much force. But the
supreme arrogance behind his assumption that she'd
take whatever he chose to give ignited Jo's fury.

She laid him flat on his back with a simple
wrestling maneuver, one she'd learned from her
brothers. Spinning, she ducked under his arm,
grabbed his wrist with both of hers, and flipped him
neatly   off   his
feet and onto his back. He hit the floor with a thud
that knocked the air from his lungs.

He was still sprawled on the floor, his face suf-
fused with disbelief, when she dug into her purse for
the title to the Sikorsky and the phone.

"I'll walk down to the helipad. Doug Brakeman

can fly me home or drive me into the city to catch a train."

"Joanna . . . !"

"Good-bye, Alex."

John Tyree Taylor died while Jo was still in the air on her way back to Washington. He was buried at Arlington National Cemetery the following Saturday morning.

The phone calls began the day after the funeral.

Chapter Fourteen

Huddled before her television that rainy October morning, Jo watched the solemn processional and service for former President Taylor. The passing of the great man saddened her, as it did much of the world.

The close-ups of Alex standing stiff-shouldered in the cold drizzle triggered emotions of a different sort.

Her anger had cooled enough to appreciate his pain. Jo had only to glimpse his rigidly controlled expression to guess at the desolation behind it. He stood a step or two away from the other dignitaries, as if distancing himself from others in his grandfather's death as he had in his own life.

Even now, after stumbling across a part of his personality she considered seriously flawed, Jo's breath caught at his sheer, physical perfection. Disdaining an umbrella, he stood bare-headed and impervious to the elements. Rain glistened on hair as sleek as coal and dampened the shoulders of his black wool topcoat. He kept his ice-blue gaze trained on the flag-draped casket, ignoring the cameras that tried to catch some flicker of his intensely private grief.

Irrationally, guilt nipped at Jo as she watched the

man who had so fascinated and infuriated her say his last farewells. Knowing how burdened Alex was with his grandfather's illness, she'd wanted to break things off gently, diplomatically. Instead, she'd tossed the man on his back and stormed out, leaving him to deal with her defection and his grandfather's death within the space of a few hours.

Some diplomat she'd make!

Wrapping her arms around her jean-clad legs, Jo propped her chin on her knees. She knew in her heart she'd made the right decision. She didn't have the makings of a politician's wife. She got in enough trouble around the squadron for shooting her mouth off. Alex would've had to hire a small army of spin doctors to work damage control every time she put her foot in it.

Sighing, she stayed glued to the television all during that gloomy morning.

As if the skies had wept on Saturday in final tribute to J. T. Taylor, Sunday dawned bright and cold and clear. Used to Wisconsin winters, the thirty-eight-degree chill invigorated Jo. Or maybe it was the sense of having stepped back from the brink of a troubled relationship that made her decide to put the MG's top down, drive by a friend's apartment, and convince Melissa Parks she wouldn't freeze her butt off during an expedition to the Eastern Shore for a last crab crawl before the season ended.

A bubbly, auburn-haired maintenance officer, Melissa buried her nose in the cowl-necked sweatshirt she wore under a windbreaker and kept Jo laughing during the drive with her scatological description of the inner workings of a Huey. They chowed down at a crab shanty overlooking the shimmering gray-blue Chesapeake. The waitress dumped steamed crustaceans by the trayful onto the brown butcher paper covering their table. Their wooden mallets flew, whacking down in reckless abandon, cracking the bright red tangle of claws, legs, and backs. Fiery spices burned in the tiny cuts on Jo's fingers made by the ragged shell shards as she dug out the delicate meat. Washed down with a local beer that pleased even her discriminating palate, the crab and lively conversation banished her lingering regret over the way things had ended with Alex.

It wasn't until she'd dropped Melissa off late that afternoon and snuggled down in front of the TV to watch the Washington Redskins take on the Dallas Cowboys that she discovered things hadn't ended quite as completely as she'd thought.

The phone rang with less than two minutes to play in the final quarter. Sure it was her brother Dave calling to crow, as he did every time her adopted 'Skins went down to ignominious defeat, she snatched up the receiver.

"Don't write them off yet. They've still got a minute plus to throw a Hail Mary, recover the ball, and take it in for a win."

A small silence greeted that bit of wishful thinking.

"I haven't written anything off, Joanna, including us."

Jo shot up, clutching the University of Wisconsin throw she'd draped over her knees.

"Alex?"

"I've missed you." The strain of the past few days

echoed in his husky voice. "More than I thought possible, given all that happened after you left."

Pity tugged at her, overlaying the harsh memories of their last meeting.

"I'm so sorry about your grandfather."

"Thank you."

His quiet grief moved her unbearably.

"I'm sorry about what happened between us in the garden room, too," she said softly.

He blew out a long breath. "Can you forgive me for that?"

"Now I can." She eased back against the couch, only peripherally aware that the football game had ended. "I was pretty pissed at the time, though."

"Yes, I formed that impression."

She had to smile at that dry understatement.

"We'll start again, Joanna. Take things easier, now that my grandfather . . . Now that I can devote all my time and attention to you."

Jo gripped the phone, her smile slipping. "I don't think that's a good idea."

"Devoting all my time to you? You're all I have now, my darling."

Guilt dug into her like a sharp, roweled spur. Doggedly, she persisted. As much as she hated to add to his inner turmoil the day after his grandfather's funeral, she had to make him understand it was over.

"No, I meant starting again. We're too different. We have different needs. I don't think we should see each other anymore."

"Of course we should. I'll send a driver for you tomorrow evening. We'll take that cruise on the Potomac I promised you."

"It's not working between us, Alex. Let it go."

"We'll make it work."

"You seem to have a problem with the word no," she replied on a small laugh, trying to make a joke of it.

He failed to see the humor. His voice dropped to a low, caressing intensity.

"I need you, my darling. I need to hear your voice, see your smile light up your face. I want to bare your beautiful breasts again and make slow, erotic love to you."

The thought of exposing herself to him another time sent a shudder rippling down Jo's spine.

"Yes, well, we all want things we can't have at times. I'm sorry, Alex. I don't want to see you anymore. Please, just accept that."

"Joanna—"

She'd had enough. "I've got an early flight tomorrow. I need to get some sleep. Good night, Alex."

That hit a nerve. Sudden, whipping anger leaped across the phone.

"Your dammed job! That's what's holding you back, isn't it? You carry this burden of misplaced loyalty to that uniform you wear."

"Misplaced?"

He ignored the warning note. "If you want to serve your country, think how much more you could accomplish as the wife of a governor, or even the President."

Irritated now, Jo didn't hold back. "If I were interested in politics instead of flying, I'd run for office, not marry into it. I don't see myself serving as someone else's shadow."

He gave a slow hiss. "That's what Katherine said. She didn't appreciate how much I needed her. I didn't *show* her how much I needed her."

Katherine again. If Jo had been searching for additional reasons to end the relationship, his strange love-hate fixation on his dead wife would have done it.

"I won't make that mistake with you, Joanna. We'll be a team. Together, we'll—"

"No, Alex! No. No. *No*."

That silenced him for several seconds.

"I'll call you tomorrow," he said finally, his voice cold and tight. "When you can discuss this more rationally."

"Don't call. Don't push. Don't—"

"Good night, Joanna."

The line went dead.

Punching the off button, Jo threw the phone into the sofa cushion. Dammit! What was his problem? What was *her* problem, that she couldn't seem to get her message across? Fuming, she tossed aside the throw rug. Her stockinged feet hit the floor with a thump.

A glance at the clock showed her it was still early, not quite nine, but she had a 6:00 A.M. flight tomorrow. She needed to get some quality sack time, as impossible as that seemed at the moment. She'd take a hot shower, she decided. Lay out her uniform for tomorrow. Try to calm down and put Alex out of her head.

The shower helped. So did the routine tasks of buffing her boots and laying out clean black cotton underwear and the black crewneck T-shirt she wore over her sports bra. She was almost ready to climb into bed when she remembered that she wanted to take her service skirt to the cleaners tomorrow. And the red and black plaid blazer, Jo recalled, padding to the closet.

Hoping the sherry she'd splashed on her sleeve in the Garden Room at BellaVista hadn't left a permanent stain, she pulled out the blazer and checked the cuff. It showed a yellowish tint at the edge, which the cleaners should be able to get out. She was folding the jacket, getting ready to toss it over the skirt on the arm of a chair, when she caught a faint rustle of paper. Sliding a hand inside the pocket, she retrieved a folded note.

Dr. Russ. In the aftermath of her eventful last meeting with Alex, she'd forgotten all about the phone number he'd slipped into her pocket.

Jo saw it when she unfolded the paper. And five words.

Call me. It's most urgent.

Jo stared down at the writing, a frown pulling at her brow. For some reason, the loops and swirls looked familiar. Where had she . . . ?

Suddenly, her heart pounded. She remembered exactly where she'd seen that distinctive scrawl before. Spinning on her heel, she darted into the spare bedroom and dug through the pile of mail and papers on her desk.

The black-and-white photo she'd found stuffed in the mailbox the night after her dinner at the White House lay at the bottom of the pile. Jo snatched it up and flipped it over. The message leaped out at her, as it had the night she'd received it.

Be careful. Very careful.

Jo swallowed a lump of surprise and confusion. The handwriting on the back of the photo matched that of the note exactly, right down to the elegant loops on the L's and the swirls on the tail of the Y.

She'd assumed the photographer . . . what was his name? Stroder. That was it. Stroder. She'd thought he'd sent the photo as some kind of snide warning that she was out of her league with Alex. Obviously, she'd thought wrong.

Dr. Russ had sent it, although Jo couldn't imagine why he'd felt compelled to warn her at that point. Or why he'd waylaid her in the hall as he had at BellaVista.

Laying the note beside the photo, Jo reached for the desk phone. A woman answered at the number Dr. Russ had scribbled.

"I'm sorry," she said after Jo had identified herself and asked to speak to the historian. "My husband went . . . uh . . ." She gave a fluttery laugh. "I seem to have forgotten where. But he'll be back tomorrow. I remember that. Shall I have him call you?"

"Yes, please."

"You'd better give me your name again, dear. I'll write it down. My memory isn't quite what it used to be these days."

Jo's answering machine was blinking when she arrived home early the next evening. Sure enough, there was a message from the professor asking her to contact him immediately.

And three from Alex.

Her mouth tight, she listened to his messages. The first was almost playful, with no reference to their argument last night. The second sounded a bit cooler. The third demanded a return call as soon she walked in the door.

Irritated all over again, Jo strode to her office and retrieved Dr. Russ's note. With the cordless phone tucked between her shoulder and ear, she wandered into the kitchen. The historian answered just as she was reaching into the fridge for a Coke.

"Hi, Dr. Russ. It's Jo West. I apologize for taking so long to call."

"I understand. These past weeks have been a . . . difficult time for all of us."

More difficult than he knew.

"I hope you're going to explain the warning you gave me at BellaVista . . . and the one you wrote on the back of that photograph you sent me."

His breath hissed out. "Can you meet me? Tonight? I must speak with you."

"You *are* speaking to me," she pointed out, rather unnecessarily, she thought.

"Some matters are best not discussed over a phone. Or between you and Alex."

"There is no me and Alex," she said sharply.

"Does he know that?"

She popped the top on her Coke, scowling at the fizz that bubbled out. "I've told him. Several times."

"We must meet," the professor pressed. "You live in Maryland, don't you? In Fort Washington? I could drive over there, or we could meet in Alexandria at . . ." He groped for a well-known area eatery. "At Gadsby's Tavern. Are you familiar with it?"

Jo wasn't particularly thrilled at the thought of battling rush-hour traffic again tonight, but the historian's urgency and the three annoying phone calls from Alex prompted her to agree.

"Yes, I know it."

They settled on seven-thirty, which gave her time to change and fight her way across the Woodrow Wilson Bridge to Alexandria.

It took her less than a half hour to exchange her green bag and boots for slimming wool slacks in a pale oatmeal, a jewel-necked black sweater, and a leather jacket that skimmed her hips and looked great when dressed up with a flowery scarf. A quick brush through her hair and she was ready to tackle the Beltway.

The night air carried a distinct chill by the time she backed the MG down the drive. Propping an elbow against the closed window, Jo toyed absently with the loose tendrils as she drove the darkened streets to Indian Head Highway.

This whole business with Alex had taken such a bizarre twist. She'd waltzed into what she'd thought was a storybook romance. Now, she was wiggling out of a decidedly uncomfortable situation.

What was it with her and relationships? Less than six months ago, her short-lived engagement to another pilot had gone sour because they'd ended up competing with each other within the squadron. Now her tenuous relationship with Alex had hit the skids.

Maybe she expected too much from a man. Maybe

she didn't know what the heck *to* expect. Maybe . . .
She grimaced. Maybe she shouldn't have cut Deke El-
liott off at the knees when he'd tried to warn her about
Alex.

She hadn't seen Deke in days. He'd flown several
overnight sorties, pulled alert, and been off for the
past two days. He didn't know she'd returned the
title to the Sikorsky or that she'd tossed Alex on his
head—literally and figuratively.

It galled her to admit Deke had been right all along.
Contrary to her blithe assertion, she hadn't kept both
hands on the controls during her tumultuous ride with
Alex. Hell, she wasn't even sure she had a handle on
the uneasy situation now.

She would, she vowed. After this meeting with Dr.
Russ, she'd cut anything and everything related to
Alexander Taylor out of her life.

With that resolution firm in her mind, she navigated the MG into the vortex of traffic converging
from I-95 and I-295 just a mile or two from the bridge.
Bumper to bumper, it inched across the Potomac.
Twenty minutes later, the MG nosed out of the traffic at the exit for Old Town, Alexandria.

Old Town was definitely one of the pleasures of an
assignment to D.C., Jo decided as she navigated the
cobblestone streets. She'd only visited the area a couple of times in the months since her arrival, once with
her folks when they'd come for a stay and once on
her own, exploring the shops. She'd fallen a little more
in love with each visit.

The city had been a thriving tobacco port back in
George Washington's day, and its past still lived in
the restored eighteenth- and nineteenth-century

homes, taverns, and iron street lamps throwing pud-
dles of light on the cobbled streets. Jo thought it so
appropriate that Dr. Russ would choose Gadsby's Tavern as a meeting place. A museum and national historical landmark as well as a popular eatery, Gadsby's
served mouthwatering colonial specialties like rum-
raisin bread pudding and hot spiced wine.

Hot spiced wine would taste good tonight, she
thought as she zipped into a parking space that mirac-
ulously opened just a few blocks down the street from
the tavern. Something to take the chill from her bones.

Locking the MG, she turned her collar up against
the brisk breeze. Dried leaves, courtesy of the towering oaks and maples lining the street, crunched under
her feet. Unlike so many urban centers, Alexandria's
sidewalks were crowded with people. Local residents,
strolling from their town houses to the area's many
fine restaurants. Tourists, peering into lighted shop
windows. Commuters, newspapers tucked under
their arms and briefcases in hand as they trudged
from the King Street Metro stop.

Jo was only a few yards from the black-shuttered
building that housed Gadsby's when Dr. Russ hailed
her from across the street.

"Captain West!"

His white hair wisped out from under a tan Bur-
burry cap reminiscent of Sherlock Holmes. A scarf in
the same plaid was tucked neatly into the neck of his
overcoat. He waved a hand, waiting for the light to
change to cross King Street and join her.

Jo jammed her hands in her pockets and shifted
from foot to foot in the chill night air. Traffic whizzed

past. Finally, the stream of cars thinned. The light flickered from green to yellow.

Tires squealed. A loose cobblestone popped as a
dark sedan raced to beat the red light. Dr. Russ
stepped off the curb as the vehicle whizzed past.

No, he didn't step. He staggered.

Jo froze, her eyes widening in alarm as the historian clutched his chest. He stumbled another step.
Two. Stopped. Clawed at his chest.

Horrified, she saw him start to pitch forward. She'd
started running before he hit the street.

"Call 911!" she shouted to a startled couple passing by. "Now! I think my friend's having a heart attack!"

Her heart pounding, she raced across the intersection. She knew CPR, knew, too, that the first few moments were critical in situations like this. She started
to drop to her knees beside the historian, only to realize that he stood as much chance of getting run over
when the light changed as dying from his attack. Jo
grabbed his arm and dragged him back to the curb.

Her breath shot out in fast, sharp puffs. A stone
cut into her knee as she slid a hand under Russ's neck
to arch it and open his air passage. She ripped away
his scarf, tore open the buttons of his heavy wool
overcoat. Folding one hand atop the other, she rose
up on both knees to start chest compressions.

She'd pushed down once, maybe twice, when she
registered the warm liquid gushing through her
clenched fists. Startled, Jo lifted her hands.

Blood dripped from her fingers.

Oh, God! She'd pressed too hard. Broken the man's
fragile ribs. Maybe pierced a lung.

Her heart caught squarely in the middle of her throat, she dropped back on her heels. What the hell did she do next? Risk puncturing more internal organs with a broken rib or continue the CPR?

It was then, only then, that Jo realized the doctor's blood pumped not from a pierced lung, but from the neat, round bullet hole in the center of his chest.

Chapter Fifteen

"I didn't hear the shot," Jo told the heavy jowled detective who'd introduced himself as Tony Ambruzzo when he'd arrived on the scene. "I didn't hear anything that sounded even close to a shot."

"The shooter must have used a silencer," the detective muttered to his partner.

Hunched sideways in the backseat of a cruiser, one heel hooked on the frame, the other planted on the street, Jo swiped her palm down the seam of her slacks. Someone . . . one of the paramedics, she thought . . . had given her a towel to wipe her hands, but blood had dried in the cracks. She could still feel its prickle, still feel the residual shock of that moment when she'd discovered the hole in Dr. Russ's chest.

More than an hour had passed since then, almost twenty minutes since Jo had watched the paramedics zip the historian's body into a plastic shroud, strap it to a gurney, and roll it into an ambulance.

Now blue and white strobe lights cut like lasers through the night. With King Street closed off by yellow crime scene tape, traffic was being detoured to the side roads. Reporters and camera crews had begun to arrive, drawn no doubt by news of the shooting gleaned from scanning police radios. The homicide detectives had shielded their witnesses from the media so far, but Jo knew she'd have to face them sooner or later. The prospect made her stomach knot.

"We'll have to wait for the ME's report to verify the bullet's angle of entry," Ambruzzo told her, spearing a glance over the cruiser's roof at the buildings on the opposite side of the street. "The shooter could have positioned himself in one of those windows, waiting for the professor."

A team from the crime scene unit was going through the buildings now, Jo knew, floor by floor, room by room. Looking for any material clues, Ambruzzo had explained. Spent shell casings, cigarette butts, candy wrappers.

"But my guess is a drive-by." The detective's gaze cut back to her. "You said a car sped through the intersection just as the light changed?"

"I didn't really pay any attention to it." Frustrated by her inability to recall any specific details, Jo swiped her itchy palm down her leg again. "It was a late model sedan. Some dark color, blue or black."

"No one else paid any attention to it, either," Ambruzzo grumbled. He'd already interviewed and released the few passersby in the vicinity at the time of the incident. "Tell me again why you were meeting Dr. Russ."

"He called me earlier this evening, wanting to set up an appointment. He said it was urgent."

"He didn't give you any clue what he wanted to talk to you about?"

"No."

She'd wracked her brain, trying to figure out what

was behind Russ's strange behavior. The only possibility that made any sense was that he wanted to warn her away from Alex. Maybe he'd uncovered Alex's predilection for rough sex. Maybe he'd just assumed she wasn't up to the rarefied circles the Taylors moved in.

"And you said he sent you a photo?"

Jo hesitated. So far she hadn't involved Alex in the discussion.

"It was a black-and-white eight-by-ten," she answered, "taken just after Alex Taylor brought me home from dinner at the White House."

Jo's name and face had clicked in Ambruzzo's mind at that point. He remembered the coverage of the incinerated Ferrari, he informed her. And the tabloid shots of her in her underwear she guessed from the speculative glance he'd run over her.

The detective shot a look at his partner before asking Jo politely, "You dine at the White House often?"

"No, only once."

"So why did the professor send you this photo?"

"I don't know. I didn't even know he was the one who'd sent it until last night, when I compared the handwriting on the back of the picture with a note he'd written me."

"I'd like to examine both the note and the photo."

"Of course."

"I'll send a patrolman out to your place tonight to pick them up. Anything else?"

Once more Jo hesitated. She couldn't imagine any connection between Dr. Russ and the photographer who'd taken that shot. Didn't even know for sure who'd captured her in such stark lines and angles. But . . .

"I think the man who took that photo was named Stroder," she said slowly. "Eric Stroder. He was killed a few weeks ago in a car-jacking."

"You don't say." Ambruzzo's pen flew across the page. "I'll check it out."

"Do you need me for anything else?"

"Not tonight, Captain. If I have any more questions, I'll call you. Hang loose, I'll get a patrolman to drive you to your car."

Jo slumped back in the cruiser's seat, knowing she wouldn't be able to escape the gauntlet of reporters for long. The media had identified her even faster than Ambruzzo had.

Sure enough, camera lights blazed in her face as the cruiser pulled away from the scene. Reporters scrambled into vans. A small convoy followed them the two blocks to her car. The questions started flying as soon as she climbed out of the black and white.

"Captain West! Can you tell us who was shot?"

Ambruzzo had already briefed reporters that he wouldn't release the name of the deceased pending notification of next of kin. Jo wasn't about to divulge the information, either. She didn't want Russ's wife to learn about his death on the local twenty-four-hours news channel.

She shouldered through the small crowd, ignoring the microphones shoved in her face.

"How do you know the deceased?"

"Any idea why he was shot?"

"When are you and Alex Taylor going to officially announce your engagement?"

That spun her around. She pinpointed the source of the question as a slender black woman muffled against the cold in a fox-trimmed coat.

"We're not engaged, officially or otherwise," she answered bluntly. "There's nothing to announce."

The reporter flashed a knowing smirk. "That's not what we hear, Captain."

"What, exactly, do you hear?"

She realized her mistake the minute the irate question slipped out. Showing even the slightest interest would only add credence to the absurd rumors.

"That you and Alex agreed you'd stay away from President Taylor's funeral because you didn't want interest in the grandson's love life to eclipse the grandfather's memorial services," the reporter replied, pouncing on her question like a hungry dog on raw meat. "Now that the funeral's over, when are you two going to share your romance with the public?"

"We're not. I mean, there is no romance."

"Then he didn't transfer the title to a new helicopter to your name? Or make a hefty donation to the foundation your brother works for?"

The woman had done her homework, Jo conceded. She also seemed to care a heck of a lot more about this supposed affair than about the fact that a man had just bled to death in the street.

Disgusted, Jo shook her head and ducked into her car. Tension crawled across her shoulders the entire drive home. Thank God she didn't have a flight scheduled tomorrow. No way she was going to sleep tonight.

*   *   *

Her first order of business when she arrived home was a quick shower. A glance at the phone on her way through the house showed no flashing message light, thank God. She wasn't ready to deal with more pressure from reporters right now.

Or from Alex.

He'd call. As soon as he heard the awful news.

For a few seconds, Jo debated whether to turn off the damned answering machine. Or better yet, unplug the phone. But the squadron had to be able to reach her. And her family, who'd no doubt hit the phones as soon as the rumors about her supposed engagement to Alex made it into the tabloids.

She'd better call them. After she cleaned up, she decided, grimacing as she caught sight of herself in the bedroom mirror. Blood had splattered across her slacks. Rust caked in the creases of her wrists.

Unzipping the slacks, she started to add them to the uniform skirt and plaid blazer she'd laid out to take to the cleaners. No. No way she'd ever be able to wear that pair again without thinking of tonight. Wadding them into a tight ball, she stuffed them into the wastebasket in the bathroom.

She was in the shower, hands braced against the tile, head bowed to the hot, pelting stream, when Jo realized she should call or visit Dr. Russ's wife. Her husband's death would no doubt traumatize her, but the woman might want to know the details of his last moments. Know, too, that he hadn't suffered for more than a few seconds.

The phone shrilled three times while she was in the shower. Above the hiss of water, Jo caught fragments of the messages left by various radio and television reporters.

Her front doorbell bonged just as she was toweling dry. It hadn't taken the media long to beat another path to her door, she thought, her mouth thinning. She ignored the chimes until a third ring reminded her that Ambruzzo had said something about sending a patrolman for the photo and note Dr. Russ had written her.

She'd learned her lesson the first time she'd flung her front door open, however. She pulled on jeans, thick socks, and a sweatshirt before she peered cautiously through the peephole.

"Deke!" Relief pouring through her, Jo fumbled with the locks. "What are you doing here?"

"I was on my way home from the base and heard your name on the news."

"They wrote that copy fast," she said grimly, waving him inside.

His hazel eyes searched her face as he pulled off his flight cap and stuffed it into a pocket of his brown leather jacket.

"Are you all right?"

"I am now that I've washed off the blood. Not mine," she added quickly as alarm flared in his face. "The man who was shot."

Leading the way to the sofa, Jo plopped down in a corner and tucked her feet under her. Deke unzipped his jacket and tossed it over the back of a chair before joining her. He must have had a late flight, she thought. Stubble shadowed his chin, and his green flight suit still carried a faint, familiar tang of aviation fuel.

"What the hell happened? The news report hinted at a drive-by shooting."

"At this point, the police don't know what it was."

"Who took the bullet?"

"A professor by the name of Martin Russ. A historian, actually. He was working on John Tyree Taylor's biography."

"You knew him?" Incredulous, Deke shoveled a hand through tobacco brown hair still flat from his helmet. "I assumed you just happened to be in the vicinity and rushed over to aid the victim."

"Actually, I was on my way to meet him."

His hand dropped. He chewed on her reply for a moment or two.

"Getting ready to add your chapter to the Taylor family history, was he?"

Fingers of heat rose in Jo's cheeks at the sardonic response. All right. Deke had pegged it. She'd gotten in over her head with Alex. She might as well admit the sorry truth.

"There isn't going to be any chapter labeled Jo West."

"Is that right?"

"That's right.

"Have you told Taylor yet?"

A shiver rippled down Jo's arms as she remembered that Dr. Russ had asked her the same thing just a few hours ago. She gave Deke the same answer she'd given the historian.

"Yes. Several times."

She pushed off the couch, not really ready to discuss her messy break-up with Alex.

"Do you want a beer?"

"That sounds good."

Almost as good as what he'd just heard, Deke thought. A deep, visceral satisfaction filled him as he stretched his legs and contemplated Jo's nicely-rounded butt until it disappeared into the kitchen.

So she'd given Taylor his walking papers? That was the best news Deke had heard all week. Hell, all year.

He rolled his shoulders, shrugging off the fatigue from the fourteen-hour day he'd just put in. Shrugging off, too, the tension that had speared him when Jo had dropped that bomb about washing away blood.

He still didn't understand her connection to the historian or what had happened tonight. But he didn't have any trouble understanding the kink in his gut when he thought she'd taken a hit. It was fear, pure and simple. The kind that comes zinging out of nowhere and hits a man when he least expects it. He'd have to think about that fear when he'd sorted out just what happened tonight.

And sorted out, too, when to make his move.

It had to be soon. That was a given. He'd lain awake too many nights thinking about the way Jo West filled out a flight suit, not to mention the laughter that played like a fiddle on Deke's heartstrings. She could put him in a sweat faster than any other woman he'd come across in his thirty-two years of looking.

He still kicked himself for standing around like a blind-drunk cowboy on a Saturday night while Taylor cut Jo out of the herd and claimed her as his own. He wouldn't make that mistake again.

That promise echoed in his head when she returned, a cold beer in each hand.

"You're not flying tomorrow?" he asked, accepting one of the bottles.

"Nope." She curled up in her corner again, tucking her toes under her. "I've got small-arms training in the morning and had planned to attend a Company Grade Officers' Council meeting tomorrow afternoon, but . . ."

"But what?"

"I'm thinking I should go see Dr. Russ's wife . . . widow." She fiddled with the bottle, peeling back a corner of the wet label. "Mrs. Russ might want a first-hand account of what happened."

"What did happen, Jo?"

"I don't know. Honestly. One minute, Dr. Russ was standing on the corner, waiting for the light to change. The next, he was lying in the street, blood pumping through a hole in his chest."

"Christ!"

"It was so weird. I didn't hear the shot, didn't even know he'd *been* shot until I rolled him over and tried to administer CPR."

Deke took a pull on his beer. He didn't much like the picture forming in his mind. From the look on Jo's face, she didn't much like it, either.

"Sounds like the shooter may have used a silencer," he said slowly.

"That's what the detective said. Which means . . ."

She peeled another strip off the label, leaving him to finish the sentence.

"Which means the killer probably wasn't some hopped-up kid out to earn his gang membership by gunning down an innocent bystander. This sounds more like a professional hit."

She nodded, her eyes somber. They always reminded Deke of the moss that grew along the creeks in his native Wyoming, dark, shining, so deep a green you could slide right into them.

"Any idea who might want to take the doc out?"

"I didn't know him well enough to hazard a guess. I only met him twice. Once at Alex's town house, and once at his grandfather's estate south of Richmond."

Deke's fist curled, the way it always did when Jo mentioned Taylor's name. It was a gut reaction, jealousy at its most primitive, uncomplicated level. A reaction he'd lived with for weeks now.

But not any longer. To hell with planning his moves. This was as good a time as any to—

The door chimes rang before he finished the tantalizing thought. Cursing under his breath, Deke almost missed the white lines that suddenly bracketed Jo's mouth.

The chimes rang again.

"It's probably a reporter," she muttered, not budging from the couch. "They were all over me earlier this evening."

"You want me to get it?"

"No. I'll handle it."

Uncurling her legs, she marched to the door. Deke set aside his beer and followed. This whole business about the shooting didn't sit right with him.

"It's a police officer," Jo announced, her eye glued to the peephole.

He noted the relieved slump to her shoulders. The evening's events had shaken her up more than she was ready to admit.

"The homicide detective said he'd send out a patrol," she said, twisting the lock. "To pick up a photo Dr. Russ had delivered to me."

"Check his ID," Deke cautioned.

"I intend to."

The cackle of static from the police cruiser's radio drifted through the screen, which Jo kept locked while she checked out the officer on the other side. He tipped a finger to his broad-brimmed hat.

"Captain West?"

"Yes."

"I'm Officer O'Brien, Alexandria Police."

Jo didn't have to ask for identification. The photo ID clipped to his jacket collar was clearly visible in the porch light.

"Detective Ambruzzo from Homicide asked me to swing by and pick up some materials at this address."

"Right." She unlatched the screen door. "Come in. They're in the other room. I'll go get them."

Deke used the time she was out of the room to request an update. "Have the police tagged any suspects yet on the shooting that Captain West witnessed?"

The officer ran a glance down Deke's uniform, snagging his name and rank from the blue-and-gold embroidered patch attached to his flight suit.

"None that I know of, Captain Elliott."

"Captain West mentioned the possibility that the shooter used a silencer."

"I'd say that was a pretty good guess. I'm told none of the witnesses in the vicinity reported hearing a shot. You might have her check with Detective Ambruzzo tomorrow, though. Sometimes these—"

He broke off as Jo rushed into the room.

"They're not there!"

Deke spun around, his stomach clenching at the sight of her white, strained face.

"The photo and the note Dr. Russ wrote me. I left them on my desk. They're both gone."

The patrolman shot her a narrow look. "Are you saying someone broke into your residence tonight?"

"The doors were locked when I came home. Nothing else is missing, that I can see. Yet the photo's gone."

She raked a hand through her damp hair, looking at once confused, angry, and shaken.

"Some bastard has a key to my house."

Chapter Sixteen

Officer O'Brien, Detective Ambruzzo, and two lab techs from the local police department left Jo's house a little after 11:00 P.M. They'd uncovered no signs of forcible entry and no trace of the missing photo and note. After dusting for prints, they advised Jo to change her locks and talk to the owner of the house about installing a security system.

Ambruzzo was the last one out the door. His heavy face wore lines of fatigue. He'd come straight to Jo's from Dr. Russ's suburban Virginia house, where he'd had to break the news of his death to his widow.

"She didn't take it well," he told Jo and Deke wearily. "My partner and I stayed with her until a neighbor showed up."

"Did she have any idea who might have killed her husband?"

"No, none, but she seemed confused about a number of matters. Her neighbor indicated she's in the early stages of Alzheimer's."

"Oh, no!" Pity tugged at Jo. A single bullet had torn apart at least two, perhaps more lives. "Does she have any children or other relatives to care for her?"

"A niece, I think, out in Ohio. The neighbor promised to get in touch with her."

"I was planning to go see Mrs. Russ," Jo murmured. "Since I was the one with her husband when he died."

"Let me know if she says anything pertinent to his murder." The detective started for the door. "I'll get on this connection between Russ and the dead photographer tomorrow."

Chewing on her lower lip, she followed him across the room. "I don't know if there is one. I'm not even one hundred percent certain Stroder snapped the shot. It just had that same in-your-face intensity of the photos he took at the scene of Alex's accident."

"Yeah, well, I might just look into that accident, too. I'll be in touch, Captain."

Jo closed the door behind him and twisted the dead bolt. Not that the damned bolt would do any good, she thought with a shiver. Whoever had waltzed into her house earlier this evening obviously had access to a set of keys.

Like most single crew members, she'd made extra house keys for friends who'd volunteered to check her mail or keep an eye on the place during her infrequent absences. Melissa Parks had a key, just as Jo had one for the maintenance officer's apartment. So did a buddy at the Pentagon, who'd camped out in the spare bedroom for a few days while waiting for his quarters on base to come available. But neither of them would walk in unannounced. Nor would they have any interest in that damned photo.

Deke had obviously reached the same conclusion. Reclaiming his beer, he offered to hang around until she got hold of a twenty-four-hour locksmith.

"Or," he added, "you could stay at my place for a few days. Until you get a security system installed and the police make some sense of Dr. Russ's murder."

Jo cocked her head, assessing the casual invitation. She hadn't missed the fierce glint in Deke's eyes when she'd told him she'd broken off with Alex. One glimpse of that savage male satisfaction had sent her scurrying into the kitchen. She was enough of a coward to shy away from the idea of severing one relationship only to plunge into another . . . and more than enough woman to actually consider it.

She wasn't going to plunge into anything tonight, though. If at all. A murder and a break-in was about all she could handle per evening.

"I'll start with the locksmith," she told him, dragging the Yellow Pages out of the hall closet.

The shrill ring of the phone caught her halfway to the sofa. Thumping the phone book down on the coffee table, Jo frowned at the cordless instrument nestled in its cradle.

"It's probably the media. They started calling before you got here."

A second ring scratched at her nerves. A third. Then a fourth. Dammit, she'd make sure she arranged for caller ID tomorrow, along with the new locks and a security system.

Finally the machine clicked on.

"Joanna, I just heard the news! Pick up."

Jo's glance jumped to Deke. His jaw squaring, he met her gaze as Alex's chocolate deep baritone poured from the answering machine.

"I know you're angry with me. I'll admit I was angry, too, but none of that matters now. All I care about is making sure you're all right. Pick up, Joanna. I know you're there."

She stared at the phone, the hairs lifting on the back of her neck. She could almost believe he *did* know she was here.

"Are you waiting for me to beg, my darling? All right, I'm not proud where you're concerned. I'll beg. I'll grovel. I'll do whatever it takes to hold you again. I'm aching to kiss those perfect breasts and feel your hot, wet juices—"

Her face flaming, Jo dived for the phone. "I'm here, Alex!"

She couldn't look at Deke. Couldn't take the hard drill of his eyes. Turning to face the wall, she hunched the phone to her shoulder.

"I appreciate your concern. I'm all right."

"Thank God. One of the reports said you were covered with blood."

The machine was still broadcasting Alex's voice over the speaker. With a quick stab, Jo punched it off.

"It wasn't my blood. It was Dr. Russ's. I tried to give him CPR but . . ." She shuddered, remembering that awful moment when she'd lifted her hands and gazed in stupefaction at the dark liquid dripping from her fingers. "He died right there in the street."

"Oh, my darling, how horrible! And so utterly senseless! We've got to put a stop to these random acts of violence."

For reasons she didn't want to think about at that moment, Jo chose not to reveal that there might not be anything random about Dr. Russ's death.

"We could make that our cause," Alex went on. "The main plank in our campaign platform. What bet-

ter memorial to Martin Russ than an all-out war on
crime?"

She scrubbed the heel of her hand across her forehead, wondering how to get through to the man. Wondering, too, what Deke was making of this one-sided
conversation. Suddenly, she was too weary to care.

"I'm tired, Alex. It's been a rough night."

"Yes, of course. Get some sleep, darling. We'll talk
tomorrow."

"No, we—"

"Good night, my love."

The connection severed. Her teeth grinding, Jo
counted to ten before hitting the Off button and turning back to Deke.

He didn't say a word. Silence stretched between
them, until a prickly irritation piled on top of Jo's
weariness.

"You don't have to wait for the locksmith," she said
brusquely. "I appreciate the offer, but it may take some
time to get one out here and it's already almost midnight."

A tightness settled around his mouth. "Make the
calls, West. I'll wait until I know you won't get any
more uninvited visitors, then I'll butt out of whatever
game it is you're playing with Taylor."

Her chin came up. "I'm not playing games, with
Alex or anyone else."

"That's not how it sounded from where I stand."

"Maybe you should try standing somewhere else
next time," she snapped

An eyebrow hooked. "Maybe I should."

She thought he'd leave then, as stung by the exchange as she was. Instead, he came around the cof-

fee table, not crowding, not pushing, but close enough for her to feel his presence.

"Let's try it from here," he said with only a faint trace of his usual, laconic twang. "I guess I'd better tell you right up front, I don't intend to beg. Or grovel. Or plead with you to talk to me over a damned phone. Whenever it happens between us, West, we won't have enough breath left for talking."

"*If* it happens, Elliot."

"It'll happen," he promised, his hands fisting at his side. "Sooner or later, it's going to happen."

That husky promise rang in Jo's ears for what was left of the short night and most of the next morning.

It was still kicking around in her head later that afternoon when she took off work early, changed into her service dress uniform, and drove over to Annandale to pay her respects to Dr. Russ's widow.

Jo found the Russ house without much difficulty. Set back from Braddock Road, the modest, white-painted brick home was separated by a screen of oaks from the trendy town houses that had sprung up all around. A curving drive wound past the front door to the detached side garage. Several vehicles lined the drive, including, Jo saw on a gulp of dismay, a midnight blue Ferrari.

She almost kept going, right on down the drive and back to Fort Washington. If she hadn't been scheduled for back-to-back sorties for the next few days, she might have done just that. But Jo was the last person to speak to Dr. Russ. She owed his widow the courtesy of a visit.

Besides, she thought as she swung her legs out of

the MG, she was darned if she'd let Alex determine her actions. She intended to live her own life, not the one he'd planned for them, and she might as well get on with it.

Mentally braced for their first meeting since Bella-Vista, she rang the bell. A frazzled-looking young woman answered—Mrs. Russ's niece, it turned out—and showed Jo inside.

"I just got here a few hours ago," she confided as she led the way to a glassed-in porch at the side of the house. "I just can't believe it. Uncle Martin, shot in the street like that!"

Jo couldn't quite believe it, either. In the bright light of afternoon, last night seemed almost like a dream, a horrible, frightening dream.

"I had to find someone to take care of the kids before I could jump on a plane," the niece rattled on, obviously still shaken by her uncle's death and hurried trip east. "I was so worried about Aunt Pat. I didn't know *how* she was going to manage without Uncle Martin to look after her, but thank goodness it's all worked out. Mr. Taylor has been so wonderful!"

Alex turned at the mention of his name, bestowing a sympathetic smile on the younger woman before shifting his gaze to Jo.

"Hello, Joanna."

He strolled forward, impeccably, impossibly elegant in a dark worsted suit, pale shirt, and striped silk tie. Jo detected the ravages of his own recent loss in the lines creasing his cheeks and mouth.

"You're sure you're all right, darling?"

With both Mrs. Russ and her niece looking on, she

chose not to remind him again she was not his darling. The poor women had enough to deal with.

"I'm fine. Excuse me, I want to offer Mrs. Russ my condolences."

Easing around Alex, she crossed a sunroom crowded with African violets in every imaginable shade of purple to the fine-boned woman seated in a chintz-covered settee.

"Mrs. Russ, I'm Joanna West."

The elderly widow seemed fascinated by the ribbons and insignia on Jo's uniform jacket. "Are you a police officer, dear?"

"No, I'm not. I'm in the Air Force."

"They came to my house last night. Police officers, I mean." Pansy eyes as deep a purple as her plants filled with tearful anxiety. "They said Martin is gone."

"Yes, he is. I'm so sorry."

"When will he come back? I get nervous when he stays away too long."

Heartsick, Jo looked to the niece.

The young woman spread her palms helplessly. "The police told her. I've told her."

With a gentle compassion that astounded Jo, Alex joined the widow on the settee and took her hands in both of his.

"Martin asked me to see that you're taken care of until he gets back, Patricia. Don't worry, you'll have someone with you all the time."

Her blue-veined fingers dug into his. "Will they help me with my violets? Martin always helps me feed my violets."

With the cruel vagary of Alzheimer's, Patricia Russ's mind cleared for an undefinable period of time.

"I developed a new variety, a strain of *pelrocosmea grandfolia*. We named it 'Russ's Joy.'" Shy and proud, she beamed at Alex. "You have to take the plant through at least three generations from leaf propagation to make sure it grows true before the African Violet Association of America will accept it."

"I didn't know that," he replied with a smile.

"Martin registered Russ's Joy for me with the AVSA. The plant has a place of honor in the front window of the living room. Would you like to see it?"

"Yes, of course."

Helping her to her feet, he tucked her <u>arm</u> in his.

"We'll be right back," she said with a vague smile at the two other women.

Her niece sighed as Mrs. Russ made her way into the other room, her slight figure dwarfed by the man at her side.

"I didn't know she was so bad. Uncle Martin had hinted that she was getting forgetful, but I didn't have any idea how much." She swallowed the tears that colored her voice. "I'll ask God's blessing on Mr. Taylor every night of my life."

Jo swung around. "Will you?"

"He's arranged for a live-in nurse/companion for my aunt. She starts tomorrow. And he paid off the mortgage. Now . . ." A hiccupy sob shook the young woman. "Now Aunt Pat can stay right here, in the house she loves so much."

He is a generous man, Jo thought. A very generous, very complicated man.

"He even took care of all Uncle Martin's papers and tapes for that book he was working on, the one about President Taylor. Mr. Taylor had them boxed up and carted off right before you got here."

Jo shot a glance at Alex's broad back, silhouetted against the bay window.

"I would have supposed the police would want to go through your uncle's papers before you disposed of them," she said slowly.

"Mr. Taylor assured me the police would have full access to them, but they needed safeguarding. Evidently they contain very private information about his family."

"Yes, I'm sure they do," Jo murmured, uncertain why Alex's preemptive move disturbed her so.

Fanatical about his privacy, it made sense that he'd ensure the intimate details about his family entrusted to a friend and biographer didn't make it into the hands of someone who might exploit or misinterpret them. The legality of who actually owned those papers and tapes didn't seem to trouble Mrs. Russ's niece.

It troubled Jo, however. Somewhere in those boxes might lie a clue to Dr. Russ's murder, or at least an explanation of the link between him and Eric Stroder.

Well, gaining access to the historian's papers wasn't her problem, she decided. Her only connection to either Russ or Stroder was Alex, and she was determined to cut that tie.

This time, she vowed, she'd leave no doubt in Alexander Taylor's mind.

He returned with Mrs. Russ a few moments later. Jo could see the widow's thoughts were on her violets, not her husband. Pulling out a business card, she passed it to the niece. It was one she'd done herself on her computer, complete with picture, mailing address, and email. Pretty spiffy, if she did say so herself.

"Here's my address and phone number. If your aunt should decide she wants to talk about your uncle's last moments, please tell her to call me."

She took leave of Mrs. Russ, who still confused her with a police officer. Alex made his farewells at the same time and accompanied her outside.

"You look tired," he said quietly, searching her face as he escorted her to the MG. "Did you get any sleep last night?"

"Not much."

She leaned a hip against the car, trying to decide whether to tell him about the missing photo. The more she shared with him, she decided, the more entangled they became. Better to let the police sort it all out.

"Come back to Georgetown with me," he urged, reaching out to tuck a wayward strand of hair behind her ear. "Let's have dinner and talk about what happened last night. What happened at BellaVista, as well."

She jerked away from his hand. How could he do this? she wondered. How could he show such patience and consideration for Mrs. Russ, and such blind obstinacy with Jo?

"No, Alex. We're not having dinner, and we're not going to talk. Not anymore."

The flat refusal took him aback. "We have to work through that misunderstanding at BellaVista and put it behind us, Joanna."

"It wasn't a misunderstanding. Not on my part,

anyway. I read your signals loud and clear. You just refused to read mine. It's over between us. You have to accept that."

"No, I don't."

This time it was Jo who blinked. "I beg your pardon?"

"It's not over, darling. It's barely begun."

He stepped closer, crowding her against the MG.

"I suggest you remember what happened last time you tried to muscle me," she warned.

"How could I forget?"

He smiled. He actually smiled! His mouth curved. The dimple in his chin almost disappeared.

"You took me by surprise. I'll be ready the next time."

For the life of her, Jo couldn't figure out what it took to get through to the man. She gave it a last, parting shot.

"There won't be a next time. Ever. Period. End of story. I'm not seeing you again after today, Alex, and I'm not answering your phone calls."

That finally seemed to penetrate his supreme self-confidence. The smile disappeared. His blue eyes bore into her with unsettling intensity, as if he wanted to see into her soul.

"Is there someone else? That other pilot I met at the picnic? What was his name? Elliot? Deke Elliott?"

His phenomenal memory shouldn't have surprised her. And she certainly shouldn't have allowed the echo of Deke's husky promise to leap into her mind. She hesitated, just for a moment. Just long enough for something ugly to ripple across Alex's face.

"Listen to me," she said with as much calm as she

could muster at that point. "What did or *didn't* happen between us had nothing to do with Deke. Only you, Alex. And me."

"Good."

He didn't touch her. Didn't move an inch closer. Yet she felt almost suffocated by his nearness.

"I won't lose you the way I lost Katherine."

Katherine. It always came back to Katherine.

"You're mine," he whispered. "All of you. Your soft skin. Your full mouth. Your slender hips. Every part of you is for my eyes only. Remember that, Joanna."

Fury and the first, faint prickling of fear brought Jo off the MG.

"Go to hell."

Yanking open the car door, she swung inside and shoved the key in the ignition. Alex was still standing in the driveway, watching her, when she peeled out onto Braddock Road.

Chapter Seventeen

The confrontation with Alex outside Dr. Russ's home left Jo angry and more determined than ever to cut the cord. She stopped by a Radio Shack on the way home and purchased a caller ID unit. A quick call to her telephone service activated the special option that afternoon.

The little device paid for itself the same evening. Alex called three times. Each time, Jo let the phone ring until the machine clicked on. The deep, sensual voice that had charmed her just a few weeks ago now sent ripples of distaste down her spine.

"I know you're there," he whispered during the last call. "Pick up, darling."

Jo's skin prickled. For an absurd moment, she glanced uneasily around the living room, wondering if the thief who'd waltzed in the other night and lifted the photograph had planted a hidden camera or some listening devices. Wondering, too, if Alex was behind that bit of larceny.

Why? Why would he want the photo? For that matter, why would he whisk away all Dr. Russ's papers before the police had a chance to go through them?

What had the historian uncovered during his poking and probing into the Taylor family history?

Hidden secrets, perhaps?

Secrets dark enough to sign his death warrant?

The idea left her feeling slightly sick. She had to get a grip. This whole business with Alex was starting to drift into the realm of the unreal.

"Talk to me, Joanna." His voice eerily floated through her thoughts.

"Not in this lifetime," she muttered to the empty, echoing house.

More than a little frazzled, she got ready for bed and set the alarm for five o'clock the next morning. That would allow her plenty of time to make her scheduled seven o'clock check ride. Like all military aircrew members, Jo was subject to periodic evaluation by the Wing standardization/evaluation team to make sure she flew by the book.

She woke to a drizzly gray dawn and a blinking light on the alarm clock. After a few groggy moments, it dawned on her that Fort Washington had suffered a power outage sometime during the night. Scooping her watch off the nightstand, Jo discovered it was six-ten.

"Well, hell!"

There was no way she could throw on her flight suit, drive the fifteen miles to the base, finish her preflighting, and make her scheduled take-off.

This was not good.

Definitely not good.

Aircraft broke down occasionally, causing delays or late take-offs. Missions were canceled or rescheduled all the time. Pilots planning on a long and successful career in the United States Air Force, however, didn't miss many showtimes.

Jo called ahead to advise Ops Control that she'd be late, which didn't earn her any brownie points with the major waiting to administer her check ride, then scrambled into her uniform and hit the road. Mercifully, traffic was light.

She aced the evaluation, but the hassle of trying to pacify the major and make up time took an edge from her satisfaction. So did the phone call she received early that afternoon.

She'd just grabbed a sandwich and a diet Coke from the vending machines and was checking the extended weather forecast for tomorrow when one of the sergeants at Ops Control patched through a call.

To her dismay, her long-distance landlord announced that he had to break her lease. He'd just received an offer he couldn't refuse for the house and land he'd inherited from his grandparents. Some huge corporation wanted to snatch up the last undeveloped section along that stretch of the Potomac.

"I'm sorry, Jo. I'll refund your deposit and this month's rent, plus pay *you* a month's rent if you'll move out by the fifteenth."

"The fifteenth of when?"

"Well . . . October."

"You're kidding! That's four days from now!"

"I know, I know. But their offer is contingent on establishing ownership of the property by that date. It has to do with tax periods or something. I didn't really catch all the legalities. Hell, I didn't catch anything after they named their price!"

"But . . ."

"I'll pay for storage for your stuff if you need to move into Bachelor Officers' Quarters temporarily."

Jo emptied her lungs on a long, exasperated breath. She wouldn't screw a fellow flier out of a fabulous deal like this, but damn! Four days to find a new place and move all her possessions?

"Okay, color me gone on the fifteenth."

"I love you! My wife loves you! Each of our three children, two dogs, and assorted frogs and turtles love you. The president of GenCorp will love you when I call him back and tell him the deal's done."

She froze, her fingers clenched on the phone. She had to fight to squeeze a single word through suddenly paralyzed vocal chords.

"Gen . . . Corp?"

"Yeah. It's some big faceless conglomerate with a ton of lawyers on the board."

GenCorp wasn't faceless to Jo. She knew exactly who headed the multinational corporation. The same man who'd transferred the title of one of their corporate helicopters to her name.

"I gotta call the lawyers right away," her landlord gushed. "I don't want to give 'em time to change their minds. Thanks, kid!"

Jo's power of speech came rushing back the moment she slammed down the phone.

"Son of a bitch!"

She didn't realized she'd practically shouted the words until she looked up to see the crew members gathered in the Ops Control center staring at her with varying expressions of surprise. Even Deke Elliot had stopped in mid-stride.

His eyes narrowing, Deke took in Jo's flushed face.

Taylor again! It had to be Taylor. No one else could raise such a storm of emotion with a single phone call.

At that moment, the pilot's active dislike of the playboy millionaire morphed into an implacable determination to break Taylor's hold over her, one way or another. The savage urge sprang from more than jealousy, he admitted, his jaw working. More than a primitive need to stake his own claim.

He hated seeing Jo played with like this. Almost as much as he hated the idea of Taylor's hands on her. Deke had lain awake a long, long time after overhearing Alex's references to her soft breasts and hot juices. It was almost as if the bastard had known he was standing there, listening. Almost as if Taylor had wanted to goad him, rub his nose in the fact that he'd scored.

Well, he'd succeeded. More than he could know. Deke was damned if he'd stand by and watch Taylor twist Jo into knots like this.

Strolling over to the still seething woman, he raked a cool glance down her face. "Got a problem, West?"

"You might say so. I'm being evicted. Four days from today."

"Didn't pay your rent?"

"I paid it," she ground out, arms crossed, angry gaze fixed on the helos lined up outside. "But it seems someone's offered to pay a lot more."

"Taylor?"

"How did you know?"

"Just an educated guess."

Her green eyes spit fire. Anger put a flush of pink in her cheeks. With a clench low in his gut, Deke reminded himself he'd yet to raise anything close to that level of emotion in Jo West. Soon, he promised silently. Soon.

He was damned if he'd prey on her while Taylor kept her so thrown off balance, but . . . soon.

"Why does lover boy want to put you out on the street? As I recall, he was ready to beg, even grovel, to get you into his arms."

The pink in her cheeks deepened to brick red. "Look, the man's obsessed, okay? I've tried to break it off a dozen times now. He won't let go."

Frowning, Deke hooked her elbow and drew her into the crew lounge. It was deserted for once, with only the mumble of news coming from the big-screen TV to disturb them.

"There are laws against stalkers, Jo."

"I know, I know." She rubbed the heel of her hand across her forehead. "I've thought about talking to the police, maybe even getting a restraining order. But I don't have any proof at this point, and the media . . ."

Her breath left on a long sigh.

"The media would eat me alive. I can see the headlines now. Dairyman's Daughter Scorned, Plots Revenge. Prince Charming Accused by Woman He Dumped."

"It won't be the first time you've made the headlines," Deke reminded her. "You can handle whatever they throw at you."

"Yeah, I guess. Maybe."

"Hey, what's this?"

Under ordinary circumstances, he wouldn't have touched her in public, not with them both in uniform anyway. He firmly believed in keeping his personal life separate and apart from his professional one. Yet the quiet desperation on her face ripped at something deep inside him. Curling a finger under her chin, he tilted it up.

"Don't tell me Super Woman's afraid of a few measly reporters?"

She laughed. It was a shaky, choking little laugh, but it lifted a boulder-sized weight from Deke's chest.

"No, not afraid. Just . . . tired of the whole awkward mess."

The weight dropped right back on his ribs. The need to shield her, to protect her, was fast becoming an obsession, every bit as compulsive as that driving Alexander Taylor. But Deke wasn't about to make the same mistakes as Taylor by pushing too hard, too fast.

"I suggested the other night that you camp out at my place until you got a security system installed. Since you're about to find yourself out on the street, I'll renew the offer."

She stared up at him, not making any effort to shield her thoughts. Deke read them effortlessly. They matched his own.

"There aren't any strings attached to the offer, West. No obligations. You come and go as you please."

She licked her lips, and it was all he could do not to kiss her right there, in the middle of the damned crew lounge. Every muscle in his body hardened, but he managed to keep his voice level.

"I'm not Taylor. I won't push you. I told you . . . when it happens between us, it happens."

This time she didn't add her zinger. No *if* it happened. Her wide, glade-green eyes registered relief, confusion, acceptance, and a spark of undisguised interest that slammed into him like a fist.

"If you're sure," she murmured.

He'd never been more sure of anything in his life.

"I'll follow you home tonight and help you pack. Maybe I can round up a few of the other guys to help, too."

Jo watched him stride away, her thoughts as chaotic as her emotions. What the heck was she doing? She'd barely escaped making a Godzilla-sized mistake with Alex, and in almost the next breath, she was moving in with Deke.

Was she crazy, or what?

What, she decided ruefully as Deke disappeared down the hall. Definitely what. Despite her broken engagement earlier this year, despite the mess with Alex, she'd decided to yield to the inevitable. As Deke seemed so fond of stating, when it happened, it happened.

Still, Jo was so gun-shy she might have backed out even then if she hadn't received two very different, very frightening documents that very day.

The first came by courier, delivered just as Jo and Deke and a half dozen buddies were about to form up the moving brigade. In answer to a call from the squadron orderly, Jo promised to join the others in the parking lot and dashed across the hangar to the administrative area.

"Joanna West?"

She eyed the uniformed courier suspiciously. "Yes."

"I've got a letter for you. I need your signature."

"What kind of letter?"

"Hey, lady, I don't read 'em, I just deliver 'em. Sign here, please."

Still wary, she checked the label on the flat cardboard envelope first. It contained her name and address, nothing more. After considerable deliberation, she signed the receipt and returned it to the courier.

Even with all that had happened during her short-lived relationship with Alex, she still wasn't prepared for the papers inside. They came with a note attached, written in a bold handwriting she recognized instantly.

> *Darling,*
> *As much as it pains me to dispossess you,*
> *the property was too choice to pass up.*
> *Please accept this with my love.*
> *Alex*

Her blood had begun a slow boil by the time she flipped to the attached lease. It was made out in her name and granted her life tenancy of a five-thousand-square-foot penthouse condo in one of the high-rise buildings on the Virginia side of the Potomac. She couldn't even begin to guess what a place like that would cost.

Spinning on one heel, Jo took off after the courier. She caught up with him in the parking lot, where Deke and her buddies had already gathered.

"Hey! You! Hold on a moment!"

Seething, she tore Alex's note and the lease into small pieces and stuffed them back in the envelope.

"Return this to the sender. I'm refusing it."

"You can't refuse it," he protested. "You've already signed for it."

"Tough. Take it back to wherever you got it."

His lip set mulishly. "It's gonna cost you, lady. The sender only paid for delivery."

Yanking down the zipper in her leg pocket, Jo grabbed the thin wallet that carried her ID and cash, pulled out a ten-dollar bill, and shoved it into his hand.

"Here."

Muttering, the courier climbed into his van and drove off, leaving Jo shaking with the force of her anger. Damn Alex! What part of *no* didn't he understand?

Deke detached himself from the others and joined her where she stood, hands curled into tight fists. "What was that all about?"

"Alex sent me a lease for a condo," she said through teeth clenched so tight they hurt. "I just sent it back."

His hazel eyes turned flinty. "I think Mr. Taylor and I will have to have a little chat."

Jo was too used to holding her own to dump her problem with Alex in someone else's lap, even Deke's. Especially Deke's.

"This isn't your fight."

"The hell it isn't."

She wanted to warn him that Alex played by his own rules, that his money and influence could burn them both if they weren't careful, but Deke didn't need warning. In his own way, he was every bit as tough and tenacious as Alexander Taylor.

"Let's get this operation under way," he said after

a moment. "I'll feel a whole lot better after we move you out of that isolated little house."

"Me, too," Jo murmured fervently.

She felt even better about it when she arrived home, unlocked the front door for the guys to carry in boxes, and found a fat letter stuffed in her mailbox.

What now? she wondered with another leap of anger. The keys to a Ferrari to match his? A marriage license with her name already filled in?

Only after she'd turned it over and noted Mrs. Martin Russ's return address did Jo start to breathe easy again. Wandering into the house, she told the guys to help themselves to a beer before tackling the daunting task ahead.

"Pack everything that isn't nailed down," she instructed, sliding a finger under the envelope flap. "I'll get changed and come—"

She broke off, shock and revulsion contorting her face as a small notebook slid into her hand. Its cover and most of its pages were warped and stained a rust red from the blood that had soaked them.

Deke was beside her in two strides. "What the hell is that?"

"I think . . ." Jo held the gory object up by a thumb and one finger. "I think it's Dr. Russ's notebook. He tore a page out of one like this at BellaVista to write me a note."

A dangerous flame leaped into Deke's eyes. "Did that sick bastard Taylor send it to you?"

"I don't know. There's no . . . Oh, here it is."

Dropping the little notebook onto the coffee table, Jo unfolded the handwritten note. The writing was so tiny and crabbed that it took her several moments to figure out Mrs. Russ's niece had authored it.

"The funeral home returned Dr. Russ's personal effects to his widow," Jo reported to Deke and the others now crowding around her. "This notebook was evidently in his pocket when he was shot."

"So why in blue blazes would Mrs. Russ send it to you?" Deke demanded.

"She gets confused. And . . ." Jo squinted at the almost indecipherable handwriting. "And she told her niece I might want to look at it, since I'm an officer of the law."

"What?"

"I wore my service dress uniform," she explained. "Mrs. Russ mistook me for a police officer. Her niece says she would have forwarded it to the police, but she had to leave to get back to Ohio right after the funeral this afternoon and couldn't find the name of the detective investigating her uncle's death."

"You'd better call Ambruzzo and tell him you have it," Deke advised.

"I will." Gingerly, Jo reclaimed the notebook. "For now, I think I'll put it in a plastic bag and slip it into my purse. I don't want it to get lost in the boxes."

Or mysteriously disappear, as Dr. Russ's note and the photo had.

She carried the gruesome little book into the kitchen and laid it on the counter. Curiosity made her lean a hip against the cupboard and lift the stained cover with the tip of one nail.

Blood had seeped through most of the paper, obliterating the inked notes. Her stomach clenching, Jo forced herself to open to a second page, then a third.

She deciphered a faint swirl here, the tail of curlicue there. Only the last few pages remained relatively legible.

And only one word leaped out to snag her by the throat.

Katherine

There, on the last page, in oversized script, double underlined. And right below, two desperate questions.

Did he kill her?
Is Captain West in danger, too?

Chapter Eighteen

Jo delivered the bloodstained notebook to Detective Tony Ambruzzo the next afternoon. A cold wind whipped at her cheeks and tore the last of the leaves from the trees lining Alexandria's streets. Brown leather jacket zipped and head ducked against the wind to keep it from dislodging her blue flight cap, Jo climbed the steps to the city offices.

A receptionist directed her to the police department. Homicide occupied a corner suite on the second floor. Alerted by a phone call from Jo earlier, Ambruzzo was waiting for her. His head shook as he slid the book out of the plastic bag onto his desk.

"I can't believe the Medical Examiner released this to the funeral director along with Russ's clothing and other personal effects."

"Mistakes happen," Jo murmured, more interested in his reaction to the historian's notes than the bureaucratic foul-ups that occurred in every profession. "Check out the last page."

With the tip of a pen, Ambruzzo flipped the pages. As Jo's had, his gaze fixed on the name inscribed in Dr. Russ's ornate handwriting.

"*Katherine*," he read softly.

The name evoked the image of the raven-haired beauty in the portrait at Chestnut Hill . . . and of the torment in Alex's eyes when he'd confessed to Jo that he'd come to hate his wife almost as much as he'd loved her.

"She was Alex Taylor's wife," she said, uneasy with the suspicions that had taken root in a dark corner of her mind, yet unable to eradicate them.

"Yes, I know."

"She died three years ago."

He nodded. "Of acute cardiomyopathy."

Smiling wryly at Jo's look of surprise, he slid open a drawer and extracted a manila folder.

"Mr. Taylor's lawyers informed me yesterday that I'll have to obtain a court order before they'll let me examine the papers and tapes removed from Dr. Russ's residence. That pissed me off—excuse me—annoyed me so much that I expanded my investigation a bit."

Digging through the folder, he pulled out a faxed report.

"I still haven't established a connection between Russ and this photographer Stroder . . . except that they both focused their attention almost exclusively on the Taylors. Russ was writing the family history. Stroder, it seems, was fascinated by Katherine."

He wasn't the only one, Jo thought.

"Reportedly, Stroder sold some twenty different photos of Katherine Taylor to various magazines before her death. He made a bundle after she died with his 'retrospectives' until Alexander Taylor slapped him with a lawsuit that tangled him up in the courts for over a year."

"What were the grounds for the lawsuit?"

"Evidently, one of the profiles hinted that all was not sunshine and happiness in the Taylor household, and that Katherine may not have died of natural causes."

Jo's chest tightened. Could it possibly be true? Could Alex have somehow engineered his wife's death?

"Taylor's lawyers suppressed the story before it got into print," Ambruzzo continued. "In the process, they convinced the judge to slap a gag order on Stroder that made him a pariah with most reputable publishers. He hadn't sold anything in years until he got lucky with those shots of you dragging Alex Taylor out of the burning Ferrari."

"But . . ."

Palms clammy, Jo struggled to subdue her own churning emotions and hang onto logic.

"If there was any reason to suspect Katherine didn't die of natural causes, wouldn't it have come out during this lawsuit?"

"The presiding judge found no grounds to exhume the body or open an investigation into her death."

She had just begun to chide herself for her creeping suspicions when Ambruzzo spurred them to a full gallop.

"Some folks wondered, of course, if the fact that the judge and John Tyree Taylor were old friends influenced the decision, but the DA chose not to pursue the matter further."

A sick feeling swirled in Jo's stomach.

"The doctors . . ." she said. "When Katherine died, they would've had to certify the cause of death."

"The attending physician was the Taylor family doctor, had been for years."

He let that sink in for a few wrenching seconds.

"I did a little research into this cardiomyopathy, by the way. It's a disease that weakens the heart muscle—the myocardium—so it can't function. The condition can be inherited or the result of long-standing hypertension. Or, as in Katherine Taylor's case, the damage can occur suddenly and traumatically from what was diagnosed at the time as a viral infection."

"At the time?"

"The ME informs me the same condition could result from ingestion of various drugs or toxins . . . some of which might not be discernible to a physician who had no reason to look for them."

"Oh, God!"

He leaned forward, his brown eyes lancing into her. "Did Taylor ever talk about his wife to you? Ever describe their relationship?"

With a feeling that she was stepping off dry land into a foul-smelling morass that could swallow her whole, Jo dipped her head in a slow nod.

"He said . . . He said Katherine told him she was bored by all the political dinners and wanted excitement. That she was going to leave him. No one knew, not even his grandfather."

"Then her heart gave out," the detective said softly.

"Then she died," Deke murmured later that evening, unknowingly paraphrasing Ambruzzo.

The remains of the pizza he'd brought home with him an hour ago littered the coffee table. Planted squarely between two man-sized sofas upholstered in hunter green corduroy, the oversized table was all that separated Deke and his temporary houseguest.

Jo hadn't yet grown comfortable with the idea of sharing Deke's spacious, fourth-floor apartment in a new high-rise a few miles north of the base. Last night had felt odd enough, with him asleep just across the hall. But her unexpected eviction, Alex's disturbing call, and the arrival of Dr. Russ's bloodstained notebook had drained her so much she'd simply helped the guys stack her boxes in Deke's basement storage area, dumped her suitcases in his spare bedroom, and crashed.

Now she was all too conscious of the way his eyes appeared more green than brown in the glow from the lamps. Conscious, as well, of the smooth glide of his throat muscles when he tilted his head back to drain the last of his beer. In jeans and a blue denim shirt with the sleeves rolled up, he looked comfortable and safe and too damned sexy for Jo's peace of mind.

Yet she felt more relaxed here with him than she had in days. Weeks. She hadn't realized how much tension she'd been carrying around on her back. Or how much Alex had gotten to her. Was still getting to her.

Somehow, telling Deke about her conversation with Ambruzzo had helped resolve some of the dark doubts that had plagued her all day. Here in the comfortable living room made homey by a mix of Air Force memorabilia and touches of Deke's native Wyoming, Dr. Russ's suspicions didn't seem quite as bizarre or absurd or frightening.

Drawing up her knees, Jo wrapped her arms

around her legs. "Ambruzzo planned to question Alex this afternoon about the papers he removed from Russ's home and the missing note and photograph. He's determined to get some answers."

"My bet is that he doesn't make it past Taylor's battery of lawyers." Deke plunked a heel on the coffee table. "And if he does, our boy will probably present a legal brief designating those papers as proprietarial to his family, a flat disclaimer of any contact with Stroder, and an airtight alibi for the time Dr. Russ was shot."

"Not to mention a sheaf of expert medical opinions on the cause of his wife's heart failure."

A shiver danced down Jo's spine. Even now, after experiencing firsthand Alex's obsessive fixation, she found it hard to believe him capable of murder.

"This is all so bizarre. Six weeks ago, Alexander Taylor was only a name to me."

Across the empty pizza carton, Deke's mouth tightened. "Six weeks from now, that's all he'll be again."

She wished that were true. If she hadn't caught the feverish glitter in Alex's eyes when he'd backed her against the MG outside the Russes' house, she might have deluded herself into believing the confident prediction.

But she'd glimpsed that dark intensity, and heard him whisper that she was his, only his. Her skin crawled with the echo of that silky warning.

"Want another beer?"

With a wrench, she dragged her thoughts from Alex. She had to get him out of her head, just as she intended to force him out of her life!

"No, thanks. I'm flying tomorrow."

"I'm not. Want to keep me company for one more?"

"Sure."

Scooping up the pizza carton, Deke balanced it in one hand and snagged the two empty beer bottles with the other.

"Did you find everything you needed last night?" he asked. "Extra blankets? Pillows? Toothpaste?"

"Mmmm," Jo replied ambiguously.

In fact, Deke was the perfect host. The linen closet in his second bathroom had been stocked with extra blankets, pillows, toothpaste, *and* a good supply of condoms. Left behind by one of his buddies passing through town, she surmised.

Or not.

A slow heat had started in her belly when she'd spied that economy-sized box of Trojans. The same slow heat that stirred now as she contemplated Deke's neat buns and long, easy stride. Beer bottles clinking, he headed for the kitchen. The phone rang when he was halfway across the room, both hands full.

"Want me to get it?" Jo asked.

"Yeah, thanks."

What a blessed relief to pick up the phone and not worry who was on the other end, she thought, stretching to reach over the arm of the sofa. Other than her parents, her boss, Detective Ambruzzo, and Ops Control, she hadn't notified anyone of her temporary change of residence.

"Bitch!"

Shock sliced through her as a voice she now recognized all too well leaped through the phone. Low and venomous, it vibrated with an anger Alex made no effort to disguise.

"I thought you said there was nothing between you and Elliot. Were you screwing him all the time you played sweet and coy with me?"

"How . . . ? How did you . . . ?"

She bit off the question, angered by her stuttering incoherence.

"How did I track you down?" he snarled. "I know every move you make almost before you make it. If I hadn't been distracted by the annoyance of Detective Ambruzzo's visit this afternoon, I would've taken steps earlier to end whatever it is that's keeping us apart and get you out of there."

Furious, she pushed off the sofa. "Dammit, *you* are what's keeping us apart, Alex. I don't love you. I don't even *like* you at this point. Keep up these calls, and I'll put your ass in jail, pal."

Her threat didn't faze him.

"Don't think you can escape me, Joanna. Don't think you can ever escape me. Elliot won't—"

A strong, tanned hand snatched the phone from hers.

"You listen to me, you sick bastard." Cold fury struck flint from Deke's eyes. "This is my phone, my place, and my woman you're harassing. If you call her once more, just once, I'll come down on you so hard and so fast you'll be sucking your dinner through a straw for the rest of your unnatural life."

He slammed the phone onto its cradle with a force that bounced it several times.

In the thunderous silence that followed, Jo's mouth opened, closed, and opened again. Of all the riotous thoughts tumbling through her head at that moment, only one emerged.

"Your woman?"

"Sorry. I figured that would grab his attention."

It had certainly grabbed hers.

"I appreciate your gallantry," she began on a testy note, rattled by the violence simmering in Deke's eyes, even more rattled as the implications of the call she'd just received sank in. "Alex may be dangerous, more dangerous than I could have imagined a few weeks ago. I can't let you put yourself in the middle of this mess."

"I've got news for you, West. We passed that point some time back."

"Hey, don't get heavy on me, Elliot. I'm just trying to spare you some of the grief I've—"

"Shut up, okay?"

"What?"

"Shut up and put your arms around me."

Her jaw dropped.

"I won't beg," he reminded her. "I won't plead. I'm telling you, just this once, to let me hold you. After that, it's anyone's guess who makes the next move."

Jo debated for all of five seconds. Then she slid her arms around his neck and kissed him.

She had to go up on tiptoe to do it. Had to fit her body to his. Even through his clothes, his shoulders felt like warm marble under her fingers. His thighs like corded steel against hers.

But his mouth . . .

His mouth was everything that she'd imagined. Hard. Hot. Delicious. Demanding. His tongue was wicked as it drew hers into a duel neither of them could win standing up.

He let her take her fill of him for several minutes,

maybe hours, before his hands clamped around her waist like a vise, banding her, lifting her. Jo felt his strength through her sweatshirt, felt the swift, greedy punch of desire his touch sparked.

The need he aroused was so raw, so different from any she'd experienced with any man, she thought on a heady rush.

Thank God!

If her fiancé . . . or Alex! . . . had loved her like this, she might have missed Deke. Might never have dug her fingers through his short, thick hair. Never have let her head fall back so he could ravage her throat. Never have caught her breath on a groan as his hands slid over her hips, cupped her rear, lifted her into him.

He was rock hard, straining against her belly. Jo felt his erection through her sweatshirt, through his jeans. Delight shot into her. Delight, and a need so intense she thought she'd melt with it.

Her breath came in short, searing pants when he pulled his head up. Nostrils flaring, cheeks flushed, he dug his hands in her hair and tipped her head back. Whatever he saw in her face curved his lips into a lopsided grin that did serious damage to Jo's entire nervous system.

"What do you say, West? Want to get naked and work up a sweat?"

As romantic proposals went, that didn't exactly top her list of all-time heart throbbers. But Deke's irreverence was so different from Alex's intensity, so light-hearted and just exactly what she needed at that moment, she couldn't help laughing.

"Sounds like a hell of a plan to me, Elliot."

Any impression that he might have been teasing

was blown away when he scooped her into his arms and started for the bedroom. Jo didn't exactly consider herself a lightweight. Nor was she used to the sensation of being carted down a hall by a male with one thing on his mind. She was adjusting to this particular mode of transportation when he dumped her on the bed.

It was a big bed, she noted, in keeping with Deke's long frame. The spread felt like cottony suede under her palms, the mattress as firm and as big as the man who stood before her, unbuttoning his shirt.

Jo had peeked into his bedroom when she'd moved in last night. She'd approved of the clean, no-frills arrangement, with a computer desk in one corner, a work-out bench in the other, and the king-sized bed taking up center stage. The painting over the bed had intrigued her. Wyoming, obviously. Deke's home, maybe. Wide open skies above grassy brown plains. Mountains smudged with purple in the distance. And she'd grinned at the pair of crossed branding irons mounted above the desk. Almost like crossed swords, she'd thought. Symbolic of another culture, a lifestyle different from any she'd experienced.

It wasn't the crossed irons that riveted her attention now, though. It was Deke. Only Deke.

He didn't waste time or unnecessary effort on finesse. Shrugging out of his shirt, he tossed it aside and unzipped his jeans with the casual grace of a man who paid little attention to the clothes he pulled on or off.

Jo's stomach hollowed at her first glimpse of his flat belly and broad chest fuzzed with gold-tipped brown hair. A faint line traced along one rib, spidery white against his saddle-leather tan.

"How did you get that scar?" she murmured, suddenly avidly curious, wanting to know everything about him.

"I got kicked by a bull calf who wasn't anxious to become a steer," he answered, grinning. "I have to admit, I felt some sympathy for the critter."

So did Jo, but only for as long as it took Deke to join her on the sueded bedspread. He stretched out beside her, his mouth sinful on hers and his hands busy on the buttons and snaps that kept her clothed.

Within moments they were naked. The sweat Deke had promised took a little longer.

But not much.

Jo splayed her hands on his shoulders, exploring the sweep of clean muscle and skin, delighting in the heat in his palm as he shaped her breast.

"You don't have any idea how many times I unzipped your flight suit, peeled it down, and did this," he muttered, contorting to fit his mouth to her nipple. "And this."

Jo gasped, arching her back as he tugged gently.

The memory of Alex's painful bite burst into her mind for an instant, then vanished forever in the exquisite sensations of Deke's mouth and teeth and tongue. Teasing. Laving. Suckling.

She couldn't have lain passive under that tender assault if she'd wanted to. Wedging a forearm between their heated bodies, she reached down. His rigid shaft, the tip already wet with the first drops of seminal fluid, filled her eager hand.

At her first stroke, Deke grunted and straightened with a jerk. His breath washed hot in her ear.

"Jo . . . !"

It was a warning, hoarse, raw. Heady with the knowledge she could wring that kind of reaction from him, she slid her hand up over the foreskin, down to the root.

In response, his fingers found her core, tested her dewy wetness, thrust home.

As quickly as that, Jo almost reached her flash point. Her womb contracted. Pleasure streaked to every corner of her body.

"Deke! Wait! I—"

She broke off, groaning aloud as the phone beside the bed shrilled.

"*Nooooooo!* Not again!"

It was Alex. With every shattered nerve in her body, she knew it was Alex. She wanted to cry. Wanted to scream with rage and frustration.

Deke didn't give her the chance to do either. With a savage oath, he rolled to the side of the bed, ripped the phone cord out of the wall, and threw the instrument across the room.

Plastic components hit wallboard, then clattered to the floor. The din was still echoing when Deke yanked open the nightstand drawer and pulled out a condom. The muscles of his back and shoulders quivered as he sheathed himself, but the grin he turned on Jo a moment later wiped every extraneous thought from her mind.

"Where were we?" he asked, as if he didn't know damned well he'd almost brought her to a climax just a few heartbeats ago. Looping her arms around his neck, Jo dragged him down atop her sweat-slicked body.

"Right about here," she said, spreading her legs in joyous welcome.

If she'd had even a hint of the devastation their joining would wreak on him, she would never have taken him into her arms so eagerly. But at that moment, with his skin flaming and his mouth hungry on hers, Jo selfishly, foolishly, believed they could control their destinies along with this glorious desire.

Chapter Nineteen

"You need to get a restraining order, Jo. Taylor's out of control."

Deke's sleep-roughened drawl caught her as she was trying to tiptoe silently past his bedroom . . . not an easy feat wearing boots and a flight suit constructed of a slick material that swished with each step. So much for trying to let him sleep while she drove in to take her early flight.

Less than twenty minutes had passed since she'd nudged aside his arm, inched her butt from the warm cradle of his thighs, and slithered out from under a tangle of blankets. She'd used those minutes to shower and dress and replay the incredible scenes from the night before a dozen or so times in her mind. Her face heated as the details came back in vivid Technicolor and thundering surround-sound.

Had she really flamed in his arms like that? Really screeched in his ear when she went over the edge the first time? The second time, thank goodness, Jo had been more prepared for the starburst of white hot pleasure. Prepared, too, for the slick steel of his body on hers and in hers and under hers.

She wasn't ready, however, for the tiny shiver of

pleasure just the sound of his voice generated in the predawn darkness . . . for the confrontation she knew would come next.

She'd planned to put it off until this evening. Planned to think through all the ramifications of Alex's call before she discussed them with Deke. She'd tried to speak to him last night, but he wasn't in a mood for talking right then. After the first touch of his hands and mouth on hers, Jo wasn't, either.

She couldn't evade the issue now, though. Deke had brought the ugly matter into the quiet of this last hour before dawn. Pushing open the door she'd pulled almost shut when she'd left him sleeping twenty minutes ago, Jo let the light from the hall spill into the room and across the bed. When she caught sight of the rumple-haired, bare-chested male propped against the headboard, her stomach clenched.

Crawling out of bed and leaving a sleeping Deke occupying more than his fair share of the mattress had been tough enough. Carrying on a rational conversation with a man who'd dragged the covers over only a minimal portion of his lap might prove even more difficult, if not downright impossible. Particularly when he stretched to flip on the bed-side lamp and the shadows retreated along with the covers.

"Sorry I woke you," she began, dragging her gaze from his lean, muscled haunches. "I tried not to make too much noise getting ready."

"The shower didn't wake me." A smile hovered around his mouth. "I've been wide awake and hurting since you squirmed out of bed. You've got some wiggle on you, West."

Something fluttered at the edges of Jo's heart. She knew darned well it was premature to think past today. And too soon after Alex to fall headlong for anyone else, even this cowboy with the killer pecs and tight buns. Yet she couldn't resist propping a shoulder against the door and soaking up the moment the way a hermit emerging from a dark cave would the sun.

"As best I recall, you made some interesting moves last night, too."

His grin kicked into a smile. "I saved a few tricky maneuvers for our next low-level pass. Want to test one or two before you hit the road?"

Was he kidding? The urge to kick off her boots, tug down a few zippers, and crawl back into bed was so powerful it dried Jo's throat.

"We'd better not," she murmured, making no effort to hide her regret. "I've already logged in one late take-off this week."

"I was afraid you'd say that." He shagged aside the covers, oblivious to his nakedness as he made for the bathroom. "Why don't you start the coffee? We'll talk about how we're going to handle Taylor as soon as I slap some water on my face."

She hoped he'd slap on some clothes as well. She was only human, after all.

Thankfully, his jeans rode low on his hips and his blue denim shirt covered most of his chest when he appeared in the kitchen some moments later.

"God, that smells great. First things first, though."

To her surprise and considerable delight he took

her mug and set it aside before caging her against the counter.

" 'Morning, West."

Water beaded at his temples. Jo traced one drop as it meandered through the stubble darkening his right cheek.

" 'Morning," she echoed, fascinated by the scrape of soft bristles against her finger, even more fascinated by the way their mouths fit when she lifted her face to his.

"I could get used to this," he murmured, trailing light kisses across her cheek to her temple.

So could she.

She pulled away before she gave in to the swamping urge to test a few more of his special maneuvers. She couldn't risk another late take-off, any more than she could risk hurting Deke.

Reclaiming her coffee, Jo nursed it in both hands for a moment while he poured himself a mug. She couldn't delay it any longer.

"You're right about Alex. He's out of hand. He's also starting to annoy me, big time."

Annoy, and frighten her just a little, although she wouldn't admit it. "I'm going to talk to Ambruzzo today about a restraining order."

"Good."

"I think I'd better load up my boxes and move out of here, too. Today."

"That's strange." His hazel eyes met hers over the rim of his mug. "I was just thinking that you ought to unpack and stay for a while."

Her heart bumped at the casual invitation. Jo

forced herself to shake her head in smiling refusal. She couldn't put Deke in the line of fire.

"I don't think that's a good idea. Not right now anyway. Alex might buy this apartment building and evict you, too."

Her attempt to make light of the situation fell flat.

"Let him buy whatever the hell he wants. Alex Taylor and his millions don't worry me, Jo."

"Well, they should," she said bluntly. "He told me once that money still talks in this town. He can make your life miserable, Deke. Trust me on this. In a few short weeks, he's turned mine upside down. That call last night . . ."

She fought back a shudder. In the dark of the evening, Alex's whispered promise that she'd never escape him had shaken her. In the stillness of the early dawn, it echoed obscenely in her head.

"He said . . . He said he knows my every move almost before I make it." A nervous laugh rasped from her throat. "For a while there, back at my house, I had almost convinced myself someone had hidden microphones or cameras in the walls. A couple of times I had the creepiest feeling I was being watched."

"Christ!" Disbelief threaded Deke's brows. "You think he's that far over the edge?"

I don't know!" Jo clutched the mug, drawing from its reassuring warmth. "It all sounds so absurd. Like a made-for-television movie. But he knew I was here last night. He said I couldn't escape him. And . . ." A lump the size of a boulder formed in her throat. "I keep thinking about Katherine."

The frightening questions scribbled on the last

pages of Dr. Russ's notebook hung over them both. For a moment, evil seemed to invade the kitchen, swirling through Jo's thoughts like a black mist.

"Alex pulled a few strings and got Sergeant Mc-Peak's little girl a kidney within a matter of hours," she reminded Deke. "Yet he couldn't buy his dying wife a heart."

"Couldn't . . . or wouldn't."

The soft comment raised goosebumps on Jo's arms. He wasn't saying anything she hadn't thought a hundred times since she'd stared down at the pages of the bloodstained notebook. Yet the idea Alex might have somehow induced Katherine's death, then held her in his arms while she gasped out her last painful breaths, made Jo feel ill . . . and wretchedly sorry for dragging Deke into this mess.

"Alex isn't going to like that crack you made last night about your phone, your apartment, and your woman."

"Tough."

"Don't underestimate him!"

"That works both ways."

At that moment, the dangerous sheen to his eyes almost convinced her Deke could handle anything Alex Taylor threw at him. Almost. The problem was, he shouldn't have to handle it.

"I thought I'd move into Bachelor Officers' Quarters on base. At least until Alex understands that my breaking things off with him had nothing to do with you."

"I don't give a shit what Taylor thinks."

"Well, I do!" she said sharply. "I don't want you caught in the cross fire."

Deke didn't trust himself to answer right away. Fury swirled in his gut. At Jo, for thinking he'd just step aside and leave her to deal with Taylor's dangerous obsession alone. At himself, for standing by all these weeks while Taylor backed her into this corner.

But mostly at the son of bitch who put that shimmer of worry and fear in her eyes.

Yet the anger flooding his veins didn't blind him to the hard, cold facts. Contrary to Jo's belief, he was far from underestimating Taylor. If the bastard could bug her house or arrange that bit of breaking and entering a few nights ago—and Deke was becoming convinced Taylor was behind both—the man was dangerous.

Carefully, he placed his coffee mug on the counter. Just as carefully, he set Jo's beside his. His hands found the warmth of her nape, his thumbs the strong line of her jaw.

"I played noble and stepped aside once while Alex Taylor made his move. This time, the guy's going to have to go through me to get to you."

"That's just what I'm afraid of." She hooked her hands on his wrists, worry rippling across her face. "I don't want you hurt."

"I'm tough. Range tough and rattlesnake mean when necessary. I'll fly cover for you, with Taylor or anyone else as long as you want me to."

She pulled in a little hiss of air.

He was pushing her. The rational half of Deke's mind acknowledged that. With everything else weighing on her right now, she wasn't ready to take what happened between them last night to the next level.

Deke could live with that. For now.

What he couldn't live with was the tight knot in his gut when he thought of Jo trying to take on the Alex Taylors of the world alone.

"Talk to Ambruzzo today as soon as you can about a restraining order," he urged.

"I will."

"I'll put a recording device on the phone this morning. Tell him we're going to tape all incoming calls. If Taylor continues to harass you, we'll have plenty of evidence to take the bastard to court."

Again, she tried to wave him off.

"If I take Alex to court, things will get nasty. Real nasty. Are you sure you want to be in the middle of all this?"

"I'm sure."

"All right, cowboy. Just don't say you weren't warned when the cowpatties hit the fan."

She rose up on tiptoe to kiss him, then ducked under his arm and grabbed her gear bag from the counter.

"In fact, I have a feeling the pace is about to pick up considerably. Ambruzzo's going to confront Alex with Dr. Russ's notebook and the information I related about his relationship with Katherine."

He followed her to the door to the attached garage, hating that he couldn't wipe the crease from between her brows, hating even more the way Taylor jerked her strings.

"When is that supposed to happen?"

"I don't know. Ambruzzo told me yesterday that he had to get a court order to examine the papers and tapes Alex had removed from Dr. Russ's residence. Maybe that notebook I gave him will expedite the process."

Deke watched her back the MG out into the early-morning darkness, his eyes thoughtful. He'd hook up that recorder to the phone, then talk to the guys in Scheduling.

Jo didn't know it yet, but they were going to fly in close formation until Taylor got the message or went down in flames.

Very close formation.

Detective Sergeant Tony Ambruzzo arrived at the Taylor Georgetown mansion a little past eleven, accompanied by a squad of uniformed officers. After reading Alex his rights and stating that he was a possible suspect in the death of Dr. Martin Russ, he directed a methodical search that took his people from basement to attic.

Coolly, Alex instructed his butler to call his lawyers, then turned his back on the proceedings. A uniformed officer stayed with him until Ambruzzo finished directing his crew. By that time, a small army of lawyers had descended on the ivy-covered town house.

Alex waited for Ambruzzo in the library, his head resting against the high back of a brocade-covered wing chair, Italian loafers propped comfortably on a footstool. In contrast, his senior attorney paced the tall-ceilinged room and began spouting legal threats the instant the detective and his partner stepped into the library.

Alex let the angry barrage continue for a few moments, wanting time to assess his adversary. He'd obtained a complete dossier on the man, knew every detail about his background on the police force, his messy divorce, and his weakness for caramel-pecan bars. He knew, too, Ambruzzo's bulldog tenacity on cases that caught his interest . . . including, it appeared, this one.

"We'll want receipts for every item you remove from the premises," Dan Stevens demanded icily.

A senior partner in the law firm that had handled Taylor business for the past decade, Stevens specialized in corporate law. He'd already consulted one of D.C.'s top criminal attorneys on the specifics in the search warrant and was ready to take on Ambruzzo and the Alexandria P.D. on behalf of his client.

"We're taking all of Dr. Russ's papers and tapes for more detailed examination," the detective replied. "I'll make sure you get a receipt."

His glance shifted to Alex. They both knew reviewing those papers was a waste of time. Ambruzzo wouldn't find anything that Alex didn't want found. Yet the detective had to go through them, just as Alex's attorney had to register a protest.

"Those papers are privileged documents," Stevens said sharply. "They were commissioned by President Taylor for use in his official biography."

"So I understand."

"His contract with Dr. Russ contained very specific provisions regarding the disposition of working papers in the event of either party's death. If any passages or excerpts about the President are leaked, the city of Alexandria will face a very lengthy, very expensive legal action."

Uninvited, the detective took the wing chair op-

posite Alex's. His partner hitched a hip on the French
Empire desk a long-ago early Taylor had bought for
the town house. The callow treatment of the price-
less antique ignited a tight spark of anger in Alex,
but he allowed no trace of it to show as Ambruzzo
picked up on the attorney's comment.

"Just out of curiosity, Mr. Taylor, did those contract provisions cover the murder of one of the parties involved?"

"I believe murder is synonymous with death," he
replied coolly.

"Not in my dictionary," the detective replied, just
as coolly.

His gaze drifted around the library, taking in the
blue velvet curtains and leather-bound rare editions.
As if by chance, his eyes caught on a striking black-
and-white photograph in a silver frame on the table
between the chairs.

"Good shot of Captain West."

"I think so."

Alex kept his face impassive as the detective lifted
the frame and tilted the photo to the light filtering
through the window.

"Was it taken by that photographer Stroder? The
one who chased you off the road a few weeks ago?"

Alex had wondered when Ambruzzo would get
around to Stroder. He permitted himself a small, tight
smile.

"That particular picture was taken by the official
White House photographer."

"Mmmm. And this is your wife?"

Despite the years, despite everything that had

passed since those awful weeks before Katherine's death, a familiar pain gripped Alex's chest.

"Yes, that's Katherine."

"Interesting that you keep photos of Joanna West and your dead wife side-by-side."

Suddenly, Alex tired of the game. It was time to cut to the chase. "What photos I choose to keep where is my business, Detective."

Hard brown eyes sliced to Alex. "Well, it's my business, too."

"How?"

Faced with that blunt challenge, Ambruzzo had no choice but to lay his cards on the table. He slid a hand into his suit pocket and produced a small piece of paper encased in plastic.

Alex recognized the spidery handwriting instantly. So they'd gotten their hands on Martin's notebook! It had been too much to believe the damned thing had been lost.

A cold lump of anger lodged in the pit of his stomach. That scrap of paper couldn't contain anything incriminating. If it had, the police would have pounced by now. Yet the idea that he'd have to go through it all again—the constant prying, the intrusive media, the speculation—infuriated him.

"Do you recognize the handwriting, Mr. Taylor?"

"Of course."

"Any idea what made Dr. Russ speculate about whether or not you killed your wife? And whether Captain West might be in danger too?"

Stevens jumped in. "You don't have to answer that!"

"I'm aware of that, Dan. I'm more than willing to do so, however."

He leaned forward, wanting Ambruzzo to feel the force of his anger.

"No, Detective, I have no idea what put those absurd notions into Martin Russ's head."

"Is it true you hated your wife?"

He dropped the question like a bomb. The ache in Alex's chest intensified. While he held his breath, waiting for it to pass, Stevens exploded.

"That's the most ridiculous thing I ever heard. Alex loved Katherine. He was devastated by her death. We all were."

Ambruzzo ignored him. Like Alex, he had fixed on the key player in their little drama.

"You told Captain West you hated your wife."

The hurt bladed into Alex, stabbing at him like a hundred vicious little daggers. He had to force air into his lungs.

"Joanna said that?"

"I believe her exact words were, 'He said he hated her as much as he loved her.'"

Cool and unmoving outside, Alex writhed inside.

"She also said you're harassing her," the detective continued, twisting the knives.

He loved Joanna! Didn't she understand? Didn't any of them understand? He loved her.

And he was coming to hate her.

"She's thinking about obtaining a restraining order."

He barely heard Ambruzzo's remark or Dan's acid retort. The awful pain buzzed in his ears. One thought, only one, forced its way through his agony.

She'd betrayed him.

Just like Katherine. *Just like his mother.* She'd betrayed him, and was now trying to desert him.

Chapter Twenty

For a few glorious days, Jo almost convinced herself it was over, that the message had finally sunk in and Alex wouldn't bother her anymore. As fall nipped the remaining leaves from the trees and the earth sparkled with morning frosts, she started to breathe easy again.

Deke put a recording device on his phone, but no threatening or harassing calls came in. A frustrated Detective Ambruzzo briefed them both on the results of his investigation, which had hit nothing but obstacles and roadblocks. He was still trying to convince the DA to petition for exhumation of Katherine Taylor's remains. Without hard evidence to support the petition, the DA wasn't willing to take on Taylor's batteries of lawyers. Even the media had been muzzled. Not a word had leaked that the police had searched Alex's residence and questioned him in regard to Martin Russ's death.

In the midst of it all, Jo and Deke had begun that slow slide into something closer than friendship, better than sex.

Not that the sex wasn't incredible! Jo had no idea she could survive that many explosive orgasms and still walk, much less fly. Every night she discovered a different facet of Deke's personality, and a new delight in his leather-smooth, rawhide-tough body.

She didn't even object very strenuously after she learned he'd arranged to fly with her whenever possible. When confronted, he merely shrugged and said he'd done it for his own peace of mind, not hers.

The more they flew together—on and off the ground—the more his companionship and easy competence as an aviator killed Jo's old worries about competition. He was, as he informed her with a grin when she reversed positions and climbed atop his naked, sweat-slicked body, a laid-back kind of guy.

The fragile cocoon they'd woven around themselves shattered early Thursday morning, not long after Deke left for a check-flight and Jo wandered into the bathroom to treat herself to a long, leisurely shower. She flipped on the lights, twisted the tap, and hummed to herself as she slipped out of the terrycloth robe she'd confiscated from Deke. The thick white material held his scent, now mixed with the musky fragrance of their love-making.

Smiling, she draped the robe on the hook next to the shower door and stepped into the blue-tiled stall. Hot water pelted down, easing the aches of a long, strenuous night.

Then, without warning, the bathroom blew up.

A sudden flash of light blazed through the window. Jo saw it in the periphery of her vision, a sword of white slashing through the shower's steamy vapor. A single heartbeat later, the frosted glass blocks in the window shattered. The shower door splintered into a thousand tiny shards. Ceramic tiles exploded only inches from her face.

She didn't have time to think, to drop or roll into a defensive ball. Didn't have time to do anything except twist violently to one side and throw up her arms to protect her head from the sharp, deadly projectiles.

Needles of pain lanced into her hip, her breast, the underside of her arm. Her ears filled with a deafening roar of fear. Of drumming water. Of bits of glass and tile crashing to the floor.

As suddenly as it began, the terror ended.

A suffocating silence descended, broken only by the pulsing water and Jo's choking gasps. Even then she huddled in the corner, her arms over her head, too stunned to comprehend what had just happened, too afraid to move in case it happened again.

At the sound of a glass shard breaking loose to tinkle to the floor, every muscle in her body contracted. Whimpering, she tried to press herself through the wall, tried to escape the explosion she was sure would follow.

A gas main! her mind screamed. The hot water heater! One of them must have gone. The whole place could still blow.

The thought galvanized her into action. Whirling, she reached through the shattered shower door, grabbed a towel, and threw it down on the carpet of broken glass and tile shards. The pieces jabbed through the towel at the soles of her feet. Ignoring the pain, she snatched up the thick terry robe and hit the bathroom door on the run.

*   *   *

"Muscle Four, this is Muscle Control."

The radio call came through Deke's headphones at the precise moment his aircraft went into total engine failure.

A sudden, startling silence screamed in the cockpit. Everything went quiet, then the Huey assumed the glide path of a homesick brick. The tachometer needle jerked from 6600 rpm and kept falling.

Deke's reaction was instant and instinctive. Jaw clamped tight, he brought the collective down to alter the pitch of the rotors and fought the urge to stomp the right pedal to the floor. He had to keep the Huey's nose pointed forward, had to maintain a minimum of 364 rpm as the reverse flow of air through the altered angle of the rotors forced the blades to keep turning.

The Huey wanted to go down. Fought to drop like an express elevator on a nonstop trip to the basement. Just as tenaciously, Deke fought to keep it in the sky. Under his flight suit, sweat pooled at the small of his back. As many times as he'd practiced this emergency maneuver, it could still put a kink in his gut.

Conditioned by hundreds of hours in the cockpit and repeated training for just this kind of emergency, Deke scanned the countryside ahead for a landing site. In a real engine failure, he knew damned well he wouldn't have many options. The site would be the one he saw between the chin bubble and his feet.

The Huey continued its rapid loss of altitude, less precipitous now as it reached six hundred feet, five hundred, four.

"Power recovery," the pilot administering the check ride instructed at one hundred feet above the ground.

With a grunt of relief, Deke gently twisted the throttle at the head of the cyclic, applying the power that had been deliberately shut off only moments before. The engine rpm increased slowly.

In a smooth coordination of arms and legs, he worked the pedals and the controls to keep the Huey in trim while the engine revved up to 6400 rpm. At that power, the bird started to fly again.

The major in the left seat jotted a note on the clipboard strapped to his knee, then gave him a thumbs up.

"Nice recovery, Elliot."

"Thanks."

Only then did Deke answer the call that had come in over his earphones just as the Huey had gone into its imitation of a dead mallard nose-diving out of the sky. Keying in his throat mike, he contacted the 1st Helo Squadron operations center.

"Muscle Control, this is Muscle Four acknowledging your earlier transmission."

"Roger, Muscle Four. Request you return to base immediately."

"Repeat, please."

"Return to base immediately."

"What's up?"

"Sorry, Captain, I don't have all the details. Just that there's been an accident, an explosion or something, at your place."

Deke's Blazer screamed to a stop just inches from one of the yellow barriers that cordoned off his apartment building. Emergency vehicles formed a solid phalanx around the high-rise. Lights flashing, radio crackling, the vehicles swarmed with police and firefighters in slickers and rubber boots. Hoses snaked like vipers from the pumpers to various hydrants.

Deke's gaze whipped to the high-rise, searching the building for signs of damage. At the sight of a shattered window four stories up, ice formed in his veins. He was through the barriers and racing around the corner to the entrance of the building before anyone could stop him.

The men gathered just outside the glass door spun around at his pounding approach.

"What the hell . . . ?"

Anger flashed across the face of a grizzled civilian with ON-SCENE COMMANDER stenciled across his blue and white helmet. Sidestepping, he blocked Deke's charge.

"You don't have any business here, Captain."

"The hell I don't."

"Get back behind the barriers."

"Not until I know what happened and find out if the woman staying in my apartment is all right."

The commander's glance darted to the name patch attached to Deke's flight suit.

"You're Elliot? Deke Elliot? Apartment four-ten?"

"I'm Elliot," he ground out. "What happened?"

"We're not sure yet. The initial 911 call reported a possible gas main leak and resulting explosion, but we haven't found any evidence of that yet. We're still—"

"Jo West," he cut in savagely. "Captain Jo West. She was in that apartment. Is she all right?"

"She's in one piece," the disaster coordinator replied grimly. "The flying glass and debris cut her up pretty bad, though. The paramedics had stopped most of the bleeding when I talked to her, but they said she'll need stitches."

An admiring glint lightened his grim expression. "That's some lady you've got there, Captain. After the explosion, she dashed next door and called 911, then helped clear the building and get everyone to a safe distance until we arrived to take charge of the scene."

"Where is she?"

The civilian scanned the emergency vehicles and nodded to a cluster of ambulances parked some yards away. "The medics wanted to transport her to the hospital, but she insisted on waiting for you. She should be over there, in one of those . . ."

Deke didn't wait to hear more. Spinning on one heel, he aimed for the nearest ambulance.

"Hey!" the on-scene commander yelled. "I need to talk to you."

"Later!"

He didn't drag in a whole breath until he found Jo. She was huddled in the back of the ambulance, wrapped in a gray blanket. Wet hair straggled down her neck as she stared through the opened rear doors at the gaping hole that was once a glass-block bathroom window.

He slowed his step, forcing air into his lungs and the hard lump of fear from his throat.

"Jo. Sweetheart, are you okay?"

Her head swung around. At the sight of a thick bandage taped to her cheek, the air he'd just sucked in slammed out of his lungs.

"Deke!"

Before he could stop her, she scrambled out of the ambulance. The blanket parted with her jerky movement. Even forewarned, he wasn't ready for the red splotches staining the front of his white robe.

His arms opened instinctively. Just as spontaneously, she fell into them. He ached to crush her to his chest, but those red stains haunted him. He settled for holding her loosely and breathing in her scent, a wrenching mixture of shampoo and plaster dust.

"I'm sorry," she muttered against his chest. "Really sorry."

"For blowing up my apartment?" He nuzzled her wet hair. "Don't sweat the small stuff, West. I can live without getting back my deposit."

What he couldn't live without was this woman. He'd suspected it for weeks. Known for sure the first time she'd welcomed him into her arms and her body. Now probably wasn't the best time to tell her, though. Especially when she braced both hands on his arms and pushed unsteadily away from his chest.

"I didn't cause the explosion."

His heart twisted. She must be in shock not to realize he'd been kidding.

"I know," he said gently. "You'd better—"

"But someone did!"

"What?"

"Someone caused the explosion." Her fingers dug into his arms. "Your apartment was the only one that took a hit, Deke. The only one!"

A second, maybe two, passed in utter silence. Not believing—not *wanting* to believe—the incredible thought that leaped into his mind, he shot another glance at the gaping hole that was once his bathroom window.

An icy fist reached into his chest and squeezed. Jo

was right. Even from this distance, the hit looked surgically precise, as though one of the Air Force's high-tech laser-guided missiles had targeted that precise spot and augered straight in.

"Jesus!"

"It was Alex." Under the thick gauze pad taped to her cheek, her face had gone paper white. "I know it was."

His first instinct was to say no way! His second, to jump in the Blazer, tear across town, and murder the bastard.

"I don't know how he did it." Jo's fingers clawed into Deke's flesh. "A high-intensity laser, maybe. I saw a flash of light right before the window shattered."

It was possible. More than possible. A man with Taylor's millions no doubt had access to technology the whiz kids at the Pentagon would salivate over.

Hard on the heels of that thought came another. If it was Taylor, if he'd gone so far off the deep end as to arrange something like this display of fireworks, he could as easily have arranged a more devastating detonation. One that would kill instead of just maim and terrorize.

This was a warning.

Or a prelude to the final act.

"We'd better talk to Ambruzzo," he said through jaws clamped tight with sudden, savage fury. "As soon as we get you to a hospital."

"The paramedics patched me up. I don't need to—"

"You're going."

Grimly, he bundled the blanket around her and steered her back into the ambulance. He'd never forgive himself for leaving her alone and unprotected this morning, or for taking the threat too lightly. He wouldn't make that mistake again.

The call came into their room at the Visiting Officers' Quarters a little past nine that night.

Jo had just slipped into a light doze, exhausted by a long day of questions with no answers and foggy from the painkillers Deke had insisted she gobble down earlier. She jerked awake, confused for a moment by the shrilling phone and the unfamiliar surroundings. Blinking, she frowned at the framed prints on the bland, cream-colored walls.

The VOQ. She was stretched out atop a bed in the VOQ at Andrews. Deke had arranged for rooms for them both. Connecting rooms, she remembered now, her frown encompassing the open door a few feet away. From the other room she heard the soft beat of a country ballad and the drum of a shower.

Oh, God! Just the patter of cascading water made her skin crawl. She'd never step into another tiled shower enclosure without cringing and waiting for the wall to blow up right beside her face.

And she'd never answer another phone without feeling the hairs on the back of her neck rise. She gritted her teeth through another long ring.

It could be her folks. Or one of her brothers. They'd all called, several times, since Deke had phoned them from the hospital where a physician's assistant had stitched the worst of Jo's cuts.

The awful fear that the caller was Alex kept her hunched in the bed, her stomach knotted.

Finally, the recording device attached to the phone

blinked red. A second later, the answering machine kicked on. Deke's terse instruction to leave a message echoed through the speaker.

The machine beeped. A silence blanked out the shower, the ballad, even the hammer of Jo's pulse.

"Hello, Joanna."

The words sounded so strange, so dragged out and electronically altered, that she didn't recognize her own name for several seconds, let alone the caller.

"Did the sound and light show this morning frighten you."

"Alex!"

It was a curse and a cry of fury. She jerked upright in bed, ignoring the pull of stitches in her left breast, and snatched up the receiver.

"These calls are being recorded. You're going down, you bastard. In flames."

His laugh echoed eerily, like a tape played at the wrong speed. Devoid of all inflection and tone, the androgynous electronic voice still managed to mock her.

"No, Joanna. You're going down. You betrayed me. I gave you a taste this morning of what to expect. Soon, very soon, you'll die."

Violent shudders raced through her, pulling at her stitches. She wanted to scream at him. Slam the receiver down. Push him out of her life once and for all. But she knew she had to get him on tape, had to get him to incriminate himself.

"Like Katherine?" she whispered.

What might have been a sigh or a slow, drawn-out hiss drifted through the phone.

"Like Katherine."

She knew then that the sophisticated equipment Alex was using to alter his voice would somehow prevent this conversation from being captured on tape. Similarly, she'd bet her last dollar there'd be no way to trace this call.

A helpless fury brought her off the bed. Ignoring the pain lancing into her hip and her breast, she stalked through the open doorway. She had to get Deke on the other extension. He could testify, back her up in court.

"Why are you doing this?"

"I told you. What's mine, I keep."

"I was never yours! Never!"

"Good-bye, Joanna."

"Wait!" she screamed. "Alex, wait!"

She was standing in the middle of the connecting bedroom, tears of fury and fear streaming down her cheeks, when Deke came pounding out of the shower.

The next days passed in agonizing tension, mounting frustration, and rage.

As Jo had guessed, a long whine buzzed through the stretch of tape that should have recorded Alex's call. Armed with another warrant, Ambruzzo searched his residences for electronic devices and his phone records for any calls to the Andrews VOQ.

Investigating officials could offer no explanation for the shattered glass-block window and shower stall in Deke's apartment except possible structural fault that caused the walls to shift and the window to implode.

Jo consulted an Air Force JAG and a civilian attorney and requested a restraining order. Alex's at-

torneys shot the request down, citing lack of any evidence of harassment or threats.

Adding insult to injury, articles started showing up
in various tabloids. As Jo had predicted, they cast her
as the woman scorned. One rag even hinted she'd
staged the small explosion in her new lover's apartment as a desperate ploy to regain Taylor's attention.

Cool, aloof, disdaining all comment, Alex somehow
managed to come across as the injured party. Maybe
because his spokesperson fed carefully tailored comments to the media and Jo refused to engage in what
she knew would be a protracted and unwinnable
headline war.

Miserable, ashamed of the fear that curled in her
belly, worried for Deke's safety, Jo felt like a tiger at
the end of a short chain. Fiercely independent for so
long, she hated this caged existence, resented having
to hunker down on base, even snapped at Deke for
enlisting other squadron members in what he labeled
the "Watch Jo Squad." Every time she left the confines of Andrews Air Force Base, she had company.

But deep in her heart she knew Alex wouldn't give
up. A final confrontation between them was inevitable,
and not even the Watch Squad could prevent it.

That truth came home a cold, damp afternoon just
a few days before Halloween. Winter had swept in
on a wind so chill it cut straight to Jo's bones as she
crossed the parking lot in front of the 1st Helo
Squadron. Gray clouds hung low in the skies, mist-
ing the roof of the hangar behind her and seeding the
wet streets for what looked to be the first ice storm
of the season.

She'd touched down early to make her appointment at the base hospital. After the medics removed the last of her stitches, she planned to meet Deke for dinner at the Officers' Club. Then, if the streets glazed as the forecasters predicted, they'd hunker in at the VOQ.

And talk, Jo decided.

They had to talk about this uneasy situation. Decide on some course of action. She was damned if she'd continue to live her life in suspended animation, nervous whenever she left the base, jumping every time the phone rang.

She'd suggested to Ambruzzo that he wire her, that she hunt Alex down and confront him face-to-face. Both the detective and Deke had vetoed that plan as too dangerous, but Jo was ready to override their votes.

Clamping a hand over her flight cap to anchor it in the whipping wind, she dashed the last few yards to the MG. A muttered curse escaped when she saw how close an oversized SUV had parked to the driver's side of her sports car. Edging between the two vehicles, she fumbled the key into the door lock.

The wind whistled through the bare tree branches, almost drowning the faint scrape of the other vehicle's side door as it slid open behind her. Jo caught the whisper of sound just a second before something cold pressed into the side of her neck.

The next instant a vicious power punch slammed through her entire system. Her legs crumpled beneath her. The world went black.

Chapter Twenty-one

Dazed, Jo struggled to part the mists swirling through her mind. Cold rolled along her skin. Her tongue felt swollen, too large for her dry mouth. She couldn't swallow, couldn't seem to lift her arm to rub the vicious ache in the side of her neck.

A distant pinging penetrated her foggy thoughts. She tried again to raise her arm, straining, shuddering with the effort. A far corner of her mind recorded an animal-like noise, half whimper, half whine. The realization that she'd uttered that pathetic sound shocked Jo out of her stupor.

She came awake then, blinking. With painful intensity, she chased the shadows from her vision and her throbbing head.

Slowly, her senses registered sights, sounds. Glass cases filled with shiny objects. A room without angles. A circular brass railing only inches from her knees. The pinging . . .

Tilting her head back on a wobbly neck, Jo followed the sound to a rounded roof high above her. In the periphery of her vision, she made out the muzzle of a cannon pointed upward.

No, not a cannon. A telescope. A huge brass telescope.

And the drumming on the domed roof was rain. Or sleet.

Yes, sleet.

Bit by bit, awareness seeped into her mind. She was at Chestnut Hill. In the observatory. And the ice storm that had been threatening when she dashed to her MG... when—hours ago?... now pelted down with a vengeance.

Somehow, fixing those facts in her head gave her the courage she needed to drop her gaze. For long moments, she stared at the tape binding her wrists to the arms of the swivel chair.

She'd occupied this same seat before, she remembered. A lifetime ago. She'd peered through the brass telescope. Laughed when Alex tried to convince her alien ships had painted contrails across a blue sky.

Alex.

Terror stabbed through Jo's chest, so sharp and so cutting she couldn't breathe. Another whimper rose in her throat.

With everything in her, she forced it down. She was damned if she'd give in to the fear that clawed at her like a living thing. Instead, she turned inward, found the tiny flame of fury that burned at her core and nursed it like a lost, freezing mountain hiker would his last canister of butane heat.

Slowly, the fear receded. A healthy rage spread through her, bringing with it a life-sustaining warmth. She allowed herself the pleasure of hating, fiercely, unrestrainedly, before she reined in her rampaging emotions.

Hate wouldn't get her out of this icy observatory alive. Rage wouldn't help her figure out how the hell to cut through the tape on her wrists.

Forcing herself to concentrate on the immediate task, she studied the bindings. Alex had taken care to remove her leather aviator's jacket before strapping her to the chair. With her one-piece flight suit zipped to the neck, she couldn't hope to wiggle her hands through the sleeves. That meant she had to break the bonds somehow.

To her disgust and shivery dismay, the reinforced nylon tape proved tougher than the cargo netting. She tried stretching, flexing, yanking, and even contorting her body to gnaw at the bonds. Alex must have anticipated just such a maneuver. He'd taped her wrists far enough back to make it impossible for Jo to get at even a single strand.

Panting and sweating now under her flight suit despite the chill of the high-domed observatory, she tried to regroup.

All right. Okay. Gnawing through the tape was out. Maybe she could cut through it somehow.

In desperation, she planted both boots flat on the floor and swung the chair from side to side to get up enough momentum for a full spin. Like a carnival ride, the swivel-mounted seat whirled around. On the second turn, Jo aimed a kick at the telescope in the wild hope of knocking out the glass lens at the viewing end. Her boot whapped against the brass and succeeded only in skewing the telescope at a cockeyed, out-of-reach angle.

"Dammit!"

Chest heaving, Jo searched frantically for other op-

tions. After long, agonizing moments, she was forced
to conclude there weren't any . . . except to wait. For
Alex. For word of her disappearance to get back to
the squadron. For someone, anyone, to climb the narrow, sloping path to the observatory.

Slumping down in the chair, she waited.

Minutes crawled by. Hours. Cold seeped under the
collar of her flight suit. Sleet pounded down on the
dome over her head.

Jo had no idea how much time passed before the
rattle of a key in a lock acted like a cattle prod. She
jerked upright, fury blazing in her heart. Fear snapped
her jaw into locked position. She was damned if she'd
give Alex the satisfaction of hearing her teeth chatter.

A blast of winter air swept in, lifting the ends that
had worked loose from Jo's French braid.

"You're awake."

His voice came from behind her. Deep, cultured,
so hateful now that it brought a bitter taste of bile
rushing into her throat. She stared straight ahead, refusing to swivel around, refusing to acknowledge his
presence by so much as a shudder.

Footsteps sounded. A measured tread. Sure. Confident. Deliberate.

He moved into her line of vision. He was bundled
against the cold in the heavy fisherman's cable-knit
sweater Jo had once admired. His hair gleamed black
and damp. Those dark-ringed eyes rested on her with
such malicious satisfaction that her fingers curved into
talons.

Reaching over the railing, he stroked the aching
spot just under her jaw. "Does your neck hurt?"

She jerked as far away from his touch as the seat would allow. "Do you care?"

"No, although I regret that I had to stun you. Almost as much as I regret the painful necessity of dragging you down here."

"You'll regret it even more if you don't let me go."

His head shook in a gentle reproof that scratched on her nerves like fingernails on a chalkboard. "I've told you repeatedly I'll never let you go."

"You can't love me," she said coldly. "Not if you want to hurt me."

"Haven't you learned that pain always accompanies love? I've experienced that pain with my mother, then with Katherine." His eyes darkened, fixing on her with an intensity that made her skin crawl. "Now you! You shouldn't have betrayed me by letting another man touch you. Or by talking to the police."

"I didn't betray you! But you've betrayed yourself this time. They'll know who snatched me. They'll come looking for me."

"They won't find you, Joanna."

With a casual carelessness that chilled her to the bone, he strolled to a work table a few feet away. Only then did she see the weapon in his hand. Fitted with both a silencer and what she guessed was an infrared target identifier, it looked deadly enough to bring down a bull moose in full charge. Her stomach curled in on itself as Alex placed the weapon on the table and dragged around a chair.

"You won't get away with it," she ground out through teeth clenched hard against her fear. "Even with your millions and your army of lawyers and your evil, twisted mind, you can't get away with killing me. Not when they already suspect you of killing Katherine and Martin Russ."

He smiled then, a twist of his lips that closed Jo's throat. "Let's not forget our friend Stroder."

Oh, God! He took some kind of perverse pleasure in his personal body count.

"Why?" she choked out. "You told me about Katherine, but Stroder and Russ?"

Fastidious as ever, Alex crossed his legs and twitched the crease of his tan slacks. When he returned his gaze to Jo, the absolute absence of remorse in his eyes hit her with the same sickening jolt as the stun gun.

"Martin kept poking his nose into matters outside his scope as my grandfather's biographer. He interviewed the maids, my drivers, even our family physician. I don't know what made him suspect I fed Katherine the toxin that damaged her heart muscle. But when he contacted Stroder, who'd developed his own theories about my wife's unfortunate demise, I knew I had to eliminate them both."

The calm admission made Jo's skin crawl. She'd never leave the observatory alive unless she took Alex down first. Just how she'd accomplish that escaped her at the moment.

"What do we do now?" she asked, hoping, praying, she'd devise some plan of her own before Alex implemented his.

"We wait." He cocked his head, listening to the rhythm of the sleet on the roof. "This ice storm gave me the perfect excuse to send the staff home so we could make our final farewells in private. Unfortunately, the storm may also delay your lover's arrival."

"Deke? You called Deke?"

His mask fell away for a moment. Hate flared briefly in his eyes, hot and venomous.

"So you admit he's your lover? That you spread your legs for Elliot?"

"My relationship with Deke has nothing to do with you! It was over between you and me before—"

He sprang out of the chair, moving so fast Jo barely had time to try to push back against the seat before he backhanded her viciously.

"Don't lie to me, you whore! You're just like Katherine! Worse. The bitch taunted me with the fact she'd taken a lover, that she intended to walk out of my life just like my mother had, but at least she didn't lie."

Blood from a cut to the tender inside lining welled in Jo's mouth. She spat it out, feeling a savage satisfaction when she hit his pants leg. If nothing else, she'd leave a little of her DNA on him.

"I'm not like Katherine, damn you! I was never like Katherine, except in your sick mind! And Deke's too smart to walk into a trap. He won't come alone!"

"He will if he wants to see you alive once more before he, too, dies."

Her bravado wilted in the face of a searing, aching regret. She'd known it! She'd sensed all along Alex would try to take his revenge on them both! Why hadn't she listened to her head instead of her heart? Why had she dragged Deke into this dark hole with her?

She could only pray he wouldn't take whatever bait had been dangled in front of him, that he'd have the sense to call Ambruzzo or the FBI or the Air Force

Office of Special Investigations instead of playing this game by Alex's rules.

Two and a half miles from the turn-off to Chestnut Hill, a Blazer coated with dirty slush from the long drive down from D.C. hit a patch of black ice and went into a skid.

"Shit!"

Fighting the urge to yank the wheel in the opposite direction, Deke steered into the turn and hit the brakes as gently as his heavy boot and gut-clenching sense of urgency allowed.

"Come on, dammit! Come on!"

No amount of coaxing, praying, or cursing could produce the traction needed to halt the spiral. With an unstoppable slide, the Blazer spun onto the shoulder. Dirt crumbled under its weight. A rear tire churned air. The Blazer tipped, slid off the edge, and slammed sideways into a tree with a crunch that rattled Deke's teeth.

Fighting a helpless fury, he shouldered open the driver's side door and clambered out to survey the damage. A single glance told him there was no way he was going to pry the passenger side door away from the white-barked ash it had wrapped itself around. Which left him one option. Only one.

He couldn't call for help. Couldn't wait to flag down a passing vehicle, even if one chanced along on this narrow, winding two-lane road. The instructions he'd received in that eerie, electronically masked voice had left no room for interpretation or deviation.

Deke had to arrive at Chestnut Hill alone, by eight P.M. If he made one call, if one alert went out over police or military nets, Taylor would know . . . and Jo would die instantly.

With any other man, Deke might have questioned an outsider's ability to tap into secure nets. But Taylor had already given them a taste of this deadly wizardry and left a gaping hole in the wall of an apartment complex. And Deke wasn't about to take any chances with Jo's life.

So he'd come alone, as instructed. Unarmed, as instructed, knowing full well he'd have to pass through an array of sophisticated metal detectors before gaining access to wherever Taylor was keeping Jo. He hadn't, however, come unprepared.

Taylor was going down.

One way or another, the bastard was going down.

The digital display on the dash showed the time. Seven-ten. He could still make it. He *would* make it! Snatching his helmet bag from the crumpled passenger seat, Deke grabbed at a tree branch to haul himself up the slick bank and took off at as fast a lope as he could manage on the icy tarmac.

He knew exactly where he was, exactly what distance he had yet to cover. Thank God he'd shelled out the extra bucks to have the civilian version of the NavStar positioning system that had guided tanks during Desert Storm installed in the Blazer.

The dark road curved ahead, lined with trees weighted down by ice. Two-point-six miles to Chestnut Hill. Fifty minutes to cover the distance and find Jo. Deke lengthened his stride, digging in his boot heels with each step to keep from slipping.

Freezing rain pelted his bare head and bounced off the shoulders of his leather jacket, but his flight suit

provided enough insulation against the cold for him
to work up a sweat. Within a few paces, his breath
puffed out in little clouds and perspiration trickled
down his neck.

He didn't kid himself. It wasn't just the insulation
properties of the Nomex that pumped sweat and
adrenaline like aortal blood. It was fear. Primitive, gut-
twisting fear.

He'd worked it out in his head, reasoned that Taylor wouldn't dispose of Jo until her lover arrived on
the scene. The only reason for bringing Deke down
was revenge against his rival . . . and to arrange for
him to share Jo's fate.

But reason and logic flew in the face of the fact
that they were dealing with a madman. One so brilliant and resourceful, he'd already gotten away with
murder once. Praying he'd read at least a portion of
Taylor's mind, Deke pounded on.

Vapor rose around his head like a cloudy plume
by the time the woods thinned, then gave way to the
rails of a white fence. He followed the rails for another half mile before spotting twin brick pillars
topped with marble pineapples. A long, winding road
led from the brick entrance to a sprawling white house
set atop a distant rise. Chestnut trees lined the road,
their naked black limbs silver-coated with ice.

The observatory, the garbled electronic voice had
instructed. Take the path behind the house. Arrive by
eight P.M. or don't arrive at all.

His breath steaming, Deke shot the cuff of his flight
suit to check his stainless steel chronometer. Nineteen-
twenty-one.

He had thirty-nine minutes to race up that sloping

road, find the damned observatory, challenge Alex Taylor on his own grounds. His face grim, Deke ripped off his gloves. Dragging down the zipper on his leather jacket, he yanked it off and dug in his helmet bag for the ceremonial knife he'd picked up as a souvenir during a visit to the Australian outback. It was nine inches long, viciously sharp, and carved entirely from bone. The razor-edged blade would cut through the toughest hide . . . and its lack of metal components defied detection by even the most sophisticated airport security devices.

His heart as icy as the bleak landscape, Deke gripped the bone handle in a white-knuckled fist.

The rattle of the observatory's door brought Jo's head up with a jerk.

Alex! she thought on twin waves of panic and loathing. He'd come back to end his macabre game. He'd intercepted Deke, sprung whatever grisly trap he'd set, and now would end the game. She allowed herself one instant of desolation, one agonizing second of despair, before she set her spine and her jaw.

For the space of that same, endless moment, absolute silence filled the domed room. Jo knew the door had opened. She could feel the cold knifing into her exposed neck. Her shoulders braced, expecting, dreading, the feel of the stun gun as well.

"Jo!"

Her heart stopped. Literally stopped. She couldn't move, couldn't breathe, until it kick-started again with such a painful jolt she gasped.

She swung the chair around, gasping again at the figure who stood in the open door. He might have stepped from the pages of a horror novel. A frozen corpse, rising from a snowy grave. Ice coated his hair. His skin was ashen. Every heaving breath his chest pushed out wreathed his head in cloudy vapor.

Fear clogged her throat. She was the bait. Alex had used her to lure this man here. He was watching! She knew it with every fiber in her body. Listening. His warped mind was giving them a final few seconds, taking sadistic pleasure in their helplessness.

"Deke! Get out of here! Now!"

"Is this place wired?" he barked, ignoring her frantic plea. "Ready to blow?"

"I don't know!"

"Has Taylor been in here?"

"Deke, you've got to—"

"Tell me, dammit! Has Taylor been in here? I want to get you out, not blow you all to hell and back by tripping some hidden device."

"Yes, he was here, but—"

She caught the movement of shadow on ice, a glint of light on steel. Her scream split the air.

"Behind you!"

Chapter Twenty-two

Deke spun around, ducking, at the same instant a shot exploded a mere inch from his ear.

Fire burned across his cheek. Cordite seared his nostrils. Eyes streaming, ears ringing from the percussion, he reacted instinctively. Lunging forward, he gutted Alexander Taylor like a fish.

One bunch of his muscles. One thrust with all the force of a savage male behind it. One vicious rip upward. That's all it took to spill a gush of hot blood and arch Taylor over in wide-eyed, unbelieving shock.

For a small eternity, they faced each other. Then slowly, so slowly, Taylor crumpled. With a kick that shattered bone, Deke knocked the gun from his hand.

Blood poured from Taylor's stomach. His mouth still gaped open in stunned disbelief. Arms curled over his belly, he drew his legs up

Swiping the tears from his stinging eyes, Deke stood over him. He'd hunted enough big game to know Taylor was breathing his last few gasps.

"Take your time, you bastard. Die slowly. Painfully. Just like your wife did."

The fallen man twitched. A groan gurgled deep in his throat. His eyes glazed, closed, flickered open.

"Just like . . . you will. You and . . . the bitch . . . who . . . betrayed . . ."

A red froth bubbled from his mouth. His lids drifted down.

Jo had always hated the cliché of the weak, helpless female who fell sobbing into her rescuer's arms. But the moment Deke sliced the tape on her wrists, she understood that clichés *became* clichés because they embodied certain fundamental truths.

She wasn't weak and she wasn't normally helpless, but she didn't even try to hold back a sob as she sprang out of the chair and into the vise of his arms. Her mouth attacked his with the same intensity his attacked hers.

They allowed themselves one moment of joy, of relief, of a fierce, elemental bonding that went beyond this place and this time. Then reality crashed down on them.

Panting, Jo pulled away. Revulsion, relief, and a fierce, primal satisfaction filled her as she surveyed the huddled form just outside the door to the observatory.

"Is he dead?"

"Yes."

Shudders racked her. That crumpled mass might so easily have been Deke. Might still be Deke. Alex's last, vicious threat rang in her head like a Klaxon.

"We've got to get out of here! I don't know what Alex planned . . ."

He shot a swift glance around the room. "My guess is another display of high-tech pyrotechnics. That seems to be his specialty."

Oh, God, not another laser light show! Not another explosion of glass and cement and deadly shards slicing through skin and muscle! Jo's insides cringed.

"He said I had to be here by eight P.M. if I wanted to see you alive."

"Eight!"

Her blood congealed in her veins. She had no idea how long she'd sat in that damned chair, but from the look on Deke's face when he yanked back his sleeve to check his watch, she guessed it had been hours.

"What time is it?"

Incredibly, he flashed her a grin. "Time to get the hell out of Dodge, West."

Jo gaped at him, stunned that he could joke at a time like this, stunned to realize she loved him because he *could* joke at a time like this.

This wasn't the moment to tell him so, she decided. Later, when she was sure the damned building wasn't going to blow up around them.

"Come on! Let's get out of here!"

By unspoken consent, they left Alex's body lying in a crumpled heap. Their breath frosting on the air, they raced along the path through the woods. The shadowy outline of the house loomed ahead of them, dark, still.

Too dark. Too still.

"Wait!"

Skidding on the ice-slick path, Jo grabbed Deke's arm with two hands and dragged him to a stop.

"Alex said . . ." Her heart hammered as she stared at the house. "He said he sent his staff home."

Surely he wouldn't booby-trap the farmhouse. Not the house he loved so much. . . .

The house where he kept so many reminders of Katherine!

The skin on the back of her neck crawled. What the hell had Alex's sick mind devised? She didn't know, couldn't know! But every instinct in her body warned her to avoid the house.

"Jo, we've got to move!"

Her frantic glance cut to the right. There, at the bottom of the hill only a hundred or so yards away. The helipad. The Sikorsky.

Cursing Alex, cursing her own remembered delight the first time he'd taken her up in the sleek bird, she yanked on Deke's arm.

"The helo!"

He hesitated for only a second before joining her for a wild plunge down the grassy slope.

"How much time?" she panted, eyes narrowed against the sleet as she scanned the long rotor blades for signs of icing.

"Six minutes."

"Christ!"

Tearing away the anchor straps and chocks, she yanked open the cockpit door and threw herself in the right seat.

Even the pounding fear that the night would explode around her at any minute couldn't break habits drilled into her from the first time she'd climbed into a cockpit. Fumbling with the safety harness, she strapped herself in and flipped on the control panel lights. Seconds later, the engine whined, a muted murmur at first, building to a full-throated pitch with the smooth precision that was the Sikorsky's hallmark.

Jo lived through two long lifetimes in the agonizing moments it took to power up to 3,400 rpm, the minimum required to lift into a hover. The thousands of preflight and engine start checklists she'd run through during her career raced through her head. Her eyes stayed glued to the instrument panel. Her boots tested the pedals. Her hand was steady on the twist-grip throttle as she beeped the power up in steady increments.

Finally, *finally!*, the bird was ready to fly. Deke knew the drill as well as she did. Twisting in his harness, he checked the side and rear of the aircraft.

"Clear to the left," he shouted, used to pitching his voice above the roar. The sound thundered in the well-insulated quiet of the S-76.

"Roger."

Jo twisted in her harness to check the right side, swung back, concentrated all her attention on coordinating all four appendages to take the helo into a hover.

The skids cleared the helipad.

The ground dropped away.

Sweat trickled between Jo's breasts as she pushed the nose forward to gain airspeed, hands and feet working in unison to counterbalance the combined effects of horizontal and vertical rotors.

Deke reached for the aerial chart book tucked conveniently into a handy pocket. "You've flown in here before. What's the closest airport?"

"Lexington. It's about ten nautical miles west northwest."

"Roger."

Steadily, Jo beeped up the power, aiming for the 90 knots of airspeed she knew the Sikorsky could handle in this kind of weather.

At 30 knots, she speared a glance over her shoulder at the dark, silent house sprawled atop its hill.

At 60, the sickening thought that they'd gotten away too easily nudged aside her relief at having gotten away at all.

Wouldn't Alex have known she'd go for the helo? Wouldn't he . . . ?

At 68 knots, the Sikorsky's tail rotor disintegrated.

The explosion rocked the aircraft. A heartbeat later, the nose pitched down and swung violently to the right.

Instantly, Jo pulled back the cyclic, fighting to keep the Sikorsky from going into a spin.

"We've got tail rotor failure! I can't get the nose up!"

Deke was already cross-checking the instruments. "You've still got engine and transmission in the green. What the hell happened?"

Teeth clenched, she spit out one word. "Alex."

She pushed Taylor out of her mind. She couldn't think about him now. Couldn't focus on anything but the vicious vibration that shook the Sikorsky.

Loss of component tail rotor was a helo pilot's worst nightmare. There was no way to train for this kind of emergency, no way to practice it except in a simulator.

And nothing anyone could do when it happened but maintain airspeed to keep from going into a spin, then ride the chopper down to the ground.

Deke understood that as well as Jo. Flipping the radio switches, he put out a distress call to any and all listeners.

"Mayday! Mayday! This is Sikorsky tail number . . ." He tore his eyes from the instruments to check the brass plate. "Victor-Able-six-three-two-two going down ten miles east southeast of Lexington VOR. Mayday! Mayday!"

He repeated the call over and over while Jo took her aircraft into its downward death spiral. She couldn't cut airspeed to slow the rate of descent. That would only increase the torque and spin the aircraft more violently to the right.

Their only hope was to find an open field, a highway, anyplace she could bring the helo in at running airspeed, like a Boeing 727 rolling in for a landing.

And they had to find it fast!

"Check the road at eight o'clock," Deke barked. "That looks like a rail fence running alongside it, which might mean open fields or pastures beyond."

Right! Pastures! If her heart hadn't been lodged firmly in her throat at that moment, Jo might have reminded him what happened the last time she made an unscheduled landing in a pasture. She only hoped the million-dollar Thoroughbreds were all tucked in some safe, dry stable for the night.

"Brace yourself," she warned. "I'm taking her in."

The toe of the skids hit first, digging furrows in the frozen earth. Then the nose. Praying, cursing, sweating, Jo fought the urge to overcorrect and applied just enough cyclic to keep the helicopter from tipping onto its side.

She couldn't prevent the downward flex of the

overhead rotor blades, however. When the Sikorsky plowed in, natural forces bowed the forty-four-foot blades. The leading blade impacted the ground, breaking off with a crack that rifled like gunfire. The second followed through on its deadly arc. Bowed low, it hit just above the left door, shattering the glass canopy, slicing the top off the cockpit.

Deke flung himself forward as far as his harness would allow. The reinforced, composite-plated seat back took most of the blow, but no amount of armor could shield his head and shoulders from the force of that deadly swipe.

Chapter Twenty-three

Jo stood at the third-floor window of the USAF Medical Center at Andrews AFB, arms folded tight around her waist. Behind her, the personnel of the ICU performed their duties amid the soft beeps and antiseptic precision of their profession. Outside the frost-steamed window, snow mantled the dark streets. The few drivers who'd braved the night plowed through two feet of fleecy white.

The snow had come in hard on the heels of the sleet that had pinged so loudly on the observatory's roof. Jo had felt the first flakes on her cheeks while she huddled in that icy field, waiting for a response to her mayday and subsequent radio calls, an unconscious Deke cradled in her arms.

The rescue team who'd arrived on the scene had taken them to Lexington, where ER doctors fought to counter the effects of that deadly, slicing blade. As soon as the Air Force received notification of the accident, the 1st Helo Squadron had scrambled a medivac chopper and brought both Deke and Jo home to Andrews and the skilled surgeons at the Malcolm Grow Medical Center.

Jo had waited six hours in the lounge outside the

surgical unit, surrounded by a gathering crowd of friends and crew members from the squadron. Forty-nine hours later, she was still waiting, this time outside the ICU.

Her family had flown in, braving the storm and threats of airport closings. Her parents, her brothers, two of her sisters-in-law. Deke's mom had arrived early yesterday afternoon, as well. All day, they'd remained at the hospital. All last night. And today.

Sometime during the endless hours, Ambruzzo and a horde of police officials had come and gone. The 89th Wing commander, General Orr, had stopped by with his wife, as had the 1st Helo Squadron commander and his wife. Advising Jo that the classes she taught at the University of Maryland had been canceled due to the storm, Eve Marshall had settled in for most of the snowy afternoon with her husband.

Now only Jo, two of her brothers, and Deke's mom kept vigil with two other pilots from the 1st. The rest of her family had dropped, exhausted, into beds at the Holiday Inn just outside the Andrews front gate. Hollow-eyed and aching from her own scrapes and bruises, Jo had refused to leave, refused even to snatch a few hours rest in the hospital bed the nurses offered. Her fear and the stinging regret of hindsight wouldn't let her sleep.

Why hadn't she listened to her instincts and stayed away from Deke? Why had she dragged him into the morass with her? She should never have moved into his apartment, even temporarily. Should never have fired Alex's twisted love/hate like that. If Deke died, as the doctors had warned he might, she'd live with a haunting guilt the rest of her life. Guilt and an aching sense of loss she was only now beginning to—

"I brought you some coffee."

Wearily, Jo turned and accepted the foam cup from her brother Jack. "Thanks."

Rubber squeaked as he angled his wheelchair to share her view of the snowy night. For long moments, neither of them spoke. Memories of another crash, another agonizing vigil, drifted through Jo's numbed mind.

"He's tough," Jack said quietly, reading her thoughts. "As tough as I was. I survived, kid. Elliot will, too."

She nodded. Through a voice made hoarse by too much coffee and too little sleep, she repeated what had become her mantra in the past two days.

"Tom says every hour he hangs in there increases his odds."

Her eldest brother had consulted with the Air Force doctors immediately upon his arrival. Tom understood the medical jargon—blunt trauma to the frontal lobe, neocortal hemorrhaging, possible damage to the right cerebral hemisphere—and translated them into stark reality. No one could assess what, if any, permanent injuries Deke had sustained until he regained consciousness.

If he regained consciousness.

That possibility, too, Tom had translated for Jo and Mrs. Elliot. Now all they could do was wait. Pray. Hope.

And talk to Deke in the dark of night.

Jo threw a glance at the clock on the wall. None of the medical staff had attempted to enforce the one ten-minute-visit-per-hour rule, but she'd tried not to abuse her access to Deke's bedside. Forty minutes had crawled by since her last visit. Forty years, it seemed.

"I'm going to check on him." She passed Jack the coffee. "Hold on to this for me, will you?"

Even after the long hours and many visits, Jo tensed as she approached the curtained unit. Deke lay unmoving, the upper half of his face and head swathed in bandages. He was breathing on his own, but a frightening array of tubes and wires linked him to monitors and IVs. One machine sounded a rhythmic click-click. Another hummed softly in counterpoint.

There were no chairs in the cubicle, but one of the nurses had rolled in a stool during Jo's last visit. Sinking down on legs rubbery from fatigue, she folded one arm on the bed rail and slipped her other hand through the supports.

"Hey, cowboy," she murmured, her fingers entwining with his. "It's still snowing out, in case you're interested. Colonel Marshall said earlier that we've shut down operations except for alert and emergency responses."

Her thumb brushed the back of his hand and wrist, gently, carefully, avoiding the IV inserted in his vein.

"Did I tell you how much I like your mother? Yeah, I think I did. She and my mom have really hit it off, by the way. They've already compared kids' ages and hours in labor birthing each one."

Propping her chin on her forearm, Jo let her lids drift down over sandpapery eyes for a moment.

"Jack—he's my next youngest brother. He was here to see you a little while ago. Jack says our mom wins the number of kids contest, but yours definitely gets the award for the longest labor. Thirty-six hours, big guy? How could you do that to your poor mother?"

She whispered whatever came into her head. There wasn't any logic to it. Only the need to maintain the fragile bond of touch and speech.

The life-support equipment pinged a soft medley in the background. Light from the nurses' station slanted across the observation area, falling just short of the bed. In the dark shadows, Jo brushed her thumb back and forth.

She had no idea when she drifted off, no idea how long she'd dozed when something woke her. Confused, she lifted her head and looked around with gritty eyes for a nurse or a relative.

Only after several dazed seconds did she realize that Deke had squeezed her fingers. So faintly she hadn't registered the pressure at first.

"Deke?" she whispered, her heart slamming against her ribs.

She didn't breathe, didn't move. Her fingers taut in his, she waited, prayed, for another faint press.

"Deke? Can you hear me?"

"I . . . hear you."

A sob tore at her throat. Jo forced it back, fought to keep from crunching his fingers with hers and shouting her delirious joy out loud.

"You . . . okay?" he rasped.

"Me?" she squeaked.

He was lying blind and immobile, and he asked about her injuries instead of his own?

"I'm fine. A few scrapes and bruises, but nothing serious."

Beneath the thick bandages, his mouth curved. "Hell of . . . a landing . . . Wonder Woman."

Oh, God! She could have held out against anything except that weak, wonderful grin. The sob she'd choked back a few seconds ago ripped free. Hot tears stung her eyes.

"It wasn't one of my best," she croaked through a tight, aching throat. "But it got us both down in one piece."

His fingers twitched. The quiver was so slight, she almost missed it in her teary, sniffling joy.

"One . . . piece?"

"Pretty much." She wouldn't lie to him. "You took a hit when the blades flexed and sliced through the canopy."

"How bad a . . . hit?"

"We don't know. They'll run more tests now that you're awake."

With infinite care, she brought the back of his hand up to her cheek.

"Your mom's here. So are my folks. And my brothers."

"All of . . . them?"

Under his mask of bandages, he managed to project the wariness of any male about to be confronted by several very large, very protective siblings of the woman who'd almost gone down in flames with him.

"All of them," she confirmed with a hiccup of shaky laughter. "Tom's one of the best neurosurgeons in the country. He's consulting with your doctors."

She hated to leave him, hated to release his hand, but she knew his mother would want to know he'd awakened, as would the medical staff.

"I better tell them you're awake."

"Not . . . yet." He drew in a slow breath. "Taylor?"

"He's dead."

When he didn't respond a frisson of worry feathered through her joy.

"Remember, Deke? Right before we ran to the Sikorsky? He fired at you, and you knifed him." She leaned over the bed rail, urging him to remember. "I played right into his hands by taking the Sikorsky up. He had it rigged and waiting for us."

"Bas . . . tard."

"Ambruzzo theorizes that Alex would have had a ready explanation for our deaths. The chopper was still in my name. Maybe he'd assert that I'd come down to Chestnut Hill to claim it, that the ice storm brought us down."

Deke lay silent. Her heart wrenching, Jo wished she could see his eyes, wished she could gauge how much he recalled. All her fears, all her bitter regret at dragging him into Alex's twisted orbit, rose up to choke her. If she'd had any energy to spare at that moment, she would have hated Alex all over again. But every thought, every emotion centered on Deke. Only Deke.

His fingers flexed, stronger now. With a little grunt that sent her pulse spiking, he tugged her forward.

"Nothing can . . . bring us . . . down, West."

She leaned over the rails, her mouth a whisper from his, her heart pulsing with joy, with hope, with love.

"You got that right, Elliot."

If you enjoyed Merline Lovelace's *Dark Side of Dawn*, you won't want to miss the exciting debut of new thriller writer Lynne Heitman. Her background in the commercial airline industry lends a chilling core of truth to *Hard Landing*, while her storytelling skill gives it the hot, pulse-pounding appeal of the best popular fiction. . . .

When Alex Shanahan becomes the new General Manager of Majestic Airlines' Boston operation, she is the spark that will set off the explosion. Her predecessor, Ellen Shepard, committed suicide, although everyone at the airline believes she was murdered. Alex's dream job quickly becomes her worst nightmare, as she is led into the minefield that is Logan Airport— and then abandoned. Alex can trust no one, not even the man she loves, when she comes too close to the truth. The only question is whether she'll live long enough to tell anyone what she's discovered.

Turn the page for a special preview of

Hard Landing

by Lynne Heitman

An Onyx paperback
on sale in April 2001

"Thoroughly engrossing suspense! *Hard Landing* combines a highly likable heroine with a cleverly twisting plot. The end result is an edge-of-your seat thriller that sweeps you up and carries you along for the ride."
—*New York Times* bestselling author, Lisa Gardner

Prologue

Angelo rolled over, reached across his wife, and tried to catch the phone before it rang again. He grabbed the receiver and held it before answering, listening for the sound of her rhythmic breathing that told him she was still asleep.

"Yeah?"

"Angie, get your ass out of bed. You gotta do something for me."

He recognized the voice immediately, but didn't like the tone. "Who's this?"

"Stop screwing around, Angie."

He switched the phone to his other ear and lowered his voice. "What the hell you doin' calling over here this time of the night? You're gonna wake up Theresa."

"I need you to find Petey."

"You gotta be kiddin' me." He twisted around to see the clock radio on his side of the bed. Without his glasses, it took a serious squint to turn the blurry red glow into individual digits. Twelve-twenty, for Peter's sake, twelve-twenty, for Pete's sake, twelve-twenty in the goddamn morning. "I got an early shift and it's raining like a sonofabitch out there. Find him yourself."

"I'm working here, Angie. I can't leave the airport."

"Never stopped you before. Call me tomorrow."

"Don't hang up on me, damn you."

The receiver was halfway to the cradle and Angelo could still hear the yelling. *"Don't you fucking hang up on me!"* But that wasn't what kept him hanging on. *"You owe me. Do you hear me? More than this, you owe me."* It was the desperation—panic even. In the thirty years he'd known him, Big Pete Dwyer had never even come close to losing control.

Angelo pulled the receiver back. With his hand cupped over the mouthpiece, he could smell the strong scent of his wife on it—the thick, sweet fragrance of her night cream mixed with the faintly medicinal smell that seemed to be everywhere in their home these days. "What the hell's the matter with you?"

"If you never do nothing else for me, Angie, you gotta do this thing for me tonight."

The old bedsprings groaned as Theresa turned. When he felt her hand on his knee, he reached down and held it between both of his, trying to warm fingers that were always so cold lately. She was awake now anyhow. "I'm listening."

"He's probably in one of those joints in Chelsea or Revere. There's gonna be some guys out looking for him. I want you to find him first."

"Are you talkin' about cops? Because I ain't gonna—"

"No. Not cops. I can't talk right now."

Big Pete had to raise his voice to be heard, and for the first time Angelo noticed the background noise. Men were shouting, work boots were scraping the gritty linoleum floor, and doors were opening and slamming shut. "What's going on over there?"

"Just do what I tell you."

"What do you want I should do with him? Bring him over to you?"

"Fuck, no. Angie, you're not getting this. Find Petey and stash him somewhere until I finish my shift. Keep him away from the airport, and don't let no one get to him before I do. No one. Do you hear?"

The line went dead. Angelo held the receiver against his chest until Theresa took it from his hand and hung it up. "What time is it?" she murmured.

"It's twelve-thirty, baby. I gotta go out for a little while."

"Who was that?"

"Big Pete needs me to find his kid."

"Again?"

"Yeah, but this time there's something hinky about it. Something's going on."

"Mmmmm . . ."

He leaned down and kissed his wife on the cheek. "Go back to sleep, babe. I'm gonna take the phone off the hook so nobody bothers you."

The big V-8 engine in Angelo's old Cadillac made the bench seat rumble. He sat with his boot on the brake, shaking the rain out of his hair and waiting for the defroster to kick in. His fingers felt as cold and stiff as his wife's had been when he tapped the finicky dome light, trying to make it come on. Where the hell were his gloves, anyway, and what was that garbage on the radio? Damn kids with their rap music, if you could even call it music. He punched a button and let the tuner scan for his big band station while he searched his pockets for gloves.

"*. . . with friends and family on that flight are advised to* *go to the Nor'easter Airlines terminal at Logan Airport, where representatives—"*

Angelo froze. What the hell . . . ? He wanted to turn up the volume, but couldn't get his hand out of his pocket. His heart started to pound as he tried to shake loose and listen at the same time.

"Again, if you've just joined us, we're receiving word—"

The scanner kicked in and rage-filled rant of a midnight radio call-in host poured out. Angelo yanked his hand free, leaned down and, god*dammi*t, cracked his forehead on the steering wheel. Still squeezing the glove in his fist, he jabbed at the tuner buttons until the solemn tones of the newscaster emerged again from the static.

". . . we know so far is that Nor'easter Airlines Flight 1704, a commuter aircraft carrying nineteen passengers and two crew members, has crashed tonight just outside of Baltimore."

Angelo put both hands on the steering wheel to keep them from shaking.

"That flight did depart Logan Airport earlier this evening. The information we have at this hour is that there are no survivors, but again, that report is unconfirmed."

The bulletin repeated as Angelo reached up and used the sleeve of his jacket to wipe the condensation from the windshield. He peered through the streaked glass and up into the black sky. There was nothing to see but a cold, spiteful rain still coming down. But he felt it. He felt the dying aircraft falling to the earth, falling through the roof of the old Cadillac. He felt it falling straight down on him.

Goddamn you, Big Pete. Goddamn you.

Chapter One

When the seat belt sign went out, I was the first one down the jetbridge. My legs wobbled, my muscles ached, and my feet felt like sausages stuffed into leather pumps that had been the right size when we'd boarded six hours earlier. All I wanted to do was get off the airplane, check into my hotel, sink into a hot bath, and forget the five hours in the air, the half hour in a holding pattern, and the interminable twenty-five minutes we'd spent delayed on the ground because, the captain had assured us, our gate was occupied.

The captain had told an airline fib.

When I'd looked out my window and down at the ramp, I'd seen no wingman on my side of the plane, which meant we hadn't been waiting for a gate—we'd been waiting for a ground crew to marshal us in, hard to imagine. It's not as if we'd shown up unexpectedly. The crew that finally did saunter out was one man short and out of uniform. I made a mental note.

At the bottom of the bridge, the door to the departure lounge was closed. I grabbed the knob and could have sworn it was vibrating. I turned the knob, pushed against the door—and it slammed back in my face. Odd. Behind me, fellow passengers from the flight stomped down the jetbridge and stood, cell phones and carry-ons in hand, blinking at me. I gave it another shot, this time putting my shoulder into it, and pushed through the obstruction, which, to my embarrassment, turned out to be a family of four—mother, father, and two small children. They'd been pinned there by a teeming mob, the size and scope of which became clear when the door swung wide, and the rumble I'd heard became a full-fledged roar.

There must have been a thousand people smashed into the departure lounge, at least twice the number that would be comfortable in that space. Judging by their faces and the combustible atmosphere, they were all supposed to be somewhere besides Logan Airport in Boston. It was Ellis Island in reverse—people trying to get out, not in.

The gate agent who had met our flight was past me before I knew it.

"Excuse me," I said, but my voice evaporated into the crowd noise. I tried again.

"Baggage claim is that way, ma'am." Without bothering to look at me, the agent pointed down the concourse, turned, and vanished into a wall of winter coats.

I stood and watched the current of deplaning passengers flow through the crowd and out to baggage claim, quiet hotel rooms, and hot baths. Technically, I could have joined them. I was anonymous in Boston, and my assignment didn't officially begin until the next day. But in the end, I did as I always did. I worked my way over to one of the check-in podiums, stowed my coat and bag in a closet, clipped on my Majestic Airlines ID, and went to work.

I spotted a senior ticket agent shuttling through the crowd from gate to gate, moving with as much authority as circumstances would allow. When I caught up with her, she was conferring with a young blonde agent at one of the podiums.

"You'll have to wait your turn," she snapped before I ever opened my mouth. "There's a line."

If there was a line at this podium, it was cleverly disguised as an angry throng. I slipped around the counter and stood next to her. "I'm not a passenger. I'm the new general manager."

She checked my badge, eyes dark with suspicion, thinking perhaps I was an impostor volunteering to be in charge of this mess.

"I'm Alex Shanahan. I came in on the Denver flight."

"The *new* GM? That didn't take long."

"What's the problem here?"

"You name it, we've got it, but basically we're off schedule. Nothing's left on time for the past two hours. In fact, nothing's left at all."

I read her name tag. "JoAnn, maybe I can help. If I could—"

"Are you *deaf*? Or are you *stupid*?"

We both turned to look across the podium at a man who was wearing an Italian suit with a silk tie that probably cost more than my entire outfit. As he berated the younger agent, she stared down at her keyboard, eyes in the locked position.

"Do you *know* how many miles I fly on this airline every year?" He pointed his phone at her and her chin started to quiver. "I *will* not sit in coach, I *will* sit in first class, and you *will* find me a seat if you have to buy someone else off this *goddamn airplane*."

Even in a lounge filled with angry people, this guy was drawing attention. I leaned across the podium so he could hear me. "Can I help you, sir?"

"Who the hell are you?"

I took him aside and listened to his patronizing rant, maintaining eye contact and nodding sympathetically so that he could see my deep concern. When he was finally out of steam, I explained that the situation was extreme and that we might not get him up front this time. I asked him to please be patient and work with us. Then I promised to send him two complimentary upgrades. Frequent fliers respond to free upgrades, the way trained seals respond to raw fish. It took a promise of five upgrades, but eventually, with one more parting shot about our "towering display of incompetence," he took my card and my apology and faded away.

I found JoAnn heading for another podium. "At least give me the number to Operations," I said, tagging after her. "I can call the agent there."

She scribbled the number on the back of a ticket envelope and handed it to me. I used my own cell phone and dialed.

"Operations-this-is-Kevin-hold-please." Kevin's Irish accent seemed far too gentle for the situation. When he came back, I told him who I was and what I needed.

"Have you talked to Danny about this?"

I plugged a finger in my non-phone ear and turned my back to the crowd. "If he's not standing there with you, Danny's too far away to be in charge right now. I need help now, Kevin. If you can't help me, someone's going to get killed up here."

There was a brief pause, then, "Go ahead."

I spoke to Kevin for five minutes, taking notes, asking questions, and getting advice. When I hung up, the noise, much like the frustration level, was on the rise and JoAnn was contemplating a call to the state troopers. I couldn't see how a couple of big guys with guns and jackboots would calm the waters, so I asked her to wait. I found a functioning microphone, pressed the button, took a deep breath and introduced myself.

The buzz grew louder.

I kicked off my shoes, climbed on top of the podium, and repeated my introduction. When people could see as well as hear me, it made all the difference.

"Ladies and gentlemen, I apologize for the inconvenience of this evening's operation. I know you're uncomfortable and you've had a hard time getting information, so that's where we're going to start. Is anyone out here booked on Flight 497 to Washington, D.C.?" A few hands shot up hopefully. Others followed more hesitantly.

"Your flight was scheduled to depart at 5:15. The aircraft just came in, and the passengers from Chicago are deplaning as I speak at Gate"—I checked my notes—"Forty-four." Heads popped up here and there as people stretched to see the gate. "We can either clean the cabin, or we can get you on board and out of town. How many of you want to leave now?" I had to smile as every hand in the place went up.

"I'm with you, people, but right now I'm asking the passengers booked to D.C. Be prepared, ladies and gentlemen, that the cabin will not be as clean as you're accustomed to on Majestic, but you'll be gone and we'll still be here." As I continued, flight by flight, the noise began to recede, the agents worked the queues, and some semblance of order began to emerge.

Four hours later, at almost ten o'clock, the last passenger boarded. I closed the door and pulled the jetbridge. The agents had either gone to punch out or to other parts of the operation, leaving the boarding lounge as littered and deserted as Times Square on New Year's Day. I was hungry, I was exhausted, I was wired, and I hadn't felt this good in almost eighteen months, not since I'd left the field. There is nothing like an epic operating crisis to get the adrenaline surging.

I shook the wrinkles out of my coat, grabbed my bags, and in my hyped-up state nearly missed what was tacked to the inside of the closet door. It had been crazy when I'd first opened this door, but even so I would have noticed a sheet of notebook-sized paper at eye level—especially this one. I took it down and stared at it. It was a crude drawing of a house with a sharply pitched roof. At the apex of the roof was a wind vane resembling a rooster. Inside the house in the attic, a woman hung from a rope, her head twisted to a grotesque angle by the coil around her throat. Limp arms dangled at her side, her tongue hung out of a gaping mouth, and her eyes, dead eyes, had rolled back in her head. My adrenaline surge receded and I felt a thickening in my chest as I read the caption.

The name Shepard, scrawled below, had been crossed out and replaced with my name—Shanahan.

"It's a message."

I jumped, startled by the sound of the voice, loud and abrupt in the now-deserted terminal. JoAnn stood behind me, arms crossed, dark eyes fixed on the drawing in my hand. "That's part of the message, and tonight's operation was the rest of it."

"What are you talking about?"

"I didn't get it until you showed up," she said, "but now it makes sense. They must have found out you were coming in tonight."

"Who?"

"The union. The boys downstairs are telling you that you may think you're in charge of this place, but you're not. And if you try to be"—she pointed to the drawing in my hand—"you're going to end up just like the last one."

"Ellen Shepard killed herself," I said.

"Yeah, right." She gave me a sour smile as she turned to walk away. "Welcome to Boston."

Look for Merline Lovelace's next riveting
novel of romantic suspense, *After Midnight*.

A unique blend of snappy humor, searing
passion, and nonstop action has made
Merline Lovelace's books internationally
beloved, and all of her storytelling talent
comes together with stunning results in

After Midnight

A Signet paperback
coming in the fall of 2001